SF   495

I0953437

SPECIAL DELIVERANCE

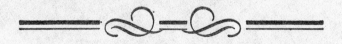

SPECIAL DELIVERANCE

Clifford D. Simak

A Del Rey Book

BALLANTINE BOOKS • NEW YORK

1

IT WAS FRIDAY AFTERNOON. The final class was finished, the last of the students walking out the door. Edward Lansing stood at his desk, gathering up his lecture notes and papers, stuffing them into his briefcase. He had the weekend free, and it felt good to have a free one—no civic or extracurricular duties chopping out a part of it. Although as yet he had not decided what he would do with it. He could drive out into the hills and have a look at the autumn color, which this weekend would reach its greatest glory. He could phone Andy Spaulding and suggest a hiking expedition. He could ask Alice Anderson to have dinner with him and let subsequent events take their course. Or he could just do nothing—hole up in his apartment, build a pleasant fire, stack the player with Mozart and do some of the reading that had been piling up.

He tucked the briefcase underneath his arm and walked out the door. The slot machine stood against the wall, halfway down the corridor. Out of sheer habit he thrust his hand into his pocket, his fingers running through the coins that he had dropped there. His fingers found a quarter and he took it out. At the slot machine he halted and inserted the quarter in the slot, reaching out to haul down on the lever. The machine chuckled at him, and the wheels in its face were spinning. Without waiting for the results, he walked away. There was no point in staying. No one ever won. At various times there would be rumors about a monstrous jackpot someone hit, but all these stories, he suspected, were no more than propaganda floated by the welfare people.

Behind him the machine ended its chuckling clatter, slamming to a stop. He turned around and looked. A pear, a lemon and an orange—for this was one of the machines made to ape those of many years ago, a circumstance calculated to appeal to the juvenile sense of humor among the undergraduates.

So he'd lost again. But that was not unusual. He could not remember ever winning. No one ever won. Perhaps (although he could not be sure of this) one played the slots out of a sense of patriotic duty, a sort of enlarged, rather nebulous civic duty. For they did provide the funding for the national welfare operation, and as a result the vicious bite of the income tax had been softened. He thought about it briefly, wondering once again if he approved or not. There was, it seemed to him, a slight moral taint to the whole idea, but, taint or not, it had worked out. He could well afford, he reminded himself, to lose a quarter now and then for the succor of the poor and a smaller income tax.

The machine blinked out, leaving him standing in the empty hall. He swung about and headed for his office. In a few minutes, after he had divested himself of the briefcase and closed the door behind him, he'd be on his way to a free weekend.

As he turned the corner he saw someone waiting for him beside his office door, leaning against the wall in that infuriating loose-jointed attitude invariably assumed by a waiting student.

He walked past the man, fumbled with his keys.

"You are waiting for me?" he asked the leaning one.

"Thomas Jackson, sir," the student said. "You left a note in my box."

"Yes, Mr. Jackson, I believe I did," said Lansing, remembering now. He held the door open and the student walked in. Following Jackson, Lansing switched on his desk light.

"The chair over there," he said, motioning to the one that stood before his desk.

"Thank you, sir," the student said.

Lansing went around his desk, pulled out his chair and sat down in it. What he wanted was in a pile of papers on the left-hand corner of the desk. He shuffled through them until he found the theme.

Glancing up at Jackson, he could see the man was nervous.

Lansing glanced out the opposite window. Beyond it lay a section of the campus mall. The afternoon, he noted, was a typical sleepy New England autumn with a mellow sun turning to molten gold the leaves of the ancient birch tree just outside the window.

He picked up the sheaf of papers in front of him and riffled through the pages, making a pretense of studying them.

"Mr. Jackson, I wonder if you'd mind discussing your paper with me?" he asked. "In many ways I find it fascinating."

The student gulped and said, "I am pleased you like it."

"It is one of the finest pieces of criticism I have ever read," said Lansing. "You must have spent a great deal of time and thought on it. That is evident. You developed an unusual feeling for one particular scene in *Hamlet* and your deductions are brilliant. There is something that puzzles me, however—some of the sources that you quote."

He laid the paper on the desk and stared at the student. The student tried to match the stare, but his eyes were glassy and soon he turned his head.

"What I want to know," said Lansing, "is who might Crawford be? And Wright? And Forbes? Well-known Shakespeare scholars, I am sure, although I've never heard of them."

The student said nothing. "What puzzles me," said Lansing, "is why you should have used the names. The paper stands on its own without them. If it had not been for them, I would have considered, although perhaps with some reluctance in view of your past scholarship, that you had finally gotten down to business and done an honest job of work. On your past record that would have seemed unlikely, but I am inclined to think I would have given you the benefit of doubt. Mr. Jackson, if this is a hoax of some sort, I fail to find much humor in it. Perhaps you have an explanation; if so, I shall listen to it."

The student spoke in a sudden flare of bitterness. "It was that damn machine!" he said.

"I don't believe I follow you. What machine?"

"You see," said Jackson, "I had to get a good mark. I knew that if I screwed up on this assignment, I would flunk the course. And I can't afford a failure. I made an honest try at it, but I couldn't hack it, so I went to the machine and—"

"I ask you again," said Lansing. "What has a machine to do with it?"

"It's a slot machine," said Jackson. "Or, rather, it looks like a slot machine, although I think it must be something else. Not too many people know of it. It wouldn't do to let it become common knowledge."

He looked beseechingly at Lansing, and Lansing asked, "If this machine is a secret thing, why are you telling me about it? I should think you would try to bluff it out. I know that if I were involved in such a conspiracy as you suggest, I would take my medicine and not reveal a word of it. I would protect the others."

Not believing the slot-machine tale, of course, not thinking for an instant there was any truth in it. Just putting pressure on the man across the desk from him, hoping that by doing so he might arrive at something like the truth.

"Well, you see, sir, it's this way," Jackson said. "You maybe think that it's a stupid hoax or that I hired someone else to write it —I don't know, you could think a lot of things and if you keep on thinking them, you'll give me a failing grade and, as I told you, I can't take another failure. If you want me to, I can explain why I can't stand much more of it. I'm on the ragged edge. So I thought if I told you the truth—you see, I'm just gambling that I can make a point or two by telling you the truth."

"Well, that is very decent of you," Lansing said. "Yes, extremely decent. But a slot machine . . ."

"It's in the Union building, sir. The Student Union."

"Yes. I know where the building is."

"Down in the basement area," said Jackson. "Just off the Rathskeller. There is a door to one side of the bar. No one ever goes in there, almost no one ever. It's a sort of storeroom, although it's not used. Not at the moment, it isn't. Maybe once it was. There are a few things in there. Things shoved in long ago and forgotten now. Over in one corner is this slot machine, or what looks like a slot machine. People who might happen to go into the room wouldn't give it a second look. It kind of huddles there, squatted in the corner. Anyone who did happen to see it would think that it was broken and—"

"Except, of course," said Lansing, "someone who knew what it really was."

"That's exactly right, sir. You mean you are believing me?"

"That's not what I said," Lansing told him. "I was simply helping you along. You were bogging down. I made the remark to put you back on track."

"Well, thank you, sir. That was kind of you. I *was* wandering a bit. You go over, sir, and put a quarter in the slot. The quarter wakes it up and it speaks to you, asking what you want, and—"

"You mean the slot machine speaks to you?"

"That's exactly right, sir. It asks you what you want and you tell it, and it tells you what it'll cost, and when you pay for it, it cranks it out for you. It can crank out a paper on almost any subject. You tell it what you want—"

"So that is what you did. Would you mind telling me how much it might have cost you?"

"Not at all. Two dollars. That's all."

"Dirt cheap," Lansing said.

"Yes, you're right, sir. It really is a bargain."

"Sitting here," said Lansing, "I'm thinking of how unfair it is that only a chosen few should know about this wondrous machine. Think of all of those hundreds sitting out there now, hunched above their desks, beating out their brains to scribble down a paragraph that has some meaning in it, when, if they only knew it, down there in the Union building there is an answer to all the problems that they face."

Jackson's face was frozen. "You don't believe me, sir. You think it's just a story. You think that I am lying."

"What did you think I'd think?"

"I really didn't know. It seems so simple to me because it really is the truth. You don't believe me when I tell the truth. I would have done better lying."

"Yes, Mr. Jackson, I think perhaps you might have."

"What are you going to do, sir?"

"Nothing at the moment. I'll give the matter some thought over the weekend. When I reach a decision, I will let you know."

Jackson rose stiffly and stalked out of the office. Lansing listened to him clumping down the hall until the sound of the clumping faded out. Then he placed Jackson's paper in a drawer and locked the desk. Picking up his briefcase, he headed for the door. Halfway there he swung about and dropped the briefcase on the desk top. Today he'd carry nothing home with him. The weekend was free, and he was going to keep it free.

Walking down the hall to the entrance that opened on the mall, he felt strange to be deprived of the briefcase. It had become a part of him, he thought. As much a part of him as his slacks and shoes. It was a part of the uniform he wore. For years he had carried it, and without it he felt slightly naked, as if it might somehow be indecent to expose himself to the public view without it clutched beneath his arm.

As he was walking down the building's broad stone steps, some-one hailed him from half a block away. He turned and saw that it was Andy Spaulding, who was hurrying up the sidewalk to inter-cept him.

Andy was an ancient and a trusted friend, but something of a windbag who at times could be slightly pompous. He was a sociol-ogist and had a good head on him, a head bubbling with ideas. The only trouble was that he never kept the ideas to himself. Whenever he could corner someone, he'd zero in on his cringing victim and talk his ideas out, clinging tightly to the lapels of the victim so that he could not get away, arguing with himself even as he expounded on that mighty tide of thought that surged within himself. But for all of this, he was a good and loyal companion, and Lansing was marginally pleased to see him.

He waited at the foot of the stairs until Andy came up.

"Let's wander over to the club," said Andy. "I'll stand you drinks."

THE FACULTY CLUB WAS on the top floor of the Student Union. The entire outer wall was a series of plate-glass windows looking out over a placid, well-tended little lake hemmed in by birch and pine.

Lansing and Andy sat at one of the tables next to the wall.

Spaulding lifted his glass and looked over it, speculatively, at Lansing.

"You know," he said, "I have been thinking the last few days how fortunate it would be if there should be visited upon us an-other medieval plague such as wiped out a third of Europe's popu-lation in the fourteenth century. Or another world war or even a second biblical flood—anything that would force us to start over once again, to erase some of the mistakes that we have made in the last thousand years or so, giving us the opportunity to arrive at some new social and economic principles. A chance to escape from mediocrity, the chance to organize ourselves more sanely. The work-and-wage system has become obsolete, it defeats itself, and still we cling to it. . . ."

"Don't you think," Lansing suggested mildly, "that the methods you suggest might prove rather drastic?"

Not meaning to argue by saying it. No one argued with Andy; he simply overrode anyone who tried. He rumbled on and on, in a voice that was just short of a monotone, marshaling his thoughts and cataloguing them, spreading them out for one to see, as one might fan out a deck of playing cards.

Not wanting to argue, not intending to, but entering into the spirit of the game, which required that at certain intervals Andy's victim or victims murmur some appropriate response.

"One of these days," said Andy, "we will suddenly realize—I have no thought how such a realization will come about—but we'll realize that our human effort so far is a futile effort because it is being pushed in the wrong direction. For centuries we have sought for knowledge, pursuing it in the name of reason, in the same reasonable manner as the ancient alchemists pursued their search for a method that would transform base metals into gold. We may find that all this knowledge is a dead end, that beyond a certain point all meaning ceases. In astrophysics we seem to be nearing that point. In a few years more, all the old and solid theories about space and time may collapse to nothing, leaving us standing in the rubble of shattered theories that we then will know are worthless and always have been worthless. There may then exist no reason to make further study of the universe. We may find that there are, in actuality, no universal laws, that the universe may operate on pure randomness, or worse. All this frantic study, all this pursuit of knowledge, not only about the universe but other things as well, has come about because we seek some advantage in it. But let us ask ourselves if we have the right to seek advantage. Basically we may have no right to expect a thing from the universe."

Lansing played the game. "You seem, this afternoon," he said, "to be more pessimistic than is your usual style."

"I am not the first," said Andy, "to indulge in this brand of pessimism, although mine is pitched from a slightly different viewpoint. There was a school of thinkers, some years ago, who advanced a similar argument. That was at a time when the cosmologists were convinced that we existed in a finite universe. At the moment the cosmological viewpoint is not that rigid. Right now we are undecided what kind of universe we're in. It may be finite, it may be infinite; no one really knows. It all depends on how much matter there may be in the universe, and estimates of the matter present fluctuate from year to year, if not from month to month. But that's neither here nor there. At the time, some years ago, when the conviction of a finite universe still obtained, the theory then was that scientific knowledge, based on a finite universe, must itself be finite. That somewhere there was a boundary to the universe and therefore a boundary to knowledge. There was only so much to be learned, and once we learned that much, that was the end of it. If knowledge was advancing and accumulating, doubling every fifteen years, as was estimated at the time, then it was said that it would not take long, perhaps a few centuries at the most, to reach a point at which the limiting factors of a finite universe would call a halt to any further accumulation of knowledge. The men of that day who supported this kind of thinking went so far as to conjure up exponential curves by which they professed to show at what point scientific and technological knowledge would finally reach an end."

"But you say," said Lansing, "that a finite universe no longer is an accepted fact—that it may be infinite."

"You miss the point," Andy rumbled. "I am not talking about the finiteness or infiniteness of the universe. I simply used it as an example to refute your charge of pessimism on my part. I was trying to explain that under other situations there were those who at times had voiced their own brands of pessimism.

"What I said to start with was that it would be a blessing should we be forced to undergo some catastrophic event that would cause us to change our thinking and to seek another way of life. For we are running down a dead-end street, and, what is more, we are running at full tilt. When we reach the dead end, we are going to pile up. Then we will come crawling back down that dead-end street, asking ourselves if there had not been a better way to do it. My point is that now, before we hit that dead end, we should stop right now and ask ourselves that question. . . ."

Andy kept on rumbling, but now Lansing blanked the rumbling out, hearing it only as a continuous mumble without words.

And this was the man, he thought, to whom he had meant to suggest a weekend hike. If he were to suggest it, more than likely Andy would agree, for this weekend his wife was in Michigan for a visit to her parents. On the hike, most probably, Andy would not be able to keep up the barrage of words and argument such as the barrage in which he was now engaged, but he'd talk; he'd talk unendingly, he would never cease his talk. On a hike an ordinary man would enjoy at least a modicum of peace and quiet, but such would not be the case with Andy. For Andy there was no such thing as peace and quiet; there was only roiling thought.

Lansing had thought, as well, that he might ask Alice Anderson to spend the weekend with him, but that had its drawbacks, too. On the last several occasions he had been with her, it had seemed he could detect in her eyes a glint of marital expectation, and that, should it come to a head, could be as disastrous as Andy's nonstop talking.

So scratch the both of them, he thought. He still could take a drive out into the hills. Or he could hole up in his apartment with the fire, the music and the reading. Perhaps, as well, there were a number of other ways in which to find enjoyment in the weekend.

He let Andy's words come in again.

"Have you ever given any thought," Andy was asking, "to historic crisis points?"

"I don't believe I ever have," said Lansing.

"History is replete with them," Andy told him. "And upon them, the sum of them, rests the sort of world we have today. It has occurred to me, at times, that there may be a number of alternate worlds . . ."

"I'm sure of it," said Lansing, not caring any longer. His friend's flight into fantasy had left him far behind. Beyond the window, the lake lay half in shadow; evening was closing in. Staring out the window at the lake, Lansing sensed a wrongness. Without knowing what it was, he knew that something had changed. Then slowly it came to him what it was: Andy had stopped talking.

He turned his head and stared at his friend across the table. Andy was grinning at him.

"I got an idea," he said.

"Yes?"

"With Mabel gone visiting her folks, why don't you and I plan something for tomorrow? I know where I can get a couple of football tickets."

"Sorry," Lansing said. "I'm all tied up."

◈ 3 ◈

LANSING STEPPED OUT OF the elevator on the first floor and headed for the door that opened on the mall. Andy, spotting an acquaintance at another table as they were leaving, had stopped to have a word with him. Doing his best not to seem to be doing so, Lansing had fled. But time was short, he told himself. The next elevator might bring Andy down, and by that time, he must be out of sight and reach. It would be like Andy, should he get hold of him again, to drag him off somewhere for dinner.

Halfway to the door he halted. The Rathskeller was just down those stairs to the right, and in an adjoining room, if Jackson had been right, was stored the fabulous slot machine. Lansing changed his course and scurried for the stairs.

He stormed mentally at himself as he went down the stairs. There'd be no storage room, and even if there were, there'd be no slot machine. Whatever had possessed Jackson to fabricate such a story he could not guess. It might have been, of course, nothing more than sheer impertinence, and while the student would be capable of that, it would stand to gain him nothing. Impertinence might be used to bait a faculty member, and there were faculty members who were often baited, who seemed to ask for it, most of them pompous fools who could benefit by a little taking down. But Lansing had always prided himself on his good relationship with his students. At times, he suspected, he was regarded as a soft touch. Thinking back on his relationship with Jackson, he realized he'd had no real trouble with him. At best Jackson had been a poor student, but that was neither here nor there. He had tried to treat the man with all courtesy and consideration, and at times had attempted to be helpful, although with a man like Jackson, he doubted that his attempts had been appreciated.

There were only a few people in the Rathskeller, most of them crowded around a table at the far side of the room. The man behind the bar was engaged in conversation with two students. When Lansing came in, no one noticed him.

There was a door opposite one end of the bar, exactly as Jackson had said. Lansing strode purposefully across the room to reach it. When he seized the knob of the door, it turned easily in his hand. He pushed the door open and stepped inside, then closed it quickly and stood with his back against it.

A single dim light bulb hung from a cord in the center of the ceiling. The room had an unfinished look, as if it were, indeed, what Jackson had said it was—a forgotten storage room. Cartons that had once held soft drinks were stacked against one wall, and a couple of filing cabinets and an ancient desk stood, not against a wall, but clustered in the center of the room. They had the look of having been placed there long ago with no attention paid them since.

In the far corner of the room stood a slot machine.

Lansing drew his breath in sharply. So far Jackson had been right. But he could have been right, Lansing reminded himself, about the room and have lied about the rest. That the slot machine stood where he had said it was afforded no proof that the rest of his story had been true.

The light was dim, and Lansing made his way with exaggerated caution across the room toward the waiting machine, alert against any unseen obstruction catching his foot and sending him sprawling.

He reached the machine and stood in front of it. It looked like any other slot machine, like any of the hundreds that lurked in corners all around the campus, waiting for the coins that finally would find their way into the fund that would care for the indigent and other unfortunates of the nation.

Lansing thrust his hand into a pocket and fingered through the coins that were there. He found a quarter, brought it out and fed it into the machine. The machine gulped it down with patent eagerness, and as it did, its face lighted up to show the cylinders with the signs upon them. It chuckled softly at him, a companionable chuckling, as if the two of them might share a joke known only to themselves.

He seized the lever and hauled it down with unnecessary force. The cylinders spun madly and twinkling lights blinked at him. Finally the cylinders stopped and nothing happened. Exactly what happened with all other slot machines, Lansing thought. It was no different from any of the others. It took your money and stood there laughing at you.

Then the machine spoke.

"What is it, sir, that you require?" it asked.

"Why, I'm not sure," said Lansing, startled. "Actually, I don't believe there is anything I need. I only came to verify the fact of your existence."

"That is unfortunate," said the slot machine. "I have many things to give. Are you sure there is nothing that you need?"

"Perhaps if you gave me some time to think about it."

"That's not possible," answered the machine. "People who come to me must have something in mind. They are not allowed to lolligag around."

"I am sorry," said Lansing.

"In any case, I am not so constructed as to give nothing for the coin you gave me," said the slot machine. "I must give you something. I'll tell you a story."

So it told Lansing a very filthy story about seven men and one woman marooned on a desert island. It was a foul story, bestial and crude and extremely obscene, with no saving social significance whatever.

Once the story was finished, Lansing, out of disgust, said nothing.

"You did not like my story?" asked the machine.

"Not overmuch," replied Lansing.

"Well, then, I've failed," said the machine. "I suspect that I misjudged you, and I cannot let it go at that. For your coin I must give you an item of some value."

It made a coughing sound and something metallic fell out of its innards into the bucket in the middle of it.

"Go ahead," said the machine. "Pick it up."

Lansing picked it up. It resembled a motel key. Two keys, one larger than the other, were attached to an oblong piece of plastic with a number and an address printed on it.

"I don't understand," said Lansing.

"Then attend most closely. Pay close attention to what I say. Are you listening?"

Lansing tried to speak, but stammered, then he said, "I am listening."

"Good. Now close attention, please. You go to the address. If you go during normal business hours, the front door will be unlocked. If you go at another time, the larger of the two keys will open it. The smaller key will open the door of room one thirty-six. Do you follow me so far?"

Lansing gulped. "Yes, I do."

"When you open the door of one thirty-six, you will find a dozen slot machines lined along a wall. Starting at the left, go to the fifth one—the fifth one: one, two, three, four, five—and insert a dollar in it. It will complete a certain transaction, and when that is done, you go to number seven and put another dollar in it. . . ."

"I put a dollar in," said Lansing. "Do I pull the lever?"

"Of course you pull the lever. Have you never played a slot machine?"

"Yes, of course I have. How could I avoid it?"

"Precisely," replied the slot machine. "Have you all of it in mind?"

"Yes, I think I have."

"Repeat it, then, to be sure you have."

Lansing repeated what the machine had told him.

"Fine," said the machine. "Keep it well in mind. I'd suggest you go very soon, so there's no chance of forgetting the instructions. You'll need two silver dollars. Do you have them by any chance?"

"I am sure I haven't."

"Well, then," said the slot machine, "here you are. We have no wish to place any roadblock in doing what we've asked of you. We are very anxious that you carry out the procedure as precisely as you're able."

Something plinked in the machine's bucket.

"Go on," urged the machine. "Go on and pick them up."

Lansing bent and picked up the two silver dollars. He put them in his pocket.

"You're sure that you have it well in mind?" asked the slot machine. "You have no questions?"

"Yes, I suppose one question. What is this all about?"

"I cannot tell you specifically," said the machine. "That would be against the rules. But I can assure you that whatever happens will be to your great advantage."

"And what would that be? *What* to my advantage?"

"That is all, Professor Lansing. That is all that I can tell you."

"How come you know my name? I didn't tell you who I was."

"I can assure you," said the machine, "that there was no need for you to tell me. I already knew you."

With that the machine clanked off, became dark and silent.

Lansing hauled off and kicked the machine. Not perhaps a kick at this machine alone, but at all the other machines that, through the years, had gulped down his quarters and then sat sneering at him.

The machine kicked back and caught him in the ankle. He did not see how it kicked him, but it did. He backed away from it. It was still sitting dark and silent.

Then Lansing turned about and went limping from the room.

4

AT HOME LANSING BUILT himself a drink and sat by a window, watching the dying of the day. The entire thing, he assured himself, was ridiculous. It could not have happened and yet he knew it had. To confirm it, he put a hand in his pocket and jingled the two silver dollars. It had been years since he had possessed a silver dollar, let alone two of them. He took them from his pocket and examined them. Both, he saw, were of recent date. Years before all the ones with an appreciable amount of silver in them had been grabbed up by speculators or coin collectors. The two keys, attached to the plastic tab, lay on a tabletop where he had tossed them. He put out a hand to pick them up, then drew it back without touching them.

Sitting quietly, with the drink in hand, not having tasted it yet, he ran all of it through his mind again and was amazed to find that he felt slightly dirty and ashamed, as if he had committed a certain kind of foulness. He tried to figure out why he felt that way, and there seemed no reason for it other than that his action in going to the room off the Rathskeller had been an action not quite normal. In all his life he had never slunk before and he had not this time, not physically at least, but in opening the door to that forgotten storeroom, he had had the sense of slinking, of performing an act that did not fit the dignity of his position as a member of the faculty of a small but well thought of—perhaps in some areas, a distinguished—college.

But that, he told himself, was not all of it. The matter of slinking, of feeling slightly dirty, was not all of it. Thinking of that, he knew that he had been holding back some factor even from himself. There was something that he didn't want to face, that he shrank from facing. The factor, he forced himself to admit, was the suspicion that he'd been had—although that was not exactly it. If it had been nothing but a joke, an infantile student prank, it would have extended no further than his slinking into the room to locate the slot machine. But the machine had talked to him— though even that, if well arranged, could have been made to come about as well by a tape, perhaps, that could have been activated when he pulled the lever.

It hadn't been that way, however. Not only had the machine talked with him, he had talked with it, had carried on a conversation with it. No student could engineer a tape that would carry on a logical conversation. And it had been logical; he had asked questions and the machine had answered; it had given him involved instructions.

So he had not imagined what had happened, and it had not been a student prank. The machine had even kicked back when he had kicked it: his ankle was still a little tender, although he no longer limped. And if it had not been a prank, no matter how ingeniously planned, then, for the love of God, what had it been?

He lifted the glass and drank down the whiskey, a thing he had never done before. He sipped at whiskey; he never drank it down. For one thing, he had no great tolerance for alcohol.

He rose from the chair and paced back and forth across the room. But pacing did nothing for him; it did not help him think. He put the empty glass on the sideboard, went back to the chair and sat down again.

So all right, he told himself, let's stop playing games, leave us quit the business of trying to protect ourself, let us drop the idea that we cannot allow ourself to look silly. Let's take it from the top and dig down to the bottom of it.

It had started with the student Jackson. None of it would have happened had it not been for Jackson. And even before Jackson, it had been Jackson's paper, a good paper, an unusually well-written paper, especially for a student such as Jackson—if it had not been for the phony sources cited. It had been the citing of the sources that had made him write the note and shove it in Jackson's mailbox. Or might he have called in the man in any case, obliquely hinting, perhaps, that he must have had some expert help to write so fine a paper? Lansing thought about that for a moment and decided that more than likely he wouldn't have. If Jackson wanted to cheat, that was not up to Lansing; Jackson would have been doing no more than cheating himself. Even if he had called him in on such grounds, the scene would have been an embarrassing and nonproductive confrontation, for there was no way in the world that cheating could be proved.

The conclusion, he told himself, was that he had been set up, most expertly set up, either by Jackson himself or by someone acting through Jackson. Jackson, it seemed to him, could not be astute enough, perhaps not energetic enough, to have set it up alone. Although there was no way to be sure. With a man like Jackson, one could never know.

And if he had been set up, no matter by whomever, what was the purpose of it?

There seemed to be no answer. Nothing that made sense. Nothing in any of it made sense.

Perhaps the way to handle it would be to forget about the entire thing, carry it no further. But could he do that, could he force himself to that course of nonaction? For the rest of his life he would wonder what it had been about; all his life he would wonder what might have happened if he had gone to the address upon the key tab and had done what the slot machine had told him.

He got up and found the bottle, picked up the glass to pour. Then he didn't pour. He put the bottle away and took the glass to the kitchen sink. He opened the refrigerator and took out an instant meal of beef and macaroni, popped it in the oven. He gagged at the thought of another meal of beef and macaroni, but what was a man to do? Certainly, at a time like this, he could not be expected to whip up a gourmet evening meal.

He went to the front door and picked up the evening paper. Deep in his easy chair, he turned on the light and opened the paper. There was little news. Congress still was piddling around with a gun-control bill and the President had forecast (again) the dire consequences if Congress should fail to approve the large military budget he had called for. The PTA still was raising hell about violence on television shows. Three new substances had been found that would cause cancer. Mr. Dithers had fired Dagwood again—not that the little twerp didn't have it coming to him. On the opinion page was a letter livid with righteous indignation because someone had messed up a crossword puzzle.

When the beef and macaroni was ready he ate it, barely tasting it, gagging it down because it was food. He unearthed a two-day-old cupcake for dessert, continued to sit at the kitchen table drinking coffee. As he drank his second cup he realized, finally, what he was doing. He was working hard at putting off something that he was going to do, no matter what, putting it off because he was not sure it was something that he should do, still responding to the nagging doubt that gnawed at him. But doubt or not, he was going to do it; he knew, without question, that finally he would do it. He'd never be able to live with himself if he didn't, all his days he would wonder what it was he had missed.

He rose from the kitchen table and went into the bedroom to get his car keys.

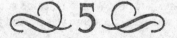

THE BUILDING STOOD ON a side street off an older business district that had lost its economic bloom some years before. A man was walking on the other side of the street a couple of blocks away, and in the mouth of an alley a dog was investigating three garbage cans, more than likely trying to make up its mind which one of the three would be the most profitable to tip over.

When Lansing tried the bigger key in the lock of the front door, it worked smoothly, and he stepped inside. A long hall, dimly lighted, ran down the length of the building. With no trouble he located 136. The smaller key worked as easily as the larger one had, and he stepped into the room. Across the room stood the dozen slot machines lined against the wall. The fifth from the left, the machine he'd met a few hours before had said. He counted from the left and strode across the room to confront number five. Fishing in his pocket, he brought out one of the silver dollars and fed it in the slot. The machine leaped into joyous life, clicking at him when he pulled the lever. The dials went spinning in that crazy fashion encountered nowhere else than in a slap-happy slot machine. One dial stopped and another jumped and then fell back and the third came to a stop with a sudden clunk. Lansing saw that the characters that had lined up on the dial were all the same. The machine made a coughing sound and a flood of golden coins, each of them the size of a dollar, came pouring from the pay-off chute. They filled the bucket and cascaded onto the floor as the golden flood still came gushing from the chute. Some of the coins struck on their rims and went rolling like glittering wheels all about the floor.

Again the dials were spinning (spinning without another dollar having been fed into the slot), and again they came thudding to a halt. This time also the symbols on the dials were all alike, and the machine, quite nonchalantly, released another gush of coins.

Lansing stood amazed and a little jittery, for this was a thing unheard of. There was no such thing, there *could* be no such thing as two jackpots in a row.

When the machine clicked off and stood dumb and stolid, he waited for a moment, half expecting it to go into its act again and produce yet another jackpot. With a machine such as this, he told himself, anything was possible; there was no end to the miracles of which it was capable.

It did not repeat itself, however, and when he was fairly sure it wouldn't, he scooped the coins out of the bucket and dropped them into a jacket pocket, then got down on hands and knees to collect those that lay scattered on the floor. One of them he held so that the light struck it fully, and he examined it. There was little doubt that it was gold. For one thing it was heavier than a silver dollar. It was a well-made coin, bright and polished, hefty and satisfying to the hand, but no such coin as he had ever seen before. On one side was engraved a cube that stood upon a cross-hatched area that probably represented ground. The other side bore the representation of what seemed to be a spindly tower. That was all. There were no words, no value designation.

He rose to his feet and stared about the room. The machine that he had talked with had told him to put the second dollar in the seventh machine. He might as well, he thought. The transaction with the fifth machine had turned out not so badly, and his luck might continue with the seventh.

He moved down the line to number seven. After he put out his hand to insert the second dollar, he pulled it back. Why take the chance? he asked himself. Maybe number five had only set him up. The Lord only knew what would happen if he played number seven. And yet, he thought, if now he should turn about and walk away with a pocketful of gold, he'd never know and he'd never quit questioning himself. He'd not have an easy moment, he would always wonder.

"The hell with it," he said aloud and dropped the dollar. The machine gulped it down and made a clanking sound, and the lights came on the dials. He chugged the lever down, and the dials began their crazy spinning. Then the lights went out and the machine went away. So did the room as well.

He stood upon a path in a woodland glen. Tall, massive trees hemmed him in, and from a little distance off he heard the liquid chatter of a singing brook. Except for the brook there was no sound, and there was nothing stirring.

And now he knew, he told himself. He might have been better off if he'd walked away from number seven, although of that there was no certainty. For this transformation to a woodland glen might be as delightful a circumstance as winning all the gold, although even as he thought it he couldn't quite bring himself to believe it.

Don't move, he told himself. Have a look around before you stir from where you're standing. And don't give in to panic—for already, in these first few seconds, he had caught the smell of panic.

He had a look around. In front of him the ground rose up, rather gently, and from the sound of it the brook could not be far away. The trees were oak and maple. Their leaves were turning color. Ahead of him a squirrel scurried across the path that angled up the hill. After the squirrel had disappeared Lansing could mark its progress by the rustling of the fallen leaves disturbed by the small tornado of its passage. Once the sound of the squirrel had faded out, the silence (except for the chatter of the brook) closed in again. Now, however, the silence did not seem so heavy. There were soft noises now—the noise of a falling leaf, the almost indiscernible scurryings as little creatures of the forest made their way about, other faint sounds that he could not identify.

He spoke to number seven and whatever (or whoever) else had operated to put him where he was.

"All right," he said, "what is this all about? If you've had your fun, let's put an end to it."

There was, however, no end put to it. The woodland glen stayed on. There was not the slightest indication that he'd been heard by number seven or, in fact, by anything.

It was unbelievable, he thought, and yet all of it had been unbelievable from the very start. This was actually no more unbelievable than that a slot machine had talked. If he ever got back, he promised himself, he'd hunt up the student Jackson and, with his bare hands alone, dismember him piece by painful piece.

If he ever got back!

Up until this moment he had thought of the situation as only temporary, subconsciously believing that any minute now he'd pop back into the room with all the slot machines lined against the wall. But what if that didn't happen? He sweated thinking of it, and the panic that had been lurking back there somewhere in the trees swooped suddenly on him and he ran. Ran unthinkingly, with reason gone to pot—running blindly, with terror riding him and no room for thinking of anything but terror.

Finally he stubbed his toe against a small obstruction in the path and went blundering into a tree, falling to the ground. He did not try to get up. He huddled where he had fallen, out of breath, gasping to pump air into his lungs.

While he lay there, some of the terror seeped away. Nothing chewed on him with long, pointed fangs. No horror drooled on him. Nothing was happening.

Regaining his breath, he pulled himself erect. He still was on the path and he saw that he had reached the top of a ridge, with the path running along the ridge. The forest was as heavy as it had been before, but the chattering brook was gone.

So now what did he do? Now that he'd caved in to panic and had, to at least some degree, recovered from it, what should be his next move? There was no point in going back to the place in the woodland glen where he first had found himself. There was a good chance, he realized, that even if he tried to do so, he might not be able to recognize it.

What he needed was information. First of all he needed to know where he was. He had to know that before he could even hope to start getting back to the college. This place, he thought, had a New England look. Somehow he had been moved in space by the slot machine, although perhaps not very far. If he could find out where he was and could find a phone, he could put in a call to Andy and ask that he pick him up. If he followed the path it was more than likely that in a little time he'd come upon some habitation.

He started along the path. It was easy to follow, for it appeared to be a trail that was used fairly often. At each turn he looked eagerly ahead, hoping that he might sight a house or meet some hiker who could tell him where he was.

The terrain looked like New England. The forest, though fairly heavy, was a pleasant forest. It had about it no hint of troll or goblin or other unpleasant denizen. And the season was the same as it had been in the place that he had come from. It had been autumn back at the college and it was autumn here, but there was one thing that bothered him a lot. Night had fallen on the campus when he had decided to hunt up the dozen slot machines, but here it still was afternoon, although by now it must be getting rather late in the afternoon.

There was another thought that bothered him. If he should fail to find a place where he could spend the night, he'd have to spend it in the open, and he was not prepared for that. He did not wear the sort of clothing that would protect him from the night-time chill, and there was no possibility of starting a fire. Since he did not smoke, he never carried matches. He looked at his watch, not realizing until he looked at it that the time it showed would mean nothing here. Not only had he been displaced in space, but apparently in time as well. While that had a scary sound to it, he was not, at the moment, too upset by it. He had other worries on his mind, and the foremost was that he might not find shelter for the night.

He had been walking for a couple of hours, or so it seemed. He wished that he had looked at his watch earlier, for while it did not tell the time of day in this place, at least it could have told him how long he'd been upon the trail.

Was it possible that he was in a wilderness area? That was the only thing he could think of that would explain the human emptiness. Under ordinary circumstances he should by now have come upon a farmhouse.

The sun was getting low in the sky and in another hour or two it would be getting dark. He started to run, then caught hold of himself. That was not the way to do it; running might bring on panic and he could not afford that now. But he did increase his pace. An hour went past, and still he had found no habitation or any sign there was anyone around. The sun was sinking into the horizon line and darkness was fast approaching.

Another half hour, he told himself, making a bargain with himself. If nothing showed up in another thirty minutes he'd have to do what he could to prepare against the night—either find some sort of natural shelter or fix up the best shelter he could.

Darkness came on more rapidly than he thought it would, and before the half hour had passed he began watching for a place to hole up in the woods. Then ahead of him he saw a gleam of light. He stopped, holding his breath, to look at it, to be certain that it was a light, to do nothing that might scare it off. He moved a few feet forward in the hope he'd get a better look at it and it was there; it was a light, there could be no doubt of it.

He moved toward it, glancing away just long enough to make sure that he was still on the path. As he moved the gleam became brighter and more certain, and he felt a surge of thankfulness welling up in him.

The forest opened into a clearing and he saw the loom of a house in the deepening dusk. The light came from several windows in one end of the building, and he saw that from a massive chimney came a thin trickle of smoke.

In the darkness he ran into a picket fence, having missed the path in his eagerness to reach the house, and cautiously felt his way along it until he came to a gate. The gate was hinged on a heavy gatepost that was taller than it needed to be. Looking up, he saw the reason for its height. A crossbeam was attached to it, and from the beam a sign hung from two lengths of chain.

Squinting at it, Lansing made out that it was an inn sign, but the night had deepened so that he could not discern the name.

6

FIVE PEOPLE, FOUR MEN and a woman, were sitting at a heavy oak table in front of a blazing fireplace. When Lansing came through the door and closed it behind him, all of them turned their heads to look at him. One of them, a grossly fat man, levered himself from his chair and waddled across the room to greet him.

"Professor Lansing, we are so glad that you have arrived," he said. "We have been worrying about you. There is still one other. We hope nothing has befallen her."

"One other? You knew that I was coming?"

"Oh, yes, some hours ago. I knew when you started out."

"I fail to understand," said Lansing. "No one could have known."

"I am your host," said the fat man. "I operate this dingy inn as best I can for the comfort and convenience of those who travel in these parts. Please, sir, come over to the fire and warm yourself. The Brigadier, I am sure, will give you his chair next to the hearth stone."

"Most happily," said the Brigadier. "I am slightly singed from sitting here so snug against the blaze."

He rose, a portly man of commanding figure. As he moved, the firelight glinted off the medals pinned upon his tunic.

Lansing murmured, "I thank you, sir."

But before he could move to take the chair, the door opened and a woman stepped into the room.

Mine Host waddled forward a step or two to greet her.

"Mary Owen," he said. "You are Mary Owen? We are so glad you're here."

"Yes, I am Mary Owen," said the woman. "And I am more glad to be here than you are to have me. But can you tell me where I am?"

"Most assuredly," said Mine Host. "You are at the Cockadoodle Inn."

"What a strange name for an inn," said Mary Owen.

"As for that I cannot say," said Mine Host. "I had no hand in naming it. It was already named when I came here. As you may note, it is an ancient place. It has sheltered, in its time, many noble folk."

"What place is this?" asked Mary Owen. "I mean the country. What is this place—what nation, what province, what country?"

"Of that I can tell you nothing," said Mine Host. "I have never heard a name."

"And I have never heard of such a thing," said Mary. "A man who knows not where he lives."

"Madam," said the man dressed all in black who stood next to the Brigadier, "it is passing strange indeed. He is not making sport of you. He told the same to us."

"Come in, come in," urged Mine Host. "Move closer to the fire. The gentlemen who have been here for some time, soaking up the heat, will make way for you and Professor Lansing. And now that we all are here, I shall go into the kitchen and see how supper's doing."

He waddled off in hurried fashion and Mary Owen came over to stand beside Lansing.

"Did I hear him call you professor?" she asked.

"Yes, I think he did. I wish he hadn't. I'm seldom called professor. Even my students—"

"But you are one, aren't you?"

"Yes, I am. I teach at Langmore College."

"I've never heard of it."

"It's a small school in New England."

The Brigadier spoke to the two of them. "Here are two chairs next to the fire. The Parson and I have held them overlong."

"Thank you, General," said Mary.

The man who had been sitting quietly opposite the Brigadier and the Parson rose and touched Lansing gently on the arm.

"As you can see," he said, "I am not a human. Would you take it unkindly if I welcomed you to our little circle?"

"Why, no—" said Lansing, then stopped to stare at the welcomer. "You are . . ."

"I am a robot, Mr. Lansing. You've not seen one before?"

"No, I never have."

"Oh, well, there are not many of us," the robot said, "and we're not on all the worlds. My name is Jurgens."

"I'm sorry I had not noticed you before," said Lansing. "Despite the fire, the room is rather dim and there was a good deal going on."

"Would you, Mr. Lansing, be, by any chance, a crackpot?"

"I don't think so, Jurgens. I have never thought about it. Why do you ask?"

"I have a hobby," said the robot, "of collecting crackpots. I have one who thinks he's God whenever he gets drunk."

"That lets me out," said Lansing. "Drunk or sober, I never think I'm God."

"Ah," said Jurgens, "that's but one road crackpottery can take. There are many others."

"I have no doubt there are," said Lansing.

The Brigadier took it upon himself to introduce all the people at the table. "I am Everett Darnley," he said. "Brigadier for Section Seventeen. The man standing next to me is Parson Ezra Hatfield, and the lady at the table is Poetess Sandra Carver. The one standing next to Mr. Lansing is the robot Jurgens. And now that we all know one another, let us take our seats and imbibe some of the pleasing liquor that has been set out for us. The three humans of us have been sampling it and it is passing good."

Lansing came around the table and sat in a chair next to Mary Owen. The table, he saw, was of solid oak and yeoman carpentry. Three flaring candles had been placed upon it, and on it as well were three bottles and a tray of mugs. Now for the first time he saw the others in the room. At a table in a far corner sat four men intent on a game of cards.

The Brigadier pulled two mugs in front of him and poured from one of the bottles. He passed one of the mugs to Mary and slid the other across the table to Lansing.

"I hope the supper now in preparation," he said, "shall prove as tasty as these potables."

Lansing tasted. The liquor went down smoothly with a comforting warmth. He settled more solidly in the chair and took a long pull at the mug.

"We had been sitting here before you came," the Brigadier said to Mary and Lansing, "wondering if, when the other two arrived—which are the two of you—they might have some idea of what *is* going on. It's apparent from what you said, Miss Owen, that you don't. How about you, Lansing?"

"Not an inkling," said Lansing.

"Our host claims that he knows nothing," said the Parson, speaking sourly. "He says he only operates the inn and that he asks no questions. Principally, I gather, because there is no one to ask questions of. I think the man is lying."

"You judge him too quickly and too harshly," said the poetess, Sandra Carver. "He has an honest and an open face."

"He looks like a pig," the Parson said. "And he allows abominations to take place beneath his roof. Those men playing cards—"

"You've been slopping up the booze," said the Brigadier, "mug for mug with me."

"Drinking is no sin," the Parson said. "The Bible says a little wine for the stomach's sake . . ."

"Pal," said the Brigadier. "This stuff isn't wine."

"Perhaps if we calmed down a bit and compared what we know of the situation," said Mary, "we might arrive at some understanding. Who exactly are we and how we got here and any thoughts we may have upon the matter."

"That is the first sensible thing that anyone has said," the Parson told them. "Has anyone objection to telling who they are?"

"I have none," said Sandra Carver, speaking so softly that the others were forced to listen closely to catch her words. "I am a certified poetess in the Academy of Very Ancient Athens and I can speak fourteen tongues, although I only write or sing in one—one of the dialects of Former Gaul, the most expressive language in the entire world. How I came here I do not entirely understand. I was listening to a concert, a new composition played by an orchestra from the Land Across the Western Sea, and in all my life I've never heard anything so powerful and so poignant. It seemed to lift me out of my corporeal body and launch my spirit into another place and when I came back again into my body, both I, my soaring spirit, and my body were in a different place, a pastoral place of astounding beauty. There was a path and I followed it and—"

"The year?" asked the Parson. "What year, pray?"

"I don't understand your question, Parson."

"What year was it? Your measurement of time."

"The sixty-eighth of the Third Renaissance."

"No, no, I don't mean that. Anno Domini—the year of Our Lord."

"What lord do you speak of? In my day there are so many lords."

"How many years since the birth of Jesus?"

"Jesus?"

"Yes, the Christ."

"Sir, I have never heard of Jesus nor of Christ."

The Parson appeared on the verge of apoplexy. His face became red and he pulled at his collar as if fighting for air. He tried to speak and strangled on his words.

"I'm sorry if I have distressed you," said the poetess. "I did it unknowingly. I would not willingly cause offense."

"It's all right, my dear," said the Brigadier. "It's only that our friend the Parson is suffering culture shock. Before all this is over he may not be the only one. I begin to catch a glint of the situation in which we find ourselves. It is, for me, entirely unbelievable, but as we go on it may become at least marginally believable, although I have the feeling that most of us may come to that realization with a great deal of difficulty."

"You are saying," said Lansing, "that all of us may come from different cultures and perhaps from different worlds, although I am not sure about the worlds." Surprised to hear himself speaking so and thinking back to the time, a few hours before, when Andy Spaulding, speculating idly and certainly meaning none of it, had prattled about alternate worlds, although, he recalled, he had blanked out the prattle.

"But we all speak English," said Mary Owen, "or we can speak English. How many languages, Sandra, did you say you spoke?"

"Fourteen," said the poetess. "Some of them rather badly."

"Lansing voiced a good preliminary grasp of what may have happened to us," said the Brigadier. "I congratulate you, sir, on your sharp perception. It may not be exactly as you say, but you may be nibbling close to truth. As to the English that we speak, let us speculate a little further. We are one little band, all speaking English. Might there not be other bands? French bands, Latin bands, Greek bands, Spanish bands—small groups of people who can get along together because they speak a common language?"

The Parson shouted, "That is sheer speculation! It is madness to suggest, to even think, of such a concept as the two of you seem to be putting together. It goes against everything that is known of Heaven or of Earth."

"The knowledge that we have of Heaven and of Earth," the Brigadier said, tartly, "is a mere pinch against the entire truth. We cannot blink our being here, and certainly our being here and the method of our coming does not square with any knowledge that we have."

"I think that what Mr. Lansing told us . . ." said Mary. "Lansing, what is your Christian name? We can't go on calling you Lansing."

"My name is Edward."

"Thank you. I think that Edward's suggestion may be a tad romantic, even visionary. But if we are to seek the knowledge of where we are and the reason for our being here, it would seem that we may be forced to strike out in some new directions in our thinking. I happen to be an engineer, and I live in a highly technical society. Any sort of thinking that projects itself beyond the known or the solidly theoretical grates upon my nerves. There is nothing in any methodolgy that I can summon up that would provide any explanation. There may be others of you who are better based to suggest an explanation. How about our robot friend?"

"I also have a technical background," said Jurgens, "but I am not aware of any methodology—"

"Why do you ask him?" shouted the Parson. "You call him a robot and that is a word that slips easily off the tongue, but when you come right down to it, he is no more than a machine, a mechanical contrivance."

"You go too far," said the Brigadier. "I happen to live in a world where mechanical contrivances have fought a war for years and have fought it intelligently and well, with an imagination that sometimes surpasses a human's."

"How horrible," said the poetess.

"You mean, I suppose," said the Brigadier, "that war is horrible."

"Well, isn't it?" she asked.

"War is a natural human function," said the Brigadier. "There is an aggressive, competitive urge in the race that responds to conflict. If this were not so, there would not have been so many wars."

"But the human suffering. The agony. The blasted hopes."

"In my day it has become a game," said the Brigadier. "As it was with many early human tribes. The Indians of the Western Continent looked upon it as a game. A young tribesman did not become a man until he'd counted his first coup. All that is manly and noble stems from war. There might have been times in the past when excessive zeal resulted in some of the consequences that you mention. Today little blood is spilled. We play it as one plays a game of chess."

"Using robots," said Jurgens.

"We don't call them robots."

"Perhaps not. Mechanicals. Mechanicals that have personal identity and the ability to think."

"That's correct. Well built, magnificently trained. They help us plan as well as fight. My staff is very heavily weighed with mechanicals. In many ways their grasp of a military situation is at times superior to mine."

"And the field of battle is littered with mechanicals?"

"Yes, of course. We salvage those we can."

"And fix them up and send them out again?"

"Why, certainly," said the Brigadier. "In war you conserve your resources very jealously."

"General," said Jurgens, "I do not think I would like to live in the kind of world you have."

"What is your kind of world? If you wouldn't want to live in my kind of world, tell me the kind of world you do live in."

"A peaceful world. A kindly world. We have compassion for our humans."

"It sounds sickening," said the Brigadier. "You have compassion for your humans. *Your* humans?"

"In our world there are few humans left. We take care of them."

"Much as it goes against my grain," said the Parson, "I'm coming to the conclusion that Edward Lansing may be right. Listening, it becomes apparent that we all *do* come from different worlds. A cynical world that regards war as a simple game—"

"It is not a simple game," said the Brigadier. "At times it is complex."

"A cynical world," said the Parson, "that regards war as a complex game. A world of poetess and poet, of music and academies. A world in which robots take kindly care of humans. And in your world, my lady, a society where a woman may become an engineer."

"And what is wrong with that?" asked Mary.

"The wrongness is that women should not be engineers. They should be faithful wives, competent keepers of the home, efficient raisers of children. These activities are the natural sphere of women."

"In my world women are not only engineers," said Mary. "They are physicists, physicians, chemists, philosophers, paleontologists, geologists, members of the board of great corporations, presidents of prestigious companies, lawyers and lawmakers, heads of executive agencies. The list could be greatly added to."

Mine Host came bustling up to the table.

"Make way," he said. "Make way for supper. I hope you'll find it to your liking."

THE MEAL WAS FINISHED, a most satisfactory one. Now, the table pushed back, they sat in front of the blazing fire. Back of them, in the other corner of the room, the card players were hunched above their table.

Lansing made a thumb over his shoulder in their direction. "What about them? They did not join us at supper."

Mine Host made a gesture of contempt. "They will not leave their play. We served them sandwiches and they continued with their game. They will not cease until early in the morning and then be up again after little sleep. Then they hold a prayer breakfast and go back to the cards."

"To whom do they pray?" asked Mary. "The gods of chance, perhaps."

Mine Host shook his head. "I do not know. I have never eavesdropped."

"It seems to me you are a most incurious man," said the Parson. "You know less of common matters than any man I have ever met. You do not know what land we're in. You do not know why we're here or what we're supposed to do."

"I tell you true," said Mine Host. "I do not know these things and I have never asked."

"Could it be true that there is no one for you to ask? No one *we* can ask?"

"I think that is a fair statement," said Mine Host.

"So we've been dumped here," said Mary, "without knowledge and without instructions. Someone, or some agency, must have dumped us here for whatever reason. Do you have the slightest idea of—"

"I have none whatsoever, my lady. I can tell you this—the other groups that have come here have left this place, following an ancient road to seek out what lies beyond."

"So there have been other groups?"

"Oh, yes. Very many of them. But at long intervals."

"And do they return?"

"Seldom. Only stragglers now and then."

"What happens when the stragglers return?"

"That I do not know. I close up for winter."

"The ancient road you speak of," said the Brigadier. "Can you tell us more of it? Where it might go or what's to be found along the way?"

"Only rumors. There are rumors of a city and rumors of a cube."

"Rumors only?"

"That is all."

"A cube?" asked Lansing.

"That is all I know," said Mine Host. "I know naught other of it. And now a matter that I hesitate to mention, but that must be done."

"What is it?" asked the Parson.

"It is the matter of payment. I must be paid for my lodging and the meals, and I run a small commissary from which you might wish to purchase food and other items before you set out upon your way."

"I have no money on me," said the Brigadier. "I seldom carry any. Had I known I was coming here, I would have obtained some cash."

"I have but a few bills and a handful of change," the Parson told Mine Host. "As are all the clergy in my country, I am very poor."

"I could write you a check," said Mary.

"I am sorry. I can accept no checks. I must have cold, hard cash."

Sandra Carver complained, "I do not understand all this. Cash and checks?"

"He is talking about money," said the Brigadier. "You must know of money."

"But I don't. Pray tell me—what is money?"

The Brigadier answered gently. "It is a token, either paper or metal, that has a stated value. It is used to pay for goods or services. You must use it, certainly, to buy what you need, your food and clothing."

"We do not buy," she said. "We give. I give my poems and my songs. Others give me food and clothing as I have need of them."

"A perfect communistic society," said Lansing.

"I see no reason for all of you to look so shocked and puzzled," Jurgens said. "Sandra's way is the only sensible way for a society to operate."

"Which means, I suppose," said the Brigadier, "that you have no money, either."

He turned to Mine Host and said, "Sorry, old chap. It seems you're out of luck."

"Hold up for a moment," said Lansing. To Mine Host he said, "Does it sometimes happen that only one member of a group carries money? Money possibly supplied by the agency that has initiated each particular wild goose chase?"

"It sometimes happens that way," said Mine Host. "As a matter of fact, it almost always happens that way."

"Then why didn't you say so?"

"Well," said Mine Host, licking his lips, "a man can never know. And he must be careful."

"Do I gather," asked the Parson, "that you, Mr. Lansing, are the treasurer for our group?"

"It would seem so," Lansing said. "I wondered at the time."

He took one of the golden coins out of his jacket pocket and flipped it to the innkeeper.

"That is honest gold," he said, not knowing if it was or not. "How far can that coin cover us?"

"Two more like this," said Mine Host, "will take care of the meal tonight, the night's lodgings and tomorrow's breakfast."

"I think, Mr. Lansing," said the Parson, "that he may be gouging you."

"I think so, too," said Lansing. "I think the one coin might cover all of it. But out of sheer generosity, I'll give you another, but no more."

Mine Host whined. "With costs going up and labor so expensive . . ."

"One more," said Lansing, holding up the second coin, "but that is all."

"All right," said Mine Host. "The next group may prove more generous."

The Parson said, "I still think it's too much."

Lansing flipped the coin, and the innkeeper grabbed it with a swoop of his flabby hand.

"It well may be too much," Lansing told the Parson, "but I do not wish him saying that we cheated him."

Mine Host got slowly to his feet. "When you wish to retire," he said, "call me and you'll be shown to your rooms."

When he was gone Mary said, "What a strange way to finance an expedition. You could have said nothing, Edward, and hung onto the money."

"It wouldn't have washed," he said. "He knew that someone had it."

"It appears, from this matter of the money," she said, "that someone sent us here."

"Or something."

"That is right. Or something. They must want us here quite badly to have paid our way."

"In that case wouldn't you think they would have told us what they wanted?"

"Yes, one would. We are dealing with strange people."

"Mr. Lansing, it may be none of our business," said the Brigadier, "but I wonder if you'd mind telling us how you got the money."

"I'd be glad to," Lansing said. "First of all, have any of you ever heard of a slot machine?"

It seemed none of them had.

"Well, then," said Lansing, "I'll tell you a tale of students and of slot machines and of an eccentric friend of mine."

He told them and they listened, paying close attention.

"I must say," said the Brigadier when Lansing had finished, "that your experience was excessively involved."

"All the time that it was happening," said Lansing, "I had the feeling that I was being taken. And yet I had to go ahead with it. My curiosity drove me to it."

"Perhaps it was a good thing that you were driven to it," said the Brigadier. "Otherwise the rest of us would have been stranded here without a penny to our name."

"It is strange," said Sandra, "how differently we were translated to this place—I through listening to music, you through the agency of these things you call slot machines."

"I was done in," said Mary, "by, of all things, a blueprint. A fellow engineer brought it to me, claiming there was something in it that he did not understand. He insisted I have a look at it, and he pointed with his finger to where he wanted me to look. It was nothing I had ever seen before and as I struggled to make some sense of it, I was caught up in the configuration that was represented on it and the next I knew I was standing in a forest. I am struck by the coincidence that both Edward and myself were trapped by another human—in his case a student, in my case another engineer. This would argue that whoever, or whatever, did this to us has agents on our worlds."

"For a time I thought," Lansing said to Mary, "that you and I might be from the same world, the same culture. Our societies seemed very much the same. But I was looking at you when I said a certain word and I could tell that you were puzzled by it. It seemed you didn't know what communistic meant."

"I know the word," she said. "I was surprised by the context in which you used it. You seemed to make it a proper noun, as if a communistic society might exist."

"On my world it does."

"There was, I am sure," said the Parson, "no human provocation for what happened to me. I saw the Glory. I had been seeking it for years. I had felt at times that I was close upon it, but each time it eluded me. And then, standing in a turnip field, I saw it, brighter and more glorious than I had thought it would be. I held up my hands to worship it, and as I did it became larger and brighter and I fell into it."

"It seems to me the evidence is clear," said the Brigadier, "that each of us is from a different world—different, but human worlds. It would seem, as well, that no further evidence is needed. The testimony of the four of you is quite sufficient. You will pardon me, I hope, if I do not join with you in telling by what strange circumstance I happen to be here."

"I, for one, would take it rather badly," said the Parson. "The rest of us have spoken fully—"

"It's all right," said Lansing, interrupting. "If the General does not want to bare his soul, it's quite all right with me."

"But in a band of brothers . . ."

"We're not brothers, Parson. There are two women here. Even in the sense you mean it, I wonder if we're brothers."

"If we are," said the robot, Jurgens, "we must prove it on the road ahead."

"If we take that road," the Parson said.

"I, for one, am taking it," said the Brigadier. "I would die of boredom, cooped up in this inn. This miserable innkeeper of ours spoke of a city up ahead. Certainly a city of any sort would offer better accommodation and entertainment, and perhaps even more instruction, than this pig sty of a place."

"He also mentioned a cube," said Sandra. "I wonder what it could be. Never before have I heard anything described simply as a cube."

THEY WERE LATE IN getting started. Breakfast had been un-
accountably delayed and there had been much haggling over the
purchase of items they would need upon the road—food, clothing,
hiking shoes, sleeping bags, belt knives, hatchets, matches, cooking gear, a long list of equipment. The Brigadier had insisted on a
gun and had become quite worked up when informed by the innkeeper that no weapons were for sale.

"That's ridiculous!" stormed the Brigadier. "Who ever heard of
an expedition starting out without an adequate defense?"

Mine Host attempted to reassure him. "There's no danger along
the way. There is no need to fear."

"How would you know that?" demanded the Brigadier. "When
we questioned you on other matters you were singularly bereft of
knowledge. Knowing nothing else, how can you be so certain that
there is no danger?"

When it came time to pay for the supplies, Lansing got down to
painful dickering. The innkeeper seemed determined to make an
extra profit to compensate for his failure at extracting a higher
price for their lodging. In his efforts Lansing was backed up vehe-
mently by the Parson, who was of the general opinion that everyone was out to gouge him.

Finally the transaction was concluded to no one's liking and
they started out.

The Brigadier led the way, with the Parson close behind him.
Mary and Sandra followed, while Jurgens and Lansing brought up
the rearguard. Jurgens carried a heavy pack that was jammed with
food. He alone of them had needed almost nothing—no food or
sleeping bag, for he neither ate nor slept. He had no need, as well,

of clothing, but he did choose a hatchet and a knife, both of which were bound by a belt about his waist.

"I am intrigued by your first words to me," Lansing said to the robot as they walked along together. "You asked me if I was a crackpot. You said you collected crackpots. Yet later on you said that in your world there are few humans left. If that is the case—"

"I made a bad joke, only," the robot told him. "I am sorry now I did. I don't actually collect humans. What I do is collect crackpot humans I find in literature."

"You make a list of crackpot characters?"

"Oh, I do more than that. I construct miniatures of them. Miniatures of the kind of humans I conceive they would have been in actual life."

"A doll collector, then?"

"More than a doll collection, Mr. Lansing. They move about and talk, they act out little scenes. It is most amusing. I use them by the hour for my entertainment. Also, I think I may get some further insight into the human condition from the interplay among them."

"Mechanical dolls?"

"I suppose you could say so. Basically mechanical. Although in some of their aspects they are biological."

"That is amazing," said Lansing, somewhat shocked. "You create living beings."

"Yes. They are alive in many different ways."

Lansing said nothing further, reluctant to expand upon the subject.

The road was little more than a trail. Occasionally the double ruts cut by wheeled vehicles could be seen, but in most places the wheel traces were obliterated by erosion, with grass and creeping vines growing over them.

For a time the road climbed through forestland that after a couple of hours of travel began to dwindle, gradually giving way to a rolling, grassy countryside, spotted with small groves of trees. The day, at first comfortably warm, grew hotter as the hour of noon approached.

The Brigadier, still in the lead, halted at a grove, carefully let himself to the ground and leaned against a tree.

As the others came up, he explained the stop. "I thought we had best halt in consideration of the ladies. The sun has proved uncommonly warm."

He hauled a large, white handkerchief from a tunic pocket and wiped his streaming face. Then he hoisted his canteen around in front of him, unscrewed the cap and gulped at the water.

"We can rest for a while," said Lansing. "If we want to take the time, we could eat some lunch."

The Brigadier responded eagerly. "A capital idea," he said.

Jurgens already had his pack open, was slicing cold meat and cheese. He found a tin of hard biscuits and opened it.

"Should I make some tea?" he asked.

"We haven't the time," said the Parson. "We should be pushing on."

"I'll rustle up some wood," said Lansing, "so we can have a fire. I saw a dead tree back a ways. Some tea would be good for all of us."

"There is no need of that," said the Parson. "We have no need of tea. We could eat cheese and biscuits as we walk along."

"Sit down," said the Brigadier. "Sit down and rest yourself. Rushing along as we have been is no way to approach a trek. You break yourself in slowly and take your time to start with."

"I'm not tired," snapped the Parson. "I need no breaking in."

"But the ladies, Parson!"

"The ladies are doing fine," said the Parson. "It's you who's caving in."

They were still bickering when Lansing went down the road to find the dead tree he had spotted earlier. It was not as far down the trail as he had thought, and he quickly settled down to work, chopping dry branches into easy lengths for carrying. It would be only a short noontime fire and not much fuel would be needed. A small armload should do.

A dry stick cracked behind him and he swung around. Mary stood a few feet from him.

"I hope that you don't mind," she said.

"Not at all, glad of company."

"It was getting uncomfortable up there—the two of them still quarreling. There'll be trouble between them, Edward, before the trip is done."

"They are two driven men."

"And very much alike."

He laughed. "They'd kill you if you told them so. Each thinks he despises the other."

"Perhaps they do. Being so much alike, perhaps they do. Do they see themselves in one another? Self-hate, perhaps."

"I don't know," said Lansing. "I know nothing of psychology."

"What do you know? I mean, what do you teach?"

"English literature. At the college I was the resident authority on Shakespeare."

"Do you know," she said, "you even look the part. You have a scholarly look."

"I think that's about enough," he said, kneeling and beginning to stack the wood on his arm.

"Can I help?" she asked.

"No, we only need enough to boil some tea."

"Edward, what do you think we'll find? What are we looking for?"

"Mary, I don't know. I don't think anyone does. There seems no reason that we should be here; no one, I think, really wants to be here. Yet here we are, the six of us."

"I've thought a lot about it," she said. "I barely got any sleep last night, wondering about it. Someone wants us here. Someone sent us here. We didn't ask to come."

Lansing rose to his feet, clutching the stack of wood piled on his arm. "Let's not fret too much about it. Not yet. We'll know more about it, maybe, in a day or two."

They went back up the road. Jurgens was striding up the hill with four canteens hanging on a shoulder.

"I found a spring," he said. "You should have left your canteens so I could have filled them, too."

"Mine is almost full," said Mary. "I've only had one little swallow out of it."

Lansing busied himself starting a fire while Jurgens poured water into a kettle and planted a forked stick by which to hang it over the blaze.

"Did you know," demanded the Parson, standing over the kneeling Lansing, "that this robot person brought along a canteen for himself?"

"What's wrong with that?" asked Lansing.

"He doesn't drink. Why do you think that he—"

"Maybe he brought it along so that you or the Brigadier could have water when your canteens are dry. Have you considered that?"

The Parson snorted in disgust, a sneering snort.

Lansing felt anger sweep quickly over him. He rose and faced the Parson deliberately. "I'm going to tell you something," he said, "and I'm saying it only once. You're a troublemaker. We don't need a troublemaker here. You keep it up and I'll wipe up the ground with you. Do you understand?"

"Hear! Hear!" cried the Brigadier.

"And you," said Lansing to the Brigadier, "keep your damn mouth shut. You've set yourself up to be the leader of this group and you are doing badly at it."

"I suppose," said the Brigadier, "you think *you* should be the leader."

"We don't need a leader, General. When your pomposity threatens to overcome you, just remember that."

A pall hung over the little band while they ate their lunch and drank the tea, then they took up the trek again, with the Brigadier still in the lead and the Parson following close upon his heels.

The rolling countryside continued, with the scattered groves of trees. It was a pleasant land, but the day was warm. Stumping on before them, the Brigadier proceeded at a slower pace than he had before they'd stopped for lunch.

The road had been climbing all the afternoon, up succeeding swales, each one higher than the last. Now, ahead of the others, the Brigadier stopped and raised a shout. The Parson loped to stand beside him and the others hurried to catch up.

The land tumbled down into a bowl, and at the bottom of the bowl stood a cube of heaven blue. Even from the ridgetop it appeared to be a massive structure. It was plain, not fancy—straight sides that rose up to a flat top. From the distance that they viewed it, it looked unadorned. But its size and intense blueness made it spectacular. The road they had been following went down the tumbled, tortured slope in angling curves and switchbacks. Once it reached the bottom of the slope, it arrowed toward the cube, but when it reached it, it swept out to run around one side of it, then continued across the bowl and went climbing up the slope beyond in a zigzag fashion.

Sandra squeaked. "It's beautiful," she said.

The Brigadier harumphed. "When the innkeeper mentioned it," he said, "I never for a moment anticipated it would be anything like this. I didn't know what to expect. A crumbling ruin, perhaps. I guess I really didn't think too much about it. I was looking forward to the city."

The Parson pulled the corners of his mouth down. "I don't like the looks of it."

"You don't like the looks of anything," said the Brigadier.

"Before we start passing opinions," said Lansing, "let us go down there and have a look at it."

It took awhile to get there. They had to follow the road because the sloping ground was too steep and treacherous to do otherwise. By following the road in all its wanderings, they traveled several times the distance between the slope's summit and its base.

The cube sat in the center of a wide, sandy area that ran all around it, a circle of sand so precise that it seemed it must have been drawn carefully by a survey team—white sand, the kind of sand that one would expect to find in a children's sandbox, a sugarlike sand that at one time might have been flattened out into a smooth surface but that now had been blown into a series of ripples by the wind.

The walls of the cube rose high. Lansing, measuring them with a careful eye, concluded they rose fifty feet or more. In them there were no breaks, nothing that would suggest a window or a door, and there was, as well, no ornamentation, no artful carving, no dedicatory plaque, no incised symbols that might announce a name by which the cube was known. Viewed close at hand the blueness of the walls held true—a celestial blue that could have represented the purest innocence. Likewise, the walls were smooth. Certainly not stone, Lansing told himself. Plastic, perhaps, although plastic seemed incongruous in this howling wilderness, or ceramic, a cube formed of the finest porcelain.

With scarcely a word spoken, the band walked around the cube, by some unspoken convention not stepping within the circle of sand that surrounded it. Back on the road again, they halted and all stood looking at the blueness.

"It's beautiful," said Sandra, drawing in her breath as a sign of continuing astonishment. "More beautiful than it seemed when we glimpsed it from the hilltop. More beautiful than you could expect anything to be."

"Amazing," said the Brigadier. "Truly amazing. But does anyone have the foggiest notion what it is?"

"It must have a function," said Mary. "The size, the mass of it would argue that. If it were merely symbolic, it would not have to be this large. And were it only symbolic, it would be placed where it could be seen from a distance, atop the highest elevation rather than being tucked away down here."

"It has not been visited recently," said Lansing. "There are no tracks in the circle of sand around it."

"If there were tracks," said the Brigadier, "they would soon be covered by the drifting sand. Even recent tracks."

"Why are we standing here, simply looking at it?" asked Jurgens. "As if we might be afraid of it."

"I think, perhaps, we are standing here because we *are* afraid of it," said the Brigadier. "It seems quite evident that it was placed here by sophisticated builders. This is no fumbling job such as might have been done by benighted heathens intent on raising a memorial to their deity. Such a great accomplishment, logic says, must be protected in some manner. Otherwise there would be graffiti scribbled all across the walls."

"There is no graffiti," Mary said. "Not a single mark upon the walls."

"Perhaps the walls are of a substance that will not take a mark," said Sandra. "Any marking device would slide right over them."

"I still think," said the robot, "that we should examine it more closely. If we moved close up to it, we might find an answer to some of the questions we are asking."

Having said that, he began to stride across the circle of sand. Lansing shouted a warning, but Jurgens made no sign that he had heard. Lansing sprang forward, sprinting to catch him. For that circle of sand, he now realized, held a subtle threat, something that all of them, with the exception of Jurgens, must have recognized as well. Jurgens was still striding ahead. Lansing closed on him, reached out a hand to grasp his shoulder. But in the instant before his fingers could close upon the shoulder, some obstruction buried in the sand caught his toe and threw him on his face.

As he struggled to his hands and knees, shaking his head to dislodge the sand that stuck to it, he heard the others shouting back of him. The Brigadier's voice boomed above all the others: "You damn fool, come back! That place could be booby trapped!"

Jurgens was almost at the wall; he had not slacked his sturdy trudging. As if, Lansing thought, the fool planned to walk head on, full tilt into it. Then, in that instant that he conceived the thought, the robot was tossed into the air, twisting backward and falling in the sand. Lansing put up his hand as if to scrub his eyes, as if to clear his vision, for in that split second when Jurgens had been tossed, he had thought he'd seen something (like a snake, perhaps, although it could not have been a snake) emerge momentarily from the sand, striking from the sand and then being there no longer, too quick for the eye to catch, no more than a flicker in the air.

Jurgens, lying on his back, now was turning over, clawing with both hands and thrusting with one leg to skid himself back from the wall. The other leg dragged limply.

Lansing leaped to his feet and ran forward. He grasped the robot by one clawing arm and started dragging him back toward the road.

"Let me," said someone, and looking up, Lansing saw the Parson standing over him. The Parson stooped, seized Jurgens about his waist and heaved him to his shoulder like a bag of grain, staggering slightly under the robot's weight.

On the road the Parson let Jurgens down. Lansing knelt beside him.

"Tell me where you hurt," he said.

"I do not hurt," said Jurgens. "I am not equipped to hurt."

"One leg was dragging," said Sandra. "The right leg. He can't use it."

"Here," said the Brigadier, "let me stand you up. Put you on your feet, see if you can bear your weight."

He hauled mightily, pulling the robot to his feet, supporting him. Jurgens tottered on his left leg, seeking to put his weight on the right. The right leg folded under him. The Brigadier eased him to a sitting position.

Mary said, "It's a mechanical problem. We can have a look at it. Or is it entirely mechanical? How about it, Jurgens?"

"I think it is mostly mechanical," said Jurgens. "There might be some biologics involved. Some biological nerve function. I can't be sure."

"If we only had some tools," said Mary. "Dammit, why didn't we think to buy some tools?"

"I have a kit of tools," said Jurgens. "A small kit. Perhaps sufficient of them."

"Well, that's better," said Mary. "Maybe we can do something for you."

"Did anyone see what happened out there?" Sandra asked.

The others shook their heads. Lansing said nothing; he could not be certain what he'd seen, if anything at all.

"Something hit me," said Jurgens.

"Did you see what it was?" Sandra asked.

"I saw nothing. I just felt the hit."

"We don't want to stay out here in the road," said the Brigadier. "It may take a while to make repairs on him. Let's find a place to camp. It's drawing on toward evening."

They found a place to camp at the edge of a grove about half a mile distant. A nearby brook supplied water. Downed trees provided wood. Lansing helped Jurgens hobble to the site, sat him down beside a tree he could lean against.

The Brigadier took over. He said to Mary, "The rest of us will get the fire going and do the cooking and whatever else needs doing. Why don't you get to work on Jurgens? Lansing can help you if you wish."

He started to walk away and then came back. He said to Lansing, "The Parson and I talked it over. Not too amiably, but we talked. That little incident back on the trail: We agreed that we'd both been out of line. I thought you'd like to know."

"Thanks for telling me," said Lansing.

"DAMMIT," SAID MARY, "THERE'S that broken ratchet, or I'd guess it's a ratchet. If only we had a replacement, he'd be as good as new."

"I sorrow to tell you," Jurgens said, "I do not carry such a part. A few ordinary parts, of course, but nothing like that. I cannot carry every part I possibly could need. I thank you, lady, for the job you've done on me. I would have been hard pressed to do it for myself."

"The leg is stiff," said Lansing. "He cannot bend the knee, and even with the repair the hip does not work too smoothly."

"I can move," said Jurgens, "but with no sprightliness. I'll be slow at best. I will hold up the march."

"I'll fix you a crutch," said Lansing. "It may take you a while to learn to use it, but once you get the hang of it, it will be of help."

"To continue this journey with you," Jurgens said, "I'd crawl on hands and knees."

"Here are your tools," said Mary. "I put them back into the case. You'd better lock them up again."

"Thank you," said Jurgens. He took the small case of tools, opened the door into his chest cavity, stored the case there and shut the door. He slapped his chest to make sure the door was closed.

"I think the coffee's ready," said Mary. "Maybe not the food, but I can smell the coffee and I want a cup. Edward, do you want to join me?"

"In a moment," Lansing said.

Squatting beside Jurgens, he watched her walk toward the fire.

"Go and get your coffee," Jurgens said. "No need to stay with me."

"Coffee can wait a while," said Lansing. "There was something that you said. That you would crawl on your hands and knees to go along with us. Jurgens, what's going on? Do you know something that we don't?"

"I know not a thing. I just want to be along."

"But why? We're a bunch of refugees. We've been hurled out of our worlds and our cultures and we don't know why we're here . . ."

"Lansing, what do you know of freedom?"

"Why, I suppose not too much. One doesn't think of freedom until he doesn't have it. Back where I came from, we had it. We didn't have to strive for it. We took it for granted. It seldom crossed our minds. Don't tell me that you—"

"Not in the way you think. In no way were the robots on my

world repressed. In a way, I suppose, we were free. But we carried a burden, a responsibility. Let me try to tell you."

"Please do," said Lansing. "You said back at the inn that you took care of your humans, which was a strange way to say it. You said there were few humans left and you took care of them."

"Before I say anything," said Jurgens, "tell me one thing. You spoke of what your friend had said—I believe you said he babbled. About alternate worlds, alternate earths splitting off from one another at certain crisis points. I believe you said that was what may have happened."

"Yes, I did. For all its madness . . ."

"And those alternate worlds each would follow its own world line. They'd exist simultaneously through time and space. Would that mean, if we indeed are from different alternate worlds, that all of us would come from the same time frame?"

"I hadn't thought of that," said Lansing, "and I don't really know. You understand that this all is supposition. But if the alternate world theory should be true and we do come from such worlds, I see no reason to believe we'd all have to be from the same time frame. Any agency that could put us here probably could be rather arbitrary about time as well."

"I am glad to hear you say that, for it has bothered me. I must come from a frame much later in time than the rest of you. You see, I existed in a world that had been deserted by the human race."

"Deserted?"

"Yes, everyone gone to other worlds circling other stars. Deep into space, I have no idea how far. The Earth, my Earth, was worn out. The environment had been ruined and natural resources gone. The last of the resources were used to build the ships that took the humans into space. They left it stripped and gutted. . . ."

"But there were humans left. Only a few of them, you said."

"There were humans left—the ne'er-do-wells, the utterly incompetent, the persistent fumblers, the idiots. The ones who were not worth the ship space they would have taken. There were robots left as well—the hopelessly obsolete, the outdated, those who had somehow escaped the scrap heap. The incompetents were left behind, both human and robot, while the others, the bright and normal humans, the sophisticated robots, went beyond the Earth to

seek a brave new life. We, the rejects of thousands of years of evolution, were left behind to make our way as best we could. And
we robots, the ones who were abandoned, have tried for centuries
to do what we could for the humans who were left. We failed—for
centuries we failed. The descendants of those pitiful humans who
were left behind have not improved in mental or moral quality
through the years. At times there would be a spark or two of
hope, two or three in a single generation might show some promise, but the promise was always lost in the morass of the gene pool.
I finally admitted to myself that the humans were breeding down,
not up, that there was no hope for them. Each generation they
grew more foul, more cruel, more worthless."

"So you were trapped," said Lansing. "Trapped by your com-
mitment to your humans."

"You say it well," said Jurgens. "You *do* understand. We were
trapped, indeed. Still we felt we must stay on, for we owed those
degenerating creatures the best that we could give them, which
was never enough."

"Now that you have broken out of your circumstance, you feel
free."

"Yes, free. More free than I have ever felt. Finally my own
man, my own robot. Is this wrong of me?"

"I don't think it's wrong. A bad job come to an end."

"Here, as you say," said Jurgens, "we don't know where we are
nor what we are supposed to do. But at least a clean slate, a starting over."

"And among people who are glad to have you."

"I'm not sure of that. The Parson does not care for me."

"Screw the Parson," Lansing said. "I'm glad that you are here.
With the possible exception of the Parson, we're all glad you are
here. You must remember that it was the Parson who came in and
carried you out when you were injured. But the fact remains that
he is a bigot."

"I'll prove myself," said Jurgens. "Even the Parson will come
to accept me."

"Was that what you were doing when you rushed up to the
wall? Trying to prove yourself?"

"I didn't think so at the time. I only thought there was something that needed to be done and I set out to do it. But I suppose I
was trying to prove—"

"Jurgens, it was a stupid thing to do. Promise me, no more stupidity."

"I'll try. Tell me when I'm stupid."

"Next time," said Lansing, "I'll clobber you with whatever comes to hand."

The Brigadier shouted at Lansing. "Come on. Supper's ready."

Lansing rose. "Won't you come with me, join the others? You can lean on me. I'll get you there."

"I think not," said Jurgens. "I have thinking that must be done."

10

LANSING WORKED AT THE forked sapling he had cut, forming a crutch for Jurgens.

The Parson got up from where he was sitting and threw some more wood on the fire.

"Where is the Brigadier?" he asked.

"He went to help Jurgens in," said Mary.

"Why should he do that? Why not leave him where he is?"

"Because it isn't right," said Mary. "Jurgens should be here with the rest of us."

The Parson said nothing, sat down again.

Sandra walked around the fire to stand beside Mary. "There's something nosing around out there in the dark," she said. "I heard it sniffling."

"It's probably the Brigadier. He went out to get Jurgens."

"It's not the Brigadier. It goes on four feet. The Brigadier doesn't sniffle."

"Some small animal," said Lansing, looking up from his work. "Whenever a campfire's built there are always some of them around. Drawn by curiosity—they have to see what is going on—or maybe snooping around on the chance they can pick up something to eat."

"It makes me nervous," said Sandra.

"All of our nerves are a bit on edge," Mary told her. "The cube . . ."

"Let's all forget about the cube right now," Lansing suggested. "With morning light we'll have a better look at it."

"I, for one, will have no better look at it," said the Parson. "It is a thing of evil."

The Brigadier came into the edge of the firelight, one arm around the lurching Jurgens.

"What's this I hear about a thing of evil?" he asked, his voice booming.

The Parson said nothing. The Brigadier eased Jurgens to the ground between Mary and the Parson.

"He can barely get along," said the Brigadier. "That leg is almost worthless. There's no way to fix it better?"

Mary shook her head. "There is a broken component in the knee and no replacement for it. Some of the hip arrangement is twisted out of shape. I was able to restore some function to the leg, but that was all. Edward's crutch will help him get around."

The Brigadier lowered himself to a place next to Lansing.

"I could swear," he said, "that when I was coming in I heard someone mention evil."

"Leave it be," Lansing curtly told him. "Let it lie."

"No need, worthy pedagogue," said the Parson, "to attempt to impose yourself between the man of cloth and the man at arms. We might as well have it out."

"All right, if you insist," said Lansing, "but be gentlemen while you're about it."

"I'm always a gentleman," said the Brigadier. "It is instinctive with me. An officer and a gentleman. That's the way it goes, the two of them together. This clownish friend of ours—"

The Parson interrupted. "I simply said the cube was a thing of evil. Perhaps my opinion only, but I am trained to make such observations and the Brigadier is not."

"How do you make it evil?" asked the Brigadier.

"Why, the very look of it to start with. And the warning strip of sand around it. Men of good will put in that warning strip and we should have honored it. The one of us who did not paid very dearly for it."

"A warning strip it may be," said the Brigadier, "planted with booby traps, one of which our metal friend encountered. But if my interpretation is correct, men of good will had nothing to do with it. If your men had been really of a deep good will, they would have built a fence around it. What you are trying to do, Parson, is to scare us off. If something holds a threat you label it evil, and that gives you the excuse to turn your back and walk away from it. My way would be to invade the strip, being very cautious, using poles or prods or whatever other means I could to unmask and disarm the booby traps. There is something about the cube that I am certain someone does not wish us to learn. Perhaps some fact of great value, and I, for one, do not propose to turn my back upon it."

"That is quite in keeping with your basic character," said the Parson, "and I'll not go a step out of my way to dissuade you. But I do feel it my solemn duty to warn you that evil forces are best left alone."

"There you go again with this talk of evil. What is evil, may I ask? How would you define an evil?"

"If you have to ask," the Parson told him, "it would be a waste of breath to attempt to tell you."

"Did anyone see exactly what happened out there when Jurgens was hurt?" asked Mary. "He himself saw nothing. He says he was hit, that something struck him a blow. But he did not see it strike."

"I saw not a thing," the Parson said, "and I was standing where I should have seen. The fact that I saw nothing convinces me more than ever that it was an evil force."

"I saw something," said Lansing, "or thought I saw something. I didn't mention it because I could not be certain. I saw, strange as it may sound, a motion. A flicker. A flicker that was gone so fast I could not be sure I'd seen it. I'm not certain even now."

"I cannot understand this talk of evil," Sandra said. "The cube is beautiful. It makes the breath catch in my throat. I sense no evil in it."

"Yet it attacked Jurgens," Mary said.

"Yes, I know. But even knowing that, I still see the beauty in it; to me there is no evil there."

"Well spoken," said the Brigadier. "There speaks our poetess—what did you call yourself, a certified poetess?"

"You are correct," Sandra said, speaking softly. "You cannot know what that means to me. Only in my world could you know the honor—almost the glory—of being certified a poetess. There are many poets, very many of them, all skilled in their profession, but very few who are certified as poets."

"I cannot imagine such a world," the Parson said. "It must be a faerie place. Many good words, perhaps, but no good works."

"You are right in saying you cannot imagine it," said Sandra. "You'd feel out of place there."

"And that," the Brigadier told the Parson, "should hold you for a while."

All of them sat in silence for a time, then Sandra said, "There it is again. There's something prowling this campfire. I hear the sniffling again."

"I hear nothing," said the Brigadier. "My dear, it's your imagination. There is nothing out there."

Another silence, then the Parson asked, "What do we do come morning?"

"We look over the cube," said the Brigadier. "We look it over well, being very careful. Then, if we find nothing that throws light on the situation, we continue on our way. Up ahead of us, if the shabby innkeeper was telling us the truth, there is a city, and it seems to me that in a city we may find more of interest than we are finding here. If we wish and it seems reasonable, we always have the option of returning to the cube and having a go at it again."

The Parson pointed to Jurgens and spoke to Lansing. "Will he be able to travel?"

Lansing held up the crutch he was working on. "It will take him awhile to get accustomed to this. It's a fairly bad job. I wish I could have done better, but there are no other materials at hand. He'll be able to travel, but he'll be slow. We'll have to match our pace to his. As I see it, there isn't any hurry."

"There might be," said the Brigadier. "We have no indication of the parameters of this expedition. There may be time limits of which we are not aware."

"Before we can begin to operate effectively," said Mary, "we must gain some clues as to why we're here. We should not pass up anything that might give us such clues. I think we should spend time with the cube until we are convinced it has nothing to offer us."

"It has been my feeling," said the Brigadier, "that in a city we might gather more information than we can out here in this barren land. In a city we'll find people we can talk with."

"If we can understand them," said Mary. "If they'll talk to us. If they don't chase us out or clap us into jail."

"Yes, there are those considerations," agreed the Brigadier.

"It's time, I think, that we should turn in," said the Parson. "We've had a long, hard day and we'll need our rest for yet another."

"I'll stand the first watch," offered the Brigadier. "After that Lansing and you, Parson, will split the remainder of the watch. You can make your own arrangements."

"There is no need of anyone standing watch," said Jurgens. "That particular chore is mine. I never sleep. I have no need of sleep. I promise that I will stay alert. You place your trust in me."

11

AFTER BREAKFAST THEY WENT across the road to the cube. The grass was still wet with dew. Jurgens had aroused them at the first light of dawn, with the oatmeal and coffee cooking.

In the slanting morning light the cube was not as blue as it had been when seen in the full light of day. It had an opal-like appearance, delicate and fragile.

"Now, it looks like porcelain," said Sandra. "It looked, at times, like porcelain when we first saw it, but now it can't be mistaken. It must be porcelain."

The Parson picked up a fist-size rock and hurled it against the cube. The rock bounced back.

"It's not porcelain," the Parson said.

"That's a hell of a way to find out," said Lansing. "The cube may remember who it was who threw the rock."

"You talk as if it may be alive," said Mary.

"I wouldn't bet it isn't."

"We're wasting time standing here and talking," said the Parson. "I'm against it, for I still think this thing is evil, but if the rest of you are set on investigating, let's investigate. The sooner we get done with it, the sooner we can get on to something else."

"That's right," said the Brigadier. "Let's go back to the grove and cut some poles. We can use them to probe the area before we move into it."

Lansing did not go with the Brigadier and Parson. He trailed along behind Jurgens, who was trying out his crutch. The robot was making awkward work of it, but after a time, Lansing told himself, he'd begin to catch the hang of it. Twice he fell and Lansing helped him up each time.

"Leave me alone," Jurgens finally told him. "You upset me, hovering over me, ready with a helping hand. I appreciate your concern but I have to work this out myself, in my own way. If I fall, I'll manage to get up."

"Okay, pal," said Lansing. "More than likely you are right."

Leaving Jurgens, he began a slow circuit of the cube, staying just outside the circle of sand. He studied the walls with care, hoping that somewhere on their surface he would see some seam, some discontinuity that might be significant. He saw nothing. The walls rose smooth and without any kind of break. The material of which they were constructed appeared to be a solid piece.

Occasionally he sneaked a look at Jurgens. The robot was not doing well, but he was sticking to the job. Once he fell, used the crutch to pull himself erect and then went on. None of the others was in sight. The Brigadier and the Parson were at the campsite, cutting poles; at times Lansing heard the sound of chopping. Mary and Sandra probably were on the other side of the cube.

He stood, looking at it, questions racing in his mind. Could it be a living space, a house in which dwelled an unknown family of beings? Could they be inside now, going about their affairs, at times some of them looking out of windows (windows?) at the strange, befuddled bipedal creatures who had stumbled on their home? Or was it, perhaps, a repository of knowledge, a library, a treasury of fact and thought wholly alien to the human mind, although not necessarily alien in itself, but the fact and thought of another branch of the human race many millennia beyond the world that he had known? Which was quite possible, he thought. The night before he and Jurgens had talked of that, of the disparity of time and might be possible in alternate worlds. It was quite apparent from what Jurgens had told him that the robot's time had been many thousands of years in the future beyond the time of Lansing's Earth. Or could the cube be a structure out of time itself, seen only dimly through the misty veil of otherwhen and otherwhere? That didn't seem to make such sense, for the cube was not difficult to see. It was as sound as anyone might wish.

He continued in his slow walk around the cube. Now that the sun was up, the day was fine. The dew had disappeared and the sky was high and blue, with no fleck of cloud to mar its depth. Plodding toward the road came the Brigadier and Parson, each of them carrying a long, trimmed pole cut from a sapling. They crossed the road and came up to him.

"You walked around it?" asked the Brigadier. "All the way around it?"

"I did," Lansing told him, "and it's the same as here. There is nothing. Not a thing at all."

"Get up close to it," said the Parson, "and one might see something that you'd miss standing out here. A close look is always better than the long look."

Lansing agreed with him. "That is right," he said.

"Why don't you go and cut a pole?" asked the Brigadier. "With the three of us, the investigation would go faster."

"I don't think I will," said Lansing. "I think it's a waste of time."

Both of them looked at him for a moment and then they turned away. The Brigadier said to the Parson, "Let's work it this way. Let's start about twelve feet apart and cover the ground outside ourselves and the ground between ourselves, overlapping. Probing with poles so that if there's something there, it will attack the poles instead of us."

The Parson nodded knowingly. "That is what I had in mind."

So they started out, the Brigadier saying, "We'll work in to the wall and when we get in next to the wall, we'll separate, you going to the left, I to the right. We'll work carefully around the wall until we meet."

The Parson did not answer and they went along, working slowly toward the wall, each one probing with his pole.

And what, Lansing wondered, if the thing, or things, that were in the sand circle were programmed or trained to snap at a living being that had invaded its domain, but at nothing else? But he said nothing and sauntered down the road, looking for Mary and Sandra. A short distance down the road he glimpsed them, coming around the cube, keeping well outside the sand circle that surrounded it.

A yelp behind him jerked him around. The Brigadier was running at full gallop through the sand circle toward the road. The pole the Brigadier carried was only half a pole. It had been sheared off cleanly in the middle and the other half of it lay on the sand against the wall. The Parson was standing stark, as if petrified, against the wall, swiveling his head around to look over his shoulder at the fleeing Brigadier. To the right of the Brigadier something flickered from the sand, so swift that there was no chance of seeing what it was, and the other half of the half pole the Brigadier was carrying flew into the air, neatly bitten off. The Brigadier bawled in terror and flung away the remainder of the pole. In a running broad jump, he cleared the last few feet of sand and piled up on the grassy surface between the sand circle and the road.

Mary and Sandra were running now to reach the fallen Brigadier while the petrified Parson still stood stiff against the wall.

The Brigadier scrambled to his feet and dusted off his tunic. Then, as if unconscious that anything had happened, he assumed the military starkness, the stiff-as-a-ramrod posture softened by a regal nonchalance that was his ordinary pose.

"My dears," he said to the two women as they pulled up in front of him, "I might say that we have some lurking force out there."

He turned about and bawled, in parade-ground thunder, at the Parson.

"Come on back," he said. "Turn about and come back slowly, probing all the way, being careful to follow the track that you made going in."

"I notice," said Lansing, "that you were not so meticulous as to follow your old trail. You broke new ground, in a manner of speaking."

The Brigadier ignored him.

Far down the road Jurgens had turned around and was coming back. He was handling the crutch somewhat better, having learned how to swing his stiffened leg, but his progress was still slow.

The Brigadier said to Lansing, "Did you see what that blighter was the last pass that it made?"

"No, I did not," Lansing told him. "It was lightning fast. Too fast for one to see."

The Parson had worked his way back along the wall and was starting down the track that he had made going to the wall, industriously using his pole to probe each inch of the way.

"A good man," the Brigadier said, approvingly. "He follows orders well."

They stood and watched the Parson inch his way along. Jurgens finally reached them and stood with them in the roadway. The Parson reached the road. With evident relief, he threw his pole to one side and came over to them.

"And now that it's all done," said the Brigadier, "perhaps we should go back to camp and regroup as best we can."

"It's not a question of regrouping," said the Parson. "It's a question of getting out of here. This place is hazardous. Well guarded, as you have good reason to know," he said, looking at the Brigadier. "I think that we should leave this place. I have no wish to stay here. I suggest that immediately we move on to the city and see what we find there. A better reception, I would hope, than we have been accorded here."

"Your sentiments," said the Brigadier, "are very much my own. I see no profit in our staying here."

"But the fact that it is so well guarded," said Mary, "must testify that there is something worth that guarding. I'm not sure we should leave here."

"Maybe, later on," said the Brigadier, "we can return, if need be. First we should see the city."

The Brigadier and the Parson moved off, heading for the camp. Sandra followed them.

Mary moved close to Lansing. "I think they're wrong," she said. "I think there's something here—perhaps what we are supposed to find."

"The trouble," Lansing told her, "is that we don't know what to find or if there's anything at all that we are supposed to seek. I am very much concerned about the whole proceedings."

"When it comes right down to that, so am I."

Jurgens came limping up the road to join them.

"How does it go?" asked Lansing.

"Rather well," the robot told him, "but I still am slow. I do not know if, with this crutch, I'll ever achieve the speed and dexterity of my former self."

"I have not the faith the Brigadier has in the city up ahead," said Mary. "If, in fact, there is a city."

"One can never know," said Jurgens. "We must wait and see."

"Let's go back to camp," said Lansing, "and cook up a pot of coffee. We can talk it over. For my part, I believe the cube may be rather promising. If we look at it hard enough, we may detect a clue that is invisible to us now, unnoticed by us now. As we see it now, it has no significance. It's misplaced. It's not the sort of structure one would expect to find sitting out here by itself. There must, however, be some reason for it. It must serve some purpose. Like you, Mary, I'd feel better if we could derive just an inkling of its purpose."

"So would I," she said. "I dislike situations that have no meaning."

"So we'll go back to camp and talk with the others," Lansing said.

When they reached the camp, they found that the others had made up their minds.

"We have consulted among ourselves," said the Brigadier. "Among the three of us. We have decided that we should push on for the city with all possible speed. The robot would hold us back, so we think that he should be left behind to make his own way as best he can. In a matter of time he will catch up with us."

"That's a stinking thing to do," said Mary. "You let him carry a full pack, mostly food—food for you, not for him since he needs none. You allowed him to do camp chores. You sent him to fill canteens with water when he drinks no water. You accepted him, perhaps not as one of us, but as a servant, and now that he's been damaged you suggest we leave him behind."

"He's naught but a robot," said the Parson. "No human, but a mere machine."

"And yet worthy to be included in this venture," said Mary,

"whatever this venture may be. And do I need to remind you that he was hand picked, as we were hand picked, by someone who thought he should be with us."

"How about you, Lansing?" asked the Brigadier. "So far you've said not a thing. How do you feel about it?"

"I stay with Jurgens," said Lansing. "I refuse to desert him. If I were the one who was crippled and unable to keep up with you, he would stay with me. Of that I'm certain."

"And I as well," said Mary. "I'm staying with the robot. You are being panicked, foolish if not panicked. In this country we should not divide our forces. Why this great hurry for the city?"

"There's nothing here," said the Brigadier. "We may find something in the city."

"Then go ahead and find it," Mary said. "Edward and I will stay with Jurgens."

Jurgens said, "Fair lady, I would not wish to become a point of controversy—"

"You shut up," said Lansing. "This is our decision. You have no voice in it."

"Then I guess there is no more to say," said the Brigadier. "We three go on, you two stay with the robot to follow us."

"How about it, Sandra?" Mary asked. "Are you throwing in with those two?"

"There seems no reason I should remain behind with you," said Sandra. "As they say, there is nothing here. Only the beauty of the cube and—"

"We can't be sure of that. Be sure there's nothing here."

"We are sure of it," said the Parson. "We have talked it over. And now that it is settled, we should make a distribution of the food supply the robot was carrying."

He took a stride toward Jurgens's pack, but Lansing moved to get between the Parson and the pack.

"Not so fast," he said. "That pack belongs to Jurgens and it stays with us."

"But share and share alike!"

Lansing shook his head. "If you're deserting us, you manage with the food you have. No more."

The Brigadier growled and stepped forward. "What do you expect to gain by this?" he asked.

"Assurance that you'll wait for us at the city. That you won't go running off. If you want any of the food, you'll wait for us."

"You know that we can take it."

"I'm not sure you can," said Lansing. "In all my life I've never struck a man, but if you force me to it, I'll fight both of you."

Jurgens hobbled up to stand beside Lansing. "Nor have I ever struck a human," he said, "but should you attack my friend, I'll stand with him."

Mary spoke to the Brigadier. "I think you had best back off. I imagine a battling robot would prove an ugly customer."

The Brigadier started to say something, then apparently thought better of it. He walked over to his own pack and hoisted it to a shoulder, slipping his arms through the straps and settling it on his back.

"Come on," he said to the other two. "We should be on our way."

The three left behind stood and watched them until the road went over a rise and the three people traveling it disappeared from sight.

12

ONCE AGAIN THEY MADE a circuit of the cube, the three of them staying close together; for now, with the others gone, they felt very much alone. They scanned the walls with care, alert to lines of color or other subtle configurations that might tell them something. Certain lines were no more than shadows that either changed or disappeared with the shifting of the light and they were left with nothing. They found three slabs of stone that had gone unnoticed, set flush against the outer circle of the sand, lying flat and so well covered with sand that they had escaped detection. Only by chance were they now detected. Four feet wide, they extended six feet or so into the circle. With the sand brushed from their surfaces, they were simple slabs of stone, albeit very smooth. They bore no dressing marks; apparently they had been split along natural geologic fracture seams. How deeply they might sink into the ground there was no way to know. The combined efforts of the two humans and the robot could not budge them from their anchorage. They discussed using a shovel to dig along the outer end of one of them in an attempt to find its depth, but decided against it—the circle was guarded by something that struck with power and swiftness, and the danger might outweigh the worth of what they'd find. The three stones were set at roughly equal distances from one another, dividing the circle into thirds.

"It's not just happenstance that they are set where they are," said Mary. "They betray an engineering knowledge. Where they are set must have some purpose or significance."

"Perhaps an aesthetic purpose," suggested Lansing. "A certain symmetry."

"Maybe, but I doubt it."

"A magic," Jurgens said. "They might respond to certain ritual, certain chants or words."

"If that's the case," said Mary, "we haven't got a chance."

Near the road they found the pole that the Parson had dropped once he'd reached safety. Lansing picked it up.

"You're not going to have a try at going in again?" asked Mary. "If I were you, I wouldn't try it."

"Nothing as foolish as that," he said, "but I just now remembered something. When I tried to run in to reach Jurgens, I tripped and fell. I'm sure something caught my toe as I was running. Let's see if we can find it."

"Maybe you just tripped."

"It's possible, but I seem to recall I stubbed my toe on something in the sand."

The tracks showed in the sand—those that Jurgens had made, covered by those of the Parson and the track that Lansing had made up to the spot on which he'd fallen. Teetering on the edge of the sand circle, Lansing reached out with the pole and probed. After several seconds the pole caught on something. Carefully Lansing lifted the pole to force up whatever the tip of the pole had caught. One corner of a board came out of the sand, and after several more attempts, Lansing managed to free the thing and sweep it toward the edge of the circle. It was a board, no more than two feet square, with a narrow strip of board (a post, perhaps?) fastened to one side of it.

Mary reached out and grasped it, pulled it free of the circle and turned it over. Crude lettering showed on it.

Lansing bent above it. "That looks like Cyrillic," he said. "Could it be Russian?"

"It *is* Russian," said Mary. "That first line with the larger letters is a danger warning. Or I think it is. It spells out a danger warning."

"How do you know? Can you read Russian?"

"To a certain extent. But this Russian is not exactly the Russian that I know. Some of the characters seem to be wrong. The bigger characters warn of danger; I am sure of that. But the writing underneath it, the smaller characters, I don't recognize."

"It had been planted out here, opposite the road," said Lansing. "Where any visitor might see it. But it must have blown over or been knocked down and the sand drifted over it. It would never have been found if I'd not stumbled over it."

"I wish I were better at reading it," she said. "My Russian is fairly limited. Sufficient to spell my way through a technical report, but that is all. Many engineers, like myself, can read some Russian; it's almost obligatory that we can. The Russians are a very technical people. It's worth some effort to try to follow what they're doing. Of course, there is a free exchange of ideas, but—"

"A free exchange with Russia?"

"Yes, of course. Why not? The same as is true of all the other technical nations."

"I suppose," he said, "that there is no reason."

He upended the sign, and using his belt knife, pounded the stake into the ground.

"It'll stay there until it blows over or falls again," he said. "For all the good it'll do."

They returned to the camp, proceeding slowly so Jurgens could keep pace with them. The sun was halfway down the western sky; they'd spent a longer time at the cube than they had thought.

The fire had burned down to a bed of gray ash, but a few coals still remained when Lansing brushed the ash away. He fed in small dry twigs until he had a blaze, then patiently built the fire up. Mary stood and watched him, saying nothing, while he worked. She knew as well as he, he thought, that there was no use staying here, that they had done as much as could be done and they might as well head for the city—if, as Mary had said, there really was a city.

By now surely he would be missed back at the college, he told himself; perhaps by now his abandoned car would have been found. How much of a stir would his disappearance cause, he wondered—perhaps no more than a ten-day wonder, a few head-lines in the press, and then he'd be forgotten, the case filed away along with all the other unsolved disappearances that popped up every year. He held his hands over the fire for its warmth. The day was warm, not chilly, but still it seemed that he felt a brush of cold.

He and the others, he and the many others who had disap-peared—had some of the others who had disappeared come this way? he wondered.

"Back at the cube," said Mary, "you seemed surprised that there should be research cooperation with the Russians. Why did you question it?"

"In my time," he told her, "the United States and some of the other nations are at odds with Russia. There was a revolution during the First World War and Russia became a communist state."

"The First War?"

"Yes, the First World War. The Second World War. The nu-clear bomb."

"Edward, in my world there were no world wars, no—what did you call it?—nuclear bomb?"

He squatted back from the fire on his heels. "So that was the crisis point between your world and mine. You had no First World War and we did. Tell me, how about the British Empire?"

"It still is sound and solid. The sun never sets on it. And you said something else. The United States, I believe. The United States of what?"

"The United States of America."

"But North America is part of the British Empire and South America a part of Spain—except for Brazil, that is."

He gaped at her.

"It's the truth," she said. "That is the way it is."

"But the American colonies revolted."

"Yes, back in the eighteenth century. The revolt was short-lived."

"So the crisis point goes back farther than the First World War."

"I'm a bit confused," she said, "but apparently it does. You told us about your friend's speculation about crisis points and alternate worlds. You didn't believe him whem he talked of it. You thought he was fantasizing and maybe he thought so, too. He was just trying to make a point. When you told us back at the inn, I thought what a pretty conceit it was, how imaginative. From what you've told me, it must be more than a conceit."

"You must have lived in a good world. Better than the one I had."

"It's solid and serene," she said. "Almost no wars, only a few little ones. The big power blocs have carved out their territories and finally, by and large, seem content with what they have. There are, of course, cries against imperialism, but no one pays attention."

"India, of course, is starving."

She shrugged. "India always starves. There are too many people."

"And Africa exploited?"

"Edward, are you for me or against me? How do you stand with the British Empire?"

"Why, not too badly. I've felt at times that we lost something big and comfortable when it fell apart after World War Two."

"It fell apart?"

"Utterly apart. Just like that."

For a moment he caught the stricken look on her face, then the face smoothed over.

"I am sorry," he said.

She said, "I'll put together supper. You get in wood for the fire. You're hungry, aren't you?"

"Ravenous," he said. "We had an early breakfast and no lunch."

"I'll help with the wood," said Jurgens. "Even stove up as I am, I still can be of help."

"Sure," said Lansing. "Come along."

After supper they built up the fire and sat around it.

"So we are learning slowly where we came from," Mary said,

"but we still have no idea where we're going. I came from a continuation of the great empires, the logical working out of the empire concept, and you from a world in which the empires have disappeared. Or was it only the British Empire that disappeared?"

"Not only the British. All nations lost at least the major part of their colonial holdings. In a sense there still are empires, although not quite the same. Russia and the United States. They aren't called empires—they're called super-powers."

"Sandra's world is harder to figure out," she said. "It sounds much like a fairyland. Like a combination of the ancient Grecian ethos, or what sentimentalists would call the Grecian ethos, and recurring Renaissances. What was it she said—the Third Renaissance? Anyhow, it sounds like an unreal world. A beautifully fuzzy world."

"We don't know about the Parson and the Brigadier," said Lansing, "except for what the Brigadier said about playing war games."

"I think he was given the impression," Mary said, "that we disapproved of his world. He tried to make it sound like knightly medieval tournaments, but I think it might be more than that."

"The Parson is the close-mouthed one," said Lansing. "That business about the Glory in the turnip patch, but that is all he told us. He kept silent after that."

"His world sounds like a dismal one," she said. "Dismal and holy. The two so often go together. But we're forgetting Jurgens."

"You'll excuse me, please," said Jurgens.

"Oh, it's all right with me," said Mary. "We were just gossiping."

"What beats the hell out of me," said Lansing, "is trying to figure out what we have in common. The one reason I can think of that we should have been pitchforked here is that all six of us are the same kind of people. But it's apparent, when you think of it, that there are few similarities among us."

"A college professor," she said, "a military man, a parson, a poetess and—how would you describe yourself, Jurgens?"

"I'm a robot. That is all. I'm not even human."

"Cut that out," said Lansing sharply. "Whatever sent us here made no distinction between a robot and the human. Which makes you one of us."

"Later it may come clear," said Mary, "this common denominator that you mention. Right now I can't seem to find it."

"We're not the only ones," said Lansing. "There have been others here before us and there may be others after us. It all spells out to a program or a project. I wish someone would tell us what kind of program or project. I'd feel more comfortable about it."

"So would I," said Mary.

Jurgens struggled to his feet and, balancing on his crutch, threw more wood upon the fire.

"Did you hear that?" asked Mary.

"I heard nothing," Lansing said.

"There's something out there in the dark. I heard it snuffling."

All of them listened. There was nothing. The dark was silent.

Then Lansing heard it—a sniffling. He held up his hand in a warning for the others to stay silent.

The sniffling stopped, then started again, a short distance from where it had been before. As if some animal had its nose against the ground, sniffing at a spoor. It stopped, then took up again, in a different place, as if whatever was doing the sniffling was circling the campfire.

Jurgens pivoted about, flailing his crutch. Lansing shook his head at him. Jurgens froze.

They listened. For long minutes there was no sniffling and they relaxed.

"You heard it?" Mary asked.

"Yes," said Jurgens. "It started right behind me."

"There was something out there, then?"

"It's gone now," said Lansing. "Jurgens scared it off."

"Sandra heard it last night," said Mary. "It's been here all the time."

"It's not unusual," said Lansing. "It's something we should expect. Wild animals are always attracted to a fire."

∽ 13 ∾

FIVE DAYS WERE REQUIRED to reach the city. The trip could have been made in two if they had not been forced to match their pace to Jurgens's.

"I should have gone back to the inn," the robot said. "I could have made it there alone. I could have stayed there and waited for you. That way I wouldn't hold you up,"

"Then what would we have done," said Lansing, "when the time came that we needed you and you weren't with us?"

"That day may never come. You may never have any need of me."

Lansing, cursing him roundly as a fool, kept the robot going.

As they progressed, the character of the country changed. The land still was rolling land, but it became more arid. The groves of trees were farther apart and smaller, both in extent and in the size of the trees, which began to tend to scrubbiness. The wind blew hot instead of cool. The little streams on which they depended for water were farther apart and smaller, often no more than trickles.

Each night the Sniffler prowled the campfire. On one occasion, the second night out, Lansing and Jurgens, armed with flashlights, went out into the darkness to seek some sign of it. There was nothing, not even tracks. The land about the fire was sandy and should have shown tracks, but there were none.

"It's following us," said Mary. "It travels along with us. Even when it isn't sniffling, I know that it's out there. It's out there watching us."

"It hasn't threatened us," said Lansing, trying to soothe her. "It means no harm. If it had meant any harm, it would have acted before now. It has had all sorts of chances."

After the first couple of days, they often sat silent around the campfire, all talked out, no longer needing to talk to keep alive the close association the trip had formed among them.

At times, in those long silences, Lansing found himself thinking back to his former life and was surprised to discover that the college where he had taught seemed a distant place and the friends he had there were friends of long ago. It has been no more than a week, he reminded himself, forcing himself to remind himself, and already there was the feel of years between this place and the college town. Nostalgia swept over him and he felt the powerful urge to turn about and retrace his steps, to get up from the campfire and go back down the trail. Although, he knew, it would not be that simple. Even should he go back, he'd be going back no farther than the inn or, perhaps, the woodland glen in which he had first found himself. There was no trail back to the college, to Andy, to Alice, to the world that he had known. Between him and his former life lay an imponderable and he had no idea what it was.

He could not go back. He must go on, for only in that way could he possibly find the way back home. There was something here that he must find, and until he found it, there was no road back home. Even when he found it, if he ever did, there still was no guarantee there would be a way back home.

It might be a foolish thing to do, but he had no choice. He must keep on. He could not drop out, as the four card players at the inn had dropped out.

He tried to conjure up a logical mechanism by which he—he and the others—had been translated to this place. The whole thing smacked of magic yet it could not be magic. Whatever had been done must have utilized the application of certain physical laws. Magic itself, if it did exist, he argued with himself, must be no more than the application of physical laws as yet unknown back in the world he'd come from.

Andy, talking over their drinks at the Faculty Club, had talked of an end to knowledge, an end to physical law. But Andy had not known or even had a glimmer of understanding about the concepts that he had talked about; he was doing no more than flapping his mouth around to produce philosophical mutterings.

Could the answer be here, he wondered, in this world where he sat beside the campfire? Might that be what he was supposed to hunt for—and if it were, and if he found it, would he recognize it? Even should he find the end of knowing, would he know it?

Disgusted with himself, he tried to wipe his mind clean of his thoughts, but they refused to go away.

They found a camping place where the other three had stopped, the cold ashes of their fire, the wrapper from a box of crackers, scattered cheese rinds, emptied coffee grounds.

The weather stayed good. At times clouds rolled up from the western horizon, but they soon cleared away. There was no rain. The rays stayed bright and warm.

On the third night out, Lansing woke suddenly from a sound sleep. He fought his way to a sitting position, pressing against a force that tried to hold him down.

In the flicker of the firelight, he saw Jurgens standing over him. The robot's hand was gripping his shoulder and he was making shushing sounds.

"What's the matter?"

"It's Miss Mary, sir. There is something wrong with her. Like a fit."

Lansing turned his head to look. Mary sat upright in her sleeping bag. Her head was tilted back so that she looked toward the sky.

He struggled out of his bed, stumbled to his feet.

"I spoke to her," said Jurgens, "and she didn't hear me. I spoke several times, asking what's the matter, what could I do for her."

Lansing strode over to her. She seemed carved in stone—stiff and straight, held in an invisible vise.

He stooped over her, cupping her face in his hands, pressing gently.

"Mary," he said. "Mary, what is wrong?"

She paid him no attention.

He slapped her with one hand, then slapped her with the other. The muscles of her face relaxed and shivered. She collapsed, reaching out for him—not for him, he knew, but for anyone.

He seized her and cradled her close against him. She was shaking uncontrollably and began to sob, soft, subdued sobbing.

"I'll make a pot of tea," said Jurgens, "and build up the fire. She needs warmth, inside and outside of her as well."

"Where am I?" she whispered.

"You're here with us. You're safe."

"Edward?"

"Yes, Edward. And Jurgens. He's making you some tea."

"I woke up and they were bending over me, looking down at me."

"Quiet," he said. "Be quiet. Rest. Relax. Take it easy. You can tell us later. Now everything's all right."

"Yes, all right," she said.

For a time she said no more. Holding her, he felt a softening of the tension that had gripped her.

Finally she straightened up, pulling away from him. She sat upright and looked at him.

"That was frightening," she said, speaking calmly. "I've never been so scared."

"It's all over now. What was it . . . a bad dream?"

"More than a dream. They were really there, hanging in the sky, bending from the sky. Let me get out of this bag and go over to the fire. You said Jurgens was making tea?"

"It's brewed," said Jurgens, "and poured for you. If I remember rightly, you use two spoons of sugar."

"That is right," she said. "Two spoons."

"Would you wish a cup as well?" Jurgens asked Lansing.

"If you please," said Lansing.

They sat together beside the fire with Jurgens crouched to one side. The wood Jurgens had piled on the fire was catching and the flames leaped high. They sipped their tea in silence.

Then she said, "I am not one of your flighty females. You know that."

Lansing nodded. "Yes, indeed, I know. You can be as tough as nails."

"I woke up," she said. "A nice, easy waking up. Not jerked out of sleep. I was lying on my back so that when I woke, I was looking straight up at the sky."

She had another sip of tea and waited, as if trying to steel herself to go on with what she had to say.

She set the cup on the ground and turned to face Lansing. "They were three," she said, "the three of them—or I think there were three of them. There could have been four. Three faces. No other parts of their body. Just faces. Big faces. Bigger than human faces, although I am sure they were human. They looked human. Three big faces in the sky, filling half the sky, looking down at me.

And I thought how silly to think that I am seeing faces. I blinked my eyes, thinking it was my imagination and they would go away. But they didn't go away. After I had blinked I could see them even better."

"Easy," said Lansing. "Take your time."

"I am easy, dammit, and I am taking my time. You're thinking hallucination, aren't you?

"No, I'm not," he said. "You saw them if you say you saw them. Hard as nails, remember?"

Jurgens hunched forward and refilled the cups.

"Thank you, Jurgens," she said. "You make splendid tea."

Then she said, "There was nothing wrong with the faces. Nothing outrageous. Quite ordinary, now that I think of it. One of them had a beard. He was the young one, the other two were old. Nothing wrong with them, I said—not to start with. Then it began to seep into me. They were looking intently at me. Interested. The way one of us would be interested if we came across an odious insect, an abominable creature of some sort, a new sort of life. As if I weren't a creature; as if I were a thing. There was, to start, what I thought might be a look of compassion for me, then I saw it wasn't—it was, rather, a mingled contempt and pity and it was the pity that hurt the most. I could almost read their thoughts. My God, they were thinking, will you look at that! And then—and then . . ."

Lansing said nothing; he sensed that it was the time to say nothing.

"And then they turned their heads away. They didn't go away. They only turned their heads away, dismissing me. As if I were beneath their notice, beneath contempt, unworthy of their pity. As if I were nothing—and, by extension, the human race was nothing. Condemning all of us to nothingness, although condemn may be too strong a word. We were not even worth their condemnation. We were a lowly form of which they would think no further."

Lansing let out his breath. "For the love of God," he said, "no wonder . . ."

"That is right. No wonder. It hit me hard. Edward, maybe my reaction—"

"Let's not talk about reactions. My reaction probably would have been as bad or worse."

"What do you think they were? Not who, but what?"

"I wouldn't know. Right now I wouldn't even guess."

"It was not my imagination."

"You have no imagination," he said. "You're a hard-headed engineer. All nuts and bolts. A realist. Two and two are four, never three or five."

"Thank you," she said.

"Later on," he said, "we'll spend hours wondering what they were, but not now. You're still too close to it. Later on."

"Another person," she said, "might have told you they were gods. Sandra would have told you that. A primitive would tell you that. The Parson would denounce them as devils thirsting for his soul. I'll tell you this much—they had the arrogance, the noncaring, the self-assurance of gods, but they weren't gods."

"Once we robots thought that humans were gods," said Jurgens. "After all, perhaps in a sense they were. You can understand why we might have thought so, for they created us. But we got over it. After a time we saw they were no more than a different life form."

"There is no need to comfort me," said Mary. "I've told you I know they aren't gods. I'm not sure there are any gods. I rather think there're not."

Lansing and Mary did not go back to their sleeping bags. Neither one of them would have slept and dawn was not far off. They sat beside the fire and talked, talking easily now. After a time Jurgens set about getting breakfast.

"Pancakes and ham," he said. "How about that?"

"That sounds fine to me," said Lansing.

"We'll have an early breakfast," said the robot, "and get an early start. Today may be the day we'll reach the city."

They did not reach the city that day, but on the late afternoon of the next.

They sighted it when they reached the crest of a high hill up which the road angled in tortuous twists and turns.

Mary drew in her breath. "There it is," she said, "but where are all the people?"

"Perhaps there aren't any," said Lansing. "It is a ruin, not a city."

It was spread out on the plain that lay below the hill—a dun-colored plain and a dun-colored city. It covered a good part of the plain that lay between the hills. It lay lifeless and inert. Nothing stirred within it.

"I never in my life," said Mary, "have seen so depressing a sight. And this was what the Brigadier was so anxious to reach. There would be people there, he said."

"You could make a living betting against the Brigadier," said Lansing.

"There is no sign of the others," said Mary. "No sign of anyone. You'd think they would have been on the lookout for us, watching the trail behind them."

"Maybe they are doing that. Maybe they'll show up soon."

"If they are still there."

"I think they still are there," said Lansing. "We'll camp up here. We'll keep the fire burning all night. They'll see the fire."

"You mean you aren't going down right now?"

"Not right now. With night coming on, I'd feel safer up here than down there in the city."

"I'm thankful for that," she said. "I could stand it in the daylight. But not now."

"There was a stream back a mile or so," said Jurgens. "I'll get the water."

"No," said Lansing, "you stay here and get some wood together. As much wood as you can. I'll get the water."

"I am glad that we are here," said Mary. "Much as I may fear that city down there, I'm glad we finally made it."

"So am I," said Lansing.

After eating they sat in a row atop the hill and watched the city. There was no movement in it. Not a single gleam of light. At any moment they expected to see one of the three who had preceded them come out of the city and wave a welcome to them, but this did not happen.

Finally, after night had closed in, Mary said, "We might as well turn in, get what sleep we can."

"Both of you will sleep," said Jurgens. "You've had hard days upon the trail."

"I hope so," Mary said.

Jurgens woke them at first light.

"The others are down there, waiting for us," he said. "They must have seen our fire."

Lansing crawled out of his bag. In the pale light of approaching dawn, he made out three figures standing just beyond the broken, tumbled city wall. One of them, the smaller one, he knew was Sandra, but the other two he could not make out. He raised both his arms and waved. All three of them waved back.

14

THE BRIGADIER STRODE FORWARD to greet them. "The long-lost lambs," he said. "We are glad to see you."

Sandra ran forward and embraced Mary. "We had been watching for you," she said. "Late last night we saw your fire. Or at least I thought it was your fire. The Parson wasn't sure."

The Parson pulled down the corners of his mouth. "In this barbarous land," he said, "one can be sure of nothing. It is a place of snares."

"The city looks deserted," said Lansing. "We would have come down late yesterday, but it had a fearsome look. We decided to wait till morning."

"It is not only deserted," said the Parson, "it is dead. It died very long ago. The buildings are crumbling of their very age."

"Still, we have found a couple of things," said the Brigadier. "What appears to have been an administration building, facing on a plaza. We've set up headquarters there, an operating base. And we have found inside it what we call a graphics tank. Mostly ruined, of course, but one corner of it—"

"In another room," said Sandra, "there is a group of statuary. The only art we've seen. Carved out of the whitest stone. And the exquisite work! It looks like statuary carved out of souls."

The Parson grunted at her. "But we have found nothing that throws a ray of light on why we're here. You," he said to the Brigadier, "were certain that we would. You were certain we would find people here. . . ."

"One meets each situation as it comes," said the Brigadier.

"You do not tear your hair nor weep nor lie down and kick your heels upon the ground when a circumstance does not meet your liking."

"Have you had breakfast?" Sandra asked.

"No," Mary told her. "When we saw you here, we came down immediately."

"Neither have we," said Sandra. "So let's go back to headquarters and all eat togther."

The Brigadier led the way and Lansing fell in step beside him.

"We'll have to go a little slowly," Mary said, "so that Jurgens can keep up."

The Brigadier turned about. "Well, all right," he said. "Jurgens, how are you getting on?"

"A little slowly," Jurgens said. "But I am all right."

The Brigadier started off again at a somewhat slower pace. "If it's not one damn thing to hold you up," he said to Lansing, "then it's another."

"You're the only one," Lansing told him, "who is in any hurry."

"It's hard to change," said the Brigadier. "I've been in a hurry all my life. Back home you had to be on your toes every blessed moment or someone would sneak up and clobber you."

"And you loved it. You loved every minute of it."

"I'll say this," said the Brigadier. "I clobbered more than ever clobbered me."

He led the way down what once had been a street, but now was little better than a trail. Many of the flat stone paving blocks that had floored the street were canted out of position, and huge blocks of stone that had fallen from buildings on either side added to the clutter. Vines and shrubs grew in the soil that had been exposed by the upheaval of the stone. In the crevices between the blocks that still remained in place grew grass and weeds.

The buildings were not tall—four and five stories for the most part. Doors and windows gaped. The stone of which the structures were built was either red or brown.

"Oxidation," said the Brigadier. "The very stone is rotting. No damage—no violent damage, that is. No sign of fire, no deliberate wrecking. The damage that you see is weathering and time. It has been looted, though. Perhaps time after time. There is virtually nothing left. At one time there were a lot of people here, but none now. The whole damn city's empty."

"You said you found something. I think you said a graphics tank. What's a graphics tank?"

"I don't know if it's one or not. I called it that. I could be wrong. Back home there are graphics tanks. You feed problems into them—"

"Military problems?"

"Well, yes, mostly military problems. A sort of war games deal. Factors are fed in and the tank works them out, showing what would happen. Showing it pictorially. That way it can be understood the better. The one we found here is ruined, for the most part dead. One small corner of it is still operating. As if you were looking out a window at another world. At times you see creatures in the picture."

"Maybe creatures that once lived here."

"I don't think so. This city is designed for humans, or approximate humans. The doors and windows are the right size. The stairs are the kind of stairs that can be climbed by humans."

The city had a creepy feeling. Despite its emptiness, something still lurked in it, something hidden, something hiding, watching and waiting. Lansing found himself closely examining each building as they came up to it, alert against the elusive flicker of something that had been watching, ducking out of sight.

"So you feel it, too," said the Brigadier. "That, dead as the place may seem, there is someone left."

"It's just natural caution on my part," said Lansing. "I'm scared by shadows."

"It may give you comfort to know that I feel much the same. As an old military person, I watch for the hidden enemy. I never go it blind. All the evidence is that the city is empty, and still I watch against the hidden enemy. I would feel better if we had some weapons. Can you imagine an expedition such as this without a weapon to its name? I still think that rascally innkeeper was lying in his teeth when he said he hadn't any."

"Maybe we don't need them," Lansing said. "So far on the trip there has been no need of them."

"That doesn't factor," said the Brigadier. "You pack a weapon a hundred miles, or a thousand, to use it only once."

A short while later they came out onto the plaza.

"That building over there," said the Brigadier, pointing. "That's where we are camped."

It was the largest building facing on the plaza and though in falling-down condition, it seemed somewhat less haggard than the others. The plaza was large, with a number of streets running into it. All around it crouched the brown-red buildings with blocks of stone that had fallen from them lying in their fronts. The building the Brigadier had indicated had one tower still standing and a broad stone stairs leading to the entrance.

"Dust lies everywhere," said the Brigadier. "On the streets, even in the center of the plaza, in the buildings, everywhere you go. It's the dust of dying stone, the wearing down of stone. In the building where we camped, we found old tracks in sheltered areas where no breeze could reach—the spoor of others who had gone before us. Other visitors, I suspect, very like ourselves. I am fairly certain one such group may be just ahead of us, for some of the tracks we found were fresh. They don't stay fresh for long. More dust settles on them, or they are blown away or covered by each little gust of wind."

Lansing looked back and saw that the rest of the band was close behind them. Jurgens was doing nobly, hobbling along at a better clip than was his usual gait. Mary and Sandra walked on either side of him and behind them came the Parson, resembling a stalking crow, with his head bent low, chin almost resting on his chest.

"I must warn you," said the Brigadier. "We must watch the Parson. He is, without doubt, a madman. He is the most cross-grained person I have ever met and there is no reason in him."

Lansing made no answer and, side by side, the two of them climbed the stairs that led up to the entrance of the building.

It was gloomy inside and there was the smell of woodsmoke. In the center of the foyer a tiny red eye gleamed at them—the burned-down campfire with a great pile of wood to one side of it— and yellow packsacks leaned against the wood. The faint flicker of firelight glinted off the polished surface of a metal cooking pot.

Even in the silence the interior of the building had a booming emptiness, and the sound of their footsteps on the floor came hollowly echoing back to them. High above their heads massive arches disappeared into a gloom that deepened into night. Wild shadows seemed to dance in the emptiness.

The others came in behind them and the conversation of Mary and Sandra, chattering at one another, set up a series of rolling, distant, booming echoes that made it seem there were a hundred hidden people talking deep inside the structure.

All of them walked together to the fire. The Brigadier stirred it up and piled on more wood. Flames began to leap, eating their way along the wood, and the shadows ran all about the walls. Lansing caught a sense of a horde of winged shapes flying high in the vault between the looming arches.

"I'll get busy with breakfast, but it will take awhile," said Sandra. "Brigadier, why don't you take the others to see the graphics tank. It's not too far away."

"Good idea," said the Brigadier. "Let me get my flashlight. Farther back it gets a little dark."

"I'll stay and help you," Mary told Sandra. "Later on I can see the tank."

The Brigadier led the way, cutting a swath before them with the flashlight. The thumping of Jurgens's crutch kept the echoes rolling back at them.

"The tank is witchery," grumbled the Parson. "It is no fit subject for anyone to look upon. I would recommend that we complete the ruin of it. A few sharp blows with the blunt end of an axe should do it."

"You try it," growled the Brigadier, "and I'll use the axe on you. The tank is one feeble remnant left to us of what, at one time, must have been a talented and sophisticated people. What it is, I do not pretend to know."

"You call it a graphics tank," said Lansing.

"I know I call it that because it's the handiest description that came to mind. But I'm sure it's more than that. I think it's a reaching out into another place, using a knowledge and a technique we have not yet thought of and that our people may never think of."

"And best we don't," the Parson said. "There are things that are better left alone. I'm convinced that throughout the universe there is a great morality—"

"A pox on your morality," said the Brigadier. "You always mumble of it. You mumble all the time. Instead of mumbling, why don't you speak out?"

The Parson did not reply.

They finally reached the graphics tank. It was located in a room in the far corner of the building. There was nothing else in the room and at first glance, the tank didn't look like much. It was a large mass that could have been described most readily as a mound of scrap. It was dead and faceless and covered by dust. Here and there the rusty red of eroding metal showed through the dust and grime.

"What I still fail to understand," said the Brigadier, "is how one small segment of it can still be operating while the rest of it is junk."

"Maybe what you are seeing," said Lansing, "is the business end of it. Maybe you are seeing all that ever could be seen—the viewing component. The rest of it may be no more than operative mechanism that still is barely hanging together. Someone stamp his foot too hard on the floor, and the last surviving connection that makes it function will crumble and then all of it goes dead."

"I hadn't thought of that," said the Brigadier. "You may be right, but I doubt you are. I think this pile of junk was, at one time, a panoramic viewing screen. What we have left is just one corner of it."

He rounded the end of the heap of junk and stopped, snapping off the flashlight.

"Have a look," he said.

What they saw was something that looked like a twenty-five-inch television screen, although the outline of the screen was jagged.

Within the jagged screen lay a haunting, red-tinted twilight world. In the foreground a clump of faceted, tumbled boulders glittered in the dim light of the unseen sun.

"Like diamonds, don't you think?" asked the Brigadier. "A clump of diamond boulders!"

"I couldn't say," said Lansing. "I have slight acquaintance with diamonds."

The diamond boulders, if they were diamonds, stood on a sandy plain with sparse vegetation, occasional clumps of wiry grass and low-growing shrubs that were scrawny and prickly and in their conformation gave the illusion of animals—strange animals, certainly, but still more animal than plant. On the distant skyline half a dozen trees were etched against the red-tinged sky, although, looking at them, Lansing could not be certain they were trees.

They were humped in a grotesque manner and their roots (if they were roots) did not go straight into the ground, but were also humped along the surface, looking somewhat like the humped posture of a traveling worm. The trees, he knew, must be huge for the details to show so sharply from so far away.

"Is that what you always see?" asked Lansing. "The scene always is the same?"

"Always the same," said the Brigadier.

A blur flickered across the screen, left to right, going very fast. For an instant, as if a camera had clicked in his brain, Lansing caught its shape. Basically it was humanoid—it had two arms, two legs, a head—but it was not human; it was very far from human. The neck was thin and long, the head small, the line of the neck extending up to the top of the skull and the head hanging down in front of the neck, both neck and head so slanted from its desperate speed that the head was almost horizontal with the ground. The outthrust jaw was massive, but the face (if there was a face at all) was tiny. The entire body was slanted forward, in the direction of its speed, both the arms and legs pumping. The arms, which were longer than a human's arms, ended in blobs that were not hands, and the one lifted foot (the other buried in the sand) ended in two claws. It seemed to be a dull gray color, but that, Lansing realized, might have been an implied coloration occasioned by the blurring speed at which it moved.

"Is this something new?" asked Lansing. "Have you seen it before?"

"We've seen it once before," said the Parson. "If not this one, another very like it."

"Running each time?"

"Each time running," said the Parson.

Lansing said to the Brigadier, "You told me creatures. You said that you'd seen creatures here. More than one, apparently."

"There is a spider thing," said the Brigadier, "that lives in the boulder clump. Probably not a spider, but that's as close an analogy as I can summon up. A spider has eight legs; this thing has more than eight, although it's hard to tell—they're always twisted up so it's impossible to count them. Usually you can see it peeking out, but it's hiding now. It's pure white, very hard to see in the diamond glitter. Every once in a while there is a three-legged egg that strolls across the screen. The body is egg-shaped, with slots running all the way around the upper end of it. Sensory organs, I assume. The three legs are hoofed and there seem to be no knee joints. It flings each leg stiffly forward as it strolls along. Cool, nonchalant, not scared of anything. Yet, so far as I can see, totally without protection of any sort at all."

"A place of horrors," said the Parson. "Something that no God-fearing man should allow himself to look upon."

❧ 15 ❧

THEY SAT AROUND THE fire, taking it easy after breakfast.

"We've explored this floor and the four floors above it," said the Brigadier, "and all we've found is the graphics tank and the statuary. All the rooms are as bare as Mother Hubbard's cupboard. Not a stick of furniture in them. Absolutely nothing left. What happened? Was it an orderly withdrawal, the city's residents moving elsewhere, taking all they owned? Or was the city looted, piece by piece? If so, who looted it? Did bands of people like us break up the furniture for firewood? That could be, for bands like ours probably have been visiting here for a long time, maybe for thousands of years. They could burn the furniture, of course, but what about the rest of it—the pots and pans, the dishes, the ceramics, the clothing, the books, the paintings, the carpeting, all the other possessions that must have been housed here? Maybe carried off as souvenirs, although I rather doubt that. It's not only here in the administration building, but everywhere we've looked. Even what appears to be private residences are bare."

"The city was a failure," said the Parson. "It was a godless city and it failed."

"It failed, I think," said Sandra, "because it had no heart. Except for the small group of statuary we found, there is no sign of art. A heartless, insensitive people who found no room for art."

"When they left," said the Brigadier, "they might have taken their art with them. Or others, coming later, could have taken it."

"Maybe this city was never meant to be permanent," said Mary. "It may never have been anything but a camping place. A place to stay while they waited for something to occur, an event they expected to occur. . . ."

"If that's the case," said the Brigadier, "they built exceedingly well. I've never heard of a camp built so solidly of stone. Another thing that puzzles me is that it had no defense of any sort. In a place like this, built so long ago, you'd expect a defensive wall. There are a few low walls here and there, outlining the perimeter of the city, but they are not continuous and not defense effective."

"We're running down hallucinations," said the Parson. "We have found nothing so far to enlighten us on why we're here. We found nothing at the cube and we've found nothing here."

"Perhaps none of us has looked deeply enough," said Jurgens.

"I doubt there is anything to find," the Parson said. "I think we're here at the irresponsible whim—"

"I cannot believe that," said the Brigadier. "For every action there is cause. In the universe there cannot be haphazard action."

"Are you sure of that?" the Parson asked.

"It stands to reason that that should be the case. You give up too easily, Parson. I'm not giving up. I'm going to rake this city clean before I quit the search. There is still the basement level in this building, and we'll have a look at that. If we find nothing there, we'll have further looks at selected targets."

"How can you be so sure that the answer's here?" asked Lansing. "There must be other places on this world."

"Because this city is the logical place. A city, one city, is the center of any civilization, the pivot point of what is going on. Where you find a concentration of people and of installations, that's where you'll find the answer."

"In which case," said Jurgens, "we should be up and looking."

"Jurgens, you are right," said the Brigadier. "We'll go down and scout the basement area, and if we find nothing there—by the way, I'm fairly sure we won't—then we'll take a hard look at the situation and decide what next to do."

"All of us had better carry torches," Sandra cautioned. "It'll be dark down there. The rest of the building is dark enough; down in the basement, it'll be really dark."

The Parson led the way down the broad flight of stairs. When

they reached the bottom of them, they instinctively huddled together, staring out into the blackness, flicking their flashlight
beams here and there, revealing corridors and gaping doorways.

"Let's split up," said the Brigadier, taking charge, "and scatter
out a bit. We'll cover more ground that way. If anyone finds anything, sing out. We'll split up by twos. Lansing, you and Jurgens
take the left-hand corridor; Mary and the Parson, the central one;
Sandra and I will take the right-hand. Each team use only one
flashlight. We have to save the batteries. We'll all meet back
here."

The Brigadier, from the way he said it, apparently expected to
be back soon.

No one questioned the Brigadier. All of them had gotten used
to his taking charge. They started out, down the corridors he had
assigned them.

Jurgens and Lansing came upon the maps in the fourth room
they visited. It would have been easy to have left without seeing
them. The basement was a depressing place. Dust lay everywhere.
As they walked, it puffed up from their feet, rising to hang in the
air. It had a dry, musty smell. Getting in his nose, it made Lansing
sneeze.

They had looked over the fourth room and, like all the other
rooms, it had been quite empty. As they were heading for the
doorway, preparatory to going to the next room, Jurgens made a
final sweep with the flashlight around the floor.

"A moment," he said. "Is there something over there on the
floor?"

Lansing looked. In the circle of light he could see an indistinct,
shadowed lumpiness.

"It's probably nothing," he said, anxious to be done with this
whole business of the basement. "Just an irregularity in the floor."

Jurgens humped forward on his crutch. "Let's be sure," he said.

Lansing watched as Jurgens hitched his way toward the lump.
The robot, balancing unsteadily, reached out with the crutch to
poke at the lump. Under the probing the lump moved and turned
over. A whiteness emerged out of the dust-covered grayness.

"We've got something," Jurgens said. "Looks like paper.
Maybe a book."

Lansing came quickly to the robot's side, knelt and tried to
wipe the dust from what Jurgens had found. It was a messy and

not too successful attempt. He picked up the lump and shook it. Dust billowed into the air, choking him.

"Let's get out of here," he said. "Find a better place to look at it."

"You haven't got it all," said Jurgens. "There's another one over there. A couple of feet to the right."

Lansing reached out and picked it up.

"That's all?" he asked.

"I think so. I don't see any more."

Quickly they retreated into the corridor.

"Hold the light close," said Lansing. "Let's see what we have."

Closer examination revealed four folded sheets—either paper or plastic. Under the coating of dust, it was hard to determine exactly what they had. Lansing thrust three of the sheets into a jacket pocket, unfolded the other. There were a number of folds, which were stiff and resisted separation. Finally the last fold came free and Lansing held out a single sheet. Jurgens shone the light upon it.

"A map," he said.

"Maybe of this place," said Lansing.

"Perhaps. We need a closer look. Where there is more light."

There were lines and strange markings and beside some of the markings strings of connected symbols that could be place names.

"The Brigadier said to sing out if we found anything."

"This can wait," said Lansing. "Let's finish with the rest of the rooms."

"But it could be important."

"It'll be just as important an hour from now as it is now."

They continued the search and found nothing. All the dusty rooms were empty.

Halfway down the corridor on their way back to the stairway, they heard the distant, booming shouting.

"Someone has found something," said Jurgens.

"Yes, I suppose so. But where?"

The shouting, hollow in the empty expanse of the basement, bounced and reverberated. It seemed to come from everywhere.

Hurrying down the corridor, they came to the foot of the stairs. There still was no possibility of determining from which direction the shouting might be coming. There were times when it sounded as if it were coming from the corridor they had just quitted.

Far down the right-hand corridor, a bouncing light glimmered.

"That's the Brigadier and Sandra," said Jurgens. "So it must be the Parson and Mary who found something."

Before they could take more than a few steps, the Brigadier was upon them.

"You're here," he panted. "It must be the Parson who is bellowing. We couldn't tell where it came from."

Together the four of them charged down the central corridor. At its far end they burst into a room far larger than any Jurgens and Lansing had found.

"You can stop the caterwauling now," called the Brigadier. "We're here. What is all the noise about?"

"We found doors," the Parson yelled.

"Well, hell, so did we," bawled the Brigadier. "All of us found doors."

"If you'll quiet down for a minute," the Parson said, "we'll show you what we have. Different kinds of doors."

Lansing, drawing up near Mary, saw along the extent of the rear wall of the room a row of circular lights—not the blinding light of a flashlight nor the dancing red light of a fire, but the softer hue of sunlight. The lights all stood about head-high from the floor.

Mary gripped his right arm with both her hands.

"Edward," she said, her voice shaking, "we've found other worlds."

"Other worlds?" he repeated, stupidly.

"There are doors," she said, "and peepholes through the doors. Look through the peepholes and you see the world."

She urged him forward and, not quite comprehending, he went along with her until they stood in front of one of the circles of light. "Look," she said, enthralled. "Look and see. That's my favorite world. I like it best of all."

Lansing moved closer and looked through the peephole.

"I call it the apple-blossom world," she said. "The blue-bird world."

And he saw.

The world stretched out before him, a quiet and gentle place with a broad expanse of grass that practically glistened in its greenness. A sparkling brook ran through the meadow in the middle distance, and now he saw that the grass was dotted with the pale blue and soft yellow of many blooming flowers. The yellow flowers looked like daffodils nodding in a breeze. The blue flowers, not so tall, half hidden in the grass, stared out at him like so many frightened eyes. On a distant hilltop stood a grove of small pink trees, covered and obscured by the astonishing pinkness of their blossoms.

"Crabapple trees," said Mary. "Crabapples bear pink blossoms."

The world had a sense of freshness, as if it might be only minutes old—washed clean by a careful springtime rain, dried and scrubbed by a solicitous breeze, burnished to its brightness by the rays of a gentle sun.

There was no more to it than the green meadow spangled by its million flowers, the brook that sparkled through the meadow and the pink of the apple trees standing on the hill. It was an uncomplicated place, a very simple place. But what it had was quite enough, Lansing told himself; it had all it needed.

He turned from the peephole to look at Mary.

"It is lovely," he said.

"I think so, too," said the Parson. For the first time since he had met the man, Lansing saw that the corners of his mouth were not turned down. His eternally anxious, puzzled face was serene.

"Some of the others," he said, shuddering. "Some of the others, but this one. . . ."

Lansing turned his attention to the door in which the peephole was located and saw that it was somewhat larger than the average door and made of what appeared to be heavy metal. Its hinges were designed to be opened outward, into the other world, and secured against inadvertent opening by heavy metal lugs that dogged it solidly in place. The lugs were held by substantial bolts set into the wall.

"This is only one of the worlds," he said. "What are the others like?"

"Not like this one," Mary said. "Go and look at them."

Lansing looked through the next peephole. It opened on an arctic scene—a vast snowfield, the veil of a raging blizzard. Through momentary breaks in the blizzard could be seen the cruel shimmer of a towering glacier. Although no cold reached him, Lansing shivered. There was no sign of any kind of life; nothing moved except the blowing snow.

The third peephole showed a barren, rocky surface partially obscured by a knee-high drift of blowing sand. The small bits of gravel on the surface seemed to have a life of their own. They rolled and scurried, urged on by the force of the wind that drove the sand. There was nothing to be seen but foreground; no middle distance or horizon. The blowing sand blotted out any depth of perception in a yellow haze.

"Yes, see," said Mary, who had moved along with him.

The next peephole was a ravening place of vicious life, a watery jungle world in which swam and crept and waddled a tangle of seething killers. For a moment Lansing was unable to separate the components of the life, getting only the impression of frantic motion. Then, bit by bit, he began to differentiate what he saw—the eaters and the eaten, the contention and the striving, the hunger and the hiding. The life forms were like nothing he had ever seen before—contorted bodies, enormous maws, lashing appendages, flashing fangs, striking claws, glittering eyes.

He turned away, sick at heart, stomach heaving. He wiped his face, as if to wipe away the hatred and abhorrence.

"I couldn't look," said Mary. "I only caught a glimpse."

Lansing felt himself shrinking in upon himself, trying to get small enough to hide, goosepimples rising on him.

"Forget it," Mary said. "Wipe it out. It's my fault. I should have warned you."

"How about the rest of them? Anything as bad as this?"

"No, this is the worst," said Mary.

"Will you look at this," said the Brigadier. "I never saw the like."

He stepped aside so that Lansing could look through the peephole. The terrain was jagged, not a single level surface, and it took a few seconds before Lansing could make out the reason. Then he saw that the entire surface of the place, if it actually had a surface, was covered by waist-high pyramids, their bases neatly fit together. There was no way of telling whether the recurring pyramids were the actual surface or whether some busybody, for whatever reason, had set the pyramids in place. Each pyramid rose to a sharp point. Any intruder, attempting to make its way through the maze, would run an excellent chance of becoming impaled.

"I must say," said the Brigadier, "that's the neatest abatis I have ever seen. Even heavy armor would have some difficulty getting through it."

"Do you think that's what it is?" asked Mary. "A fortification?"

"It could be," said the Brigadier, "but I see no logic for it. There is no strongpoint I see that it might be guarding."

That was true. The field of pyramids was all that could be seen. They continued to the horizon and there was nothing else.

"I don't suppose we'll ever know," said Lansing, "what it really is."

The Parson said, behind them, "There's a way to know. Unbolt the lugs and open the door and walk out into . . ."

"No," the Brigadier insisted, positively, "that's the one thing we can't take a chance on doing. Those doors could be traps. Open one of them and take one step beyond the threshold and you may find there's no longer any door, that you've stepped into the world with no way to get back."

"You have no trust in anything," said the Parson. "You call everything a trap."

"It is my military training," said the Brigadier, "and it stands me in good stead. It has saved me from a lot of foolish moves."

"There's just one more," Mary told Lansing, "and it's the saddest thing. Don't ask me why it's sad. It just is, that's all."

It was sad. Face pressed against the peephole, he saw the deep darkness of a woodland glen. The trees that grew along the hillside that shut in the glen were angular and crooked—deformed trees that gave the impression of very aged men hobbling, for there was no movement, no wind to stir the trees. And that, thought Lansing, might be a part of the sadness, forever being frozen in an agony of motion. Deeply embedded, mossy boulders loomed among the trees, and down in the bottom of the deep ravine, Lansing knew, there would be running water, but it would not run with a happy sound. Yet he could not pin down the sadness of the scene—depressing, yes, it was a depressing place, but *why* should it be so sad?

He turned away and looked at Mary. She shook her head at him. "Don't ask me," she said. "I have no idea."

16

THEY HAD BUILT UP the fire to give some warmth and comfort—warmth, for the sun was going down and it was chilly inside the building. Now they sat around and talked.

"I would like to think," said the Brigadier, "that the doors might hold the answer to what we're looking for, but I can't bring myself to think so."

"It's quite apparent to me," said the Parson, "that they are doors to other worlds. If we essayed to enter them . . ."

"I've told you," said the Brigadier, "that the doors are traps. Start messing around with one of them and you may find there's no way of coming back."

"Apparently," Mary began, "the people who occupied this city were much concerned with other worlds. Not only do we have the doors, but there's the graphics tank. What still can be seen in it must be another world."

"What we don't know," said Sandra, "is whether they are other actual worlds or landscapes of the mind. It has occurred to me that all of it may be no more than art—perhaps from our point of view a rather unconventional art form, but we can't pretend to know all the forms that art might take."

"That sounds to me like utter nonsense," said the Brigadier. "No artist in his right mind would force a viewer to peek through a hole to see what he had created. He'd want to hang it on a wall where everyone could see it, everyone at once."

"You're approaching the whole concept from a narrow viewpoint," Sandra told him. "How are you to know what an artist wants or what medium he would choose to work in? Perhaps the peephole method might be the one way he could bring a viewer close to what he'd done. Forcing the viewer to concentrate upon the art itself, shutting him off from all outside distractions. And the moods—did you notice that each of the peepholes had a well-established mood, each one different, each one appealing to a different emotional perception? In that way alone it could be the truest form of art."

"I still don't think it's art," said the Brigadier, being stubborn. "I think they are doors to other worlds and we'd best keep away from them."

"It seems to me we're neglecting one thing," said Mary. "The maps that Edward and Jurgens found. As far as I can see, none of them is a map of this place. Maybe they are maps of other places that we should know about. Perhaps even maps of some of the worlds we saw through the doors. If that's the case, there must be a way of going into them and getting back again."

"That may well be true," said the Brigadier, "but to do that you'd have to know *how* to do it, and we don't."

"The maps may represent other parts of this world we're on," said Jurgens. "We may not recognize them as such because we have seen but a small portion of this world."

"It seems to me," said Lansing, reaching for the maps, "that there is one that could be of this part of the world. Yes, here's the one." He unfolded the map and spread it out on the floor. "Look, here's something that could be this city. A cross-hatched area that might be a conventional sign for a city, and what seems to be a road leading from it, the trail we followed. And, here, this black square could be the inn."

The Brigadier hunched forward to study the map.

"Yes, there is something that could be the city," he said, "and a line connecting it with another point that could be the inn. But what about the cube? There's nothing there to represent the cube. Certainly the mapmaker would not have missed the cube."

"Maybe the map was made before the cube was built," said Jurgens.

"That could be true," said Sandra. "The cube looked new to me."

"We'll have to ponder on it awhile longer," said the Brigadier. "What we're doing now is talking off the tops of our heads, saying whatever comes to mind. Maybe all of us should give further thought to the situation, then we can talk again."

The Parson rose slowly to his feet. "I'm going for a stroll," he said. "A breath of fresh air may serve to clear the head. Does anyone want to go along with me?"

"I think I would," said Lansing.

Outside, in the plaza, the shadows were deepening. The sun was now gone and soon night would be closing in. The jagged, broken outlines of the buildings surrounding the plaza rose dark against the sunset sky. Walking along beside the Parson, Lansing felt, for the first time, the ancient aura of the place.

The Parson must have experienced the same sensation, for he said, "This place is half as old as time and it bears down upon one. As if it is possible to feel the weight of centuries resting on one's shoulders. Time has eroded its very stones. It is becoming one with the land on which it stands. Had you, Mr. Lansing, noticed that?"

"I think I have," said Lansing. "There's an unusual feel to it."

"It is a place," the Parson said, "where history has run down, where it has fulfilled itself and died. The city now stands as a reminder that all things of the flesh are fleeting, that history itself is no more than illusion. Such places as this are left for men to contemplate upon their failures. For this world is a failure. It seems to me it must have failed in many ways, more than other worlds."

"Perhaps you are right," said Lansing, not knowing what else he might say.

The Parson ceased his talk and strode along, hands clasped behind his back, head held high, but turning at intervals to survey the plaza.

Then he spoke again. "We must watch the Brigadier closely. The man is raving mad, but mad in such a reasonable, human way that it requires some discernment to come upon his madness. He's opinionated and stubborn. There is no reasoning with him. He can be wrong in more ways than any man I have ever met. It is because he has a military mind. Have you ever noticed that all military men are very narrow-minded?"

"In my time," said Lansing, "I have known few military men."

"Well, they are," the Parson said. "In their minds there's but one way to do a thing. Their minds are cerebral rule books and they live according to their book. They wear invisible blinders that will let them see neither left nor right, but only straight ahead. I think the two of us should keep close watch on the Brigadier. If we don't, he'll lead us into trouble. That's the nub of the trouble, actually. He must be the leader. He has a phobia about leading. Certainly you have noticed that."

"Yes, I have," said Lansing. "If you recall, I spoke to him about it."

"So you did," the Parson said. "He reminds me, in a way, of a neighbor I once had. The neighbor lived across the street from me and just down the street dwelled a devil. It was a nice neighborhood and you'd never expect to find a devil living there, but there was. I think few other people recognized him, but I did and I suspect that the neighbor that I speak of did as well, although we never talked about it. But the point I want to make is that the neighbor, even recognizing the devil for what he was, which I am sure he did, was neighborly with the devil. He'd say good morning to him when he met him on the street and would even stop and chat with him. I am certain there was nothing sinister in what they said to one another. They simply stopped to pass the time of day. But wouldn't you have thought that, knowing who the devil was, my neighbor would not have associated with him? If I had mentioned the matter to this neighbor, indicating my belief that he should not associate with a known devil—which I never did, of course—he would, I am sure, have informed me that he was a tolerant man, that he held no prejudice against Jews or black people or Papists or any other different sorts of people and that, having no bias against these, he could not be biased against the devil that lived on the selfsame street.

"It seems to me that in the universe there must be moral law, that there are things that are right and others that are wrong and that it is incumbent upon each of us to distinguish between right and wrong. If we are to be a moral people, we must know these distinctions. And I am not talking about the narrowness of religious views, which I must admit oftentimes are narrow, but about the whole spectrum of our human conduct. While I would not agree with it, I am well aware that certain people hold the opinion that a man may be virtuous even though he subscribes to no religion. I do not agree with this because it seems to me that a man needs the bulwark of his faith, his own personal, affirmed faith, to stand foursquare for the right, or what he perceives to be the right."

The Parson stopped and turned about to stand face to face with Lansing. "I talk in this wise," he said, "but it may be from pure habit and for no other reason. At home, in my turnip patch and in that white house fronting on a sedate green street, sedate despite the devil down the block, I knew my mind. I could be as positive and as self-assertive and self-righteous as any other man. In my small parish church, also sedate and white, exactly like my house, I could stand up and recite for my parishioners the right and wrong of any matter, no matter how important or how trivial it might be. But now I don't know. Now some of that solid self-assurance has been stripped from me. I was sure before; I am sure no longer."

He stopped talking and looked owlishly at Lansing. "I don't know why I'm saying this to you," he said. "You, of all people. Do you know why I am saying this to you?"

"I can't imagine why you should," said Lansing. "But if you want to talk at me, I'm quite content to listen. If it helps you any, I'll be glad to listen."

"Don't you feel it, too? The abandonment?"

"I can't say I have," said Lansing.

"The emptiness!" cried the Parson. "The nothingness! This horrible place, this equivalent of Hell! That is what I have always said, that is what I've told my people—that Hell is not a catalogue of tortures nor of misery, but an absence, a losing, a lostness, the end of love and faith, of a man's respect of self, of the strength of belief—"

Lansing shouted at him, "Man, pull yourself together! You can't let this place get to you. Don't you think that all of us—"

The Parson threw up his hands toward Heaven and cried out in a bellowing voice, "My God, why have you abandoned me? Why, oh, Lord—"

From the hills above the city another bellowing voice, another anguished cry was raised in answer to him. The anguished cry had in it a loneliness that caught at the heart with icy hands, a loneness and a lostness that made the blood run cold. It bayed and sobbed and wept across the city that had been deserted for millennia. It rang against the cruelty of the sky that looked down upon the city. It was a cry such as might be made by a thing without a soul.

Sobbing, head held between his hands, the Parson started running toward the camp. He went at a long-legged, frantic, bounding gallop. At times he staggered and seemed about to fall, but each time he caught himself to remain erect and continued running.

Lansing, with no hope of catching him, loped earnestly after him. At the edge of his mind was a tiny thankfulness that there was no chance of catching him. Once caught, what could one do with him?

And all the time the monstrous wailing from the hills beat against the sky. Up there something horrible was crying out its heart. Lansing felt the awful coldness of its pain gripping at his chest, as if a great fist had grabbed him and was slowly squeezing. He gasped, not with his running, but from the cold fist that had him in its clutch.

The Parson reached the front of the building and went pounding up the stairs. Running after him, Lansing halted just outside the firelit circle. The Parson was huddled on the floor, close by the fire, his legs pulled up tight against his body, his head bent forward to meet his knees, his arms wrapped about himself, assuming a fetal position as protection against the world.

The Brigadier was kneeling beside him, while the others stood off and watched in horror. At the sound of Lansing's footsteps, the Brigadier looked up, then rose from his place beside the Parson.

"What happened out there?" asked the Brigadier in a thunderous voice. "Lansing, what did you do to him?"

"You heard the wailing?"

"Yes, we wondered what it was."

"He was frightened by the wailing. He put his hands up to his ears and ran."

"Pure funk?"

"I think pure funk. He's been in a bad way for some time. He talked out there with me, terribly disjointed talk that had little logic in it. I tried to quiet him down, but he threw up his hands and cried out that God had abandoned him."

"Incredible," said the Brigadier.

Sandra, who had taken the place beside the Parson that the Brigadier had left, rose to her feet and put her hands up to her face. "He's rigid," she said. "He's all tied up in knots. What can we do for him?"

"Leave him alone," said the Brigadier. "He'll come around all by himself. If not, there's nothing we can do."

"A good stiff drink might do him no harm," suggested Lansing.

"How do we give it to him? I'll give you odds his teeth are clenched. You'd have to break his jaw to get it down him. Later on, perhaps."

"How horrible for this to happen to him," Sandra said.

"He's been working up to it," said the Brigadier, "ever since we started."

"Do you think he can pull out of it?" asked Mary.

"I've seen cases such as his," said the Brigadier, "in combat situations. Sometimes they come out of it; other times they don't."

"We should try to keep him warm," said Mary. "Has anyone a blanket?"

"I have two of them," said Jurgens. "I brought them in case of an emergency."

The Brigadier pulled Lansing to one side. "That wailing from the hills, was it fairly bad? We heard it in here, of course, but it was muffled."

"It was fairly bad," said Lansing.

"But you stood up under it?"

"Well, yes. But I wasn't under an emotional strain. He was. He's been under it some time. He had just finished telling me how God had abandoned him when that thing up there cut loose."

"Funk," said the Brigadier, disgusted. "Shameless, unadulterated funk."

"The man couldn't help it. He lost control."

"A big, loud-mouthed religious bully," the Brigadier said, "who finally got cut down to size."

Mary said, angrily, "You sound as if you're glad it happened."

"Well, not that," said the Brigadier, "not that at all. But faintly disgusted. Now we have two cripples to haul along with us."

"Why don't you just line them up and shoot them?" Lansing asked. "Oh, pardon me, I keep forgetting. You haven't a gun."

"The thing that none of you understands," said the Brigadier, "is that on a venture such as ours, toughness is the key. You must be tough to make it."

"You're tough enough," said Sandra, "to make up for all the rest of us."

"You do not like me," said the Brigadier, "and that's all right with me. No one ever likes a tough commanding officer."

"It just happens," Mary told him, "that you're not our commanding officer. All of us could get along most handsomely without you."

"I think it's time," said Lansing, "that we all knock it off. I've said some harsh things of you, Brigadier, and meant every word I said. But I'm willing to withdraw them if you will forget them. If we keep on squabbling like this, the venture, as you call it, will come to no good end."

"Admirable," said the Brigadier. "Spoken like a man. Lansing, I am glad you are on my side."

"I don't believe I'm on your side," said Lansing, "but I'm willing to do my best to get along with you."

"Listen," said Sandra. "Be quiet, all of you, and listen. I think the wailing's stopped."

They were quiet and listened, and it had.

17

WHEN LANSING WOKE IN the morning, all the rest were still asleep. Underneath the huddled blankets, the Parson had uncoiled a bit. He was still in a semifetal position, but not tied up in quite so hard a knot.

Jurgens squatted beside the fire, watching a bubbling pot of oatmeal. The coffee was set off to one side, on a small bed of raked-out coals, keeping warm.

Lansing crawled out of his sleeping bag and squatted beside Jurgens.

"How is our man?" he asked.

"He rested fairly easily," said Jurgens. "The last few hours he's been all right. Earlier he had a spell of shakes, quivering all over. No use calling anyone, for no one could have done anything for him. I watched over him and made sure that he kept covered. Finally he quit shaking and drifted off to sleep. You know, Lansing, we could have brought along some medicine. Why didn't someone think of that?"

"We do have some bandages and painkillers and disinfectants," said Lansing, "but I suppose that was all that was available. It wouldn't do us much good if we had other medicines. Not one of us has a shred of medical knowledge. Even if we had medicines, we'd not know how to use them."

"It seemed to me," said Jurgens, "that the Brigadier was uncommonly rough on him."

"The Brigadier was scared," said Lansing. "He has problems of his own."

"I don't see any problems for him."

"He's assumed the responsibility of watching after us. The kind of man he is, it's quite natural for him. He worries about everything we do, every step we take. He acts like a mother hen. It's not easy for him."

"Lansing, we can look out for ourselves."

"I know, but he doesn't think so. He probably blames himself for what happened to the Parson."

"He doesn't even like the Parson."

"I know. No one likes the Parson. He is hard to get along with."

"Then why did you go walking with him?"

"I don't know. Maybe I was sorry for him. He seems so much alone. No man should be as alone as he is."

"You're the one," said Jurgens, "who takes care of all of us. Without showing it, you take care of all of us. You have told no one about me, not about what I told you. Who I am and where I came from."

"When Mary asked you, you begged to be excused. I figured then that you wanted no one else to know."

"But I told *you*. You see what I mean. I told you. I trusted you. I don't know why, but I thought it was all right. I wanted you to know."

"Maybe because I have a father-confessor image."

"It's more than that," said Jurgens.

Lansing got up and walked to the entrance. On the stairs outside, he stopped and looked about the plaza. It was a peaceful scene. Although the east was brightening, the sun was not up yet. In the thin light of early dawn, the buildings that surrounded the plaza showed pink rather than the red they would become when the sun came up. A tang of cold hung in the air, and somewhere among the ruins a lone bird was cheeping.

A footstep sounded behind him and Lansing turned. The Brigadier was coming down the steps.

"The Parson seems little better," he said.

"Jurgens told me," said Lansing, "that he had the shakes early on, but quieted down and seemed to be sleeping for the last few hours."

"He presents a problem," said the Brigadier.

"So?"

"We must be about our work. We must comb the city. I'm convinced there's something here that must be found."

"Let's take just a few minutes," said Lansing, "and try to think things through. We have never really tried to think the situation through. You're convinced, I suppose, that somewhere there is a key that will free us from this place, let us go back to where we came from."

"No," said the Brigadier. "No, I don't think that. I don't think we ever will be able to go back to where we came from. The road back home is closed to us. But there must be a road to somewhere else."

"You think, perhaps, that we are here, were brought here by some strange agency to work out a puzzle, to find our way to a place the agency wants us to go but insists we find on our own. Like rats running a maze?"

The Brigadier looked at him narrowly. "Lansing, you are playing the devil's advocate. Why should you do that?"

"Perhaps because I have no idea of why we're here or what we're supposed to do, if anything."

"So you propose that we loll back and wait for events to take their course?"

"No, I don't propose that. I think we have to look for some way out, but I haven't the foggiest what we should be looking for."

"Neither do I," said the Brigadier, "but we have to look none the less. And that's why I say we have a problem. All of us should be out there looking, but we can't leave the Parson alone. Someone must stay with him, and that cuts down our force. We lose not one person, but two."

"You're right," said Lansing. "The Parson can't be left alone. I think Jurgens would be willing. He still has trouble getting around."

"Not Jurgens. We need him with us. He has a good head on his shoulders. He doesn't say much, but he's a thoughtful one. He has a good eye. He notices things."

"All right. Take him along. I'll stay."

"Not you. I need you. Do you think Sandra would be agreeable to staying? She's not of much value in the field. At best she's a fuzzy-headed creature."

"You could ask her," Lansing said.

Sandra agreed to remain behind with the Parson, and after breakfast the others started out. The Brigadier had the expedition well planned.

"Lansing, you and Mary take that street over there and go down its length. If you reach the end of it, then go to the next street over and come back. Jurgens and I will take this street and do the same."

"What will we be looking for?" asked Mary.

"For anything unusual. For anything that catches the eye. Even a hunch. It pays to follow hunches. I wish we had the time and people to make a house-by-house survey, but that's impossible. We'll have to pick our shots."

"It sounds haphazard to me," said Mary. "From you I would have expected a more logical plan."

Mary and Lansing walked down the street that had been indicated. Often the way was partially blocked by fallen masonry. There was nothing unusual to see. The houses were dowdy stone buildings, much the worse for wear and, for the most part, indistinguishable from one another. They appeared to be residences, although there could be no certainty of that.

They entered and explored a few houses, which were not at all unusual, since it seemed that exploring none was a shirking of their duty, and found nothing. The rooms were bare and depressing, coated with dust unmarked by any sign of recent intrusion. Lansing tried to imagine the rooms inhabited by happy, cheerful folks with words spoken and laughter ringing out, but found it was impossible to conjure up such images and finally gave up. The city was dead, the houses dead, the rooms dead. They had died too long ago to harbor ghosts. They had lost all memory. Nothing was left.

"It seems hopeless to me," said Mary, "this blind searching for some unknown factor. Even if it should be here, and there's no evidence that it is, it could take years to find. If you ask me, I think the Brigadier's insane."

"Perhaps not insane," said Lansing. "Simply a man driven by an insane purpose. Even when we were at the cube, he was certain that what we were looking for would be found in the city. At that time, of course, he was thinking of the city in different terms. He was thinking we would find people here."

"But not finding them, wouldn't it seem reasonable he should change his thinking?"

"Perhaps it would be reasonable for you and me. We can admit mistakes; we can adjust to changing situations. But not the Brigadier. He plans a course of action and he follows it. If he says a thing is so, then it is so. He will not change his mind."

"Knowing this, what do we do about it?"

"We play along with him. We travel a few more miles with him. Maybe the time will come, not too long from now, when he'll become persuaded."

"I'm afraid we'll have to wait too long."

"If so," said Lansing, "then we'll decide what to do."

"Knocking in his silly head would be my first suggestion."

He grinned at her, and she smiled back.

"Maybe," she told him, "that's a shade too vicious. But there are times I like to think of it."

They had been sitting on a slab of stone and as they rose to go on, Mary spoke sharply. "Listen. Is that someone screaming?"

For a moment they stood rigid, side by side, then the sound that Lansing had not heard at first came again—faint, far off, thinned by distance, the sound of a woman screaming.

"Sandra!" Mary cried and started to run down the street toward the plaza. She was running lightly, as if her feet were winged, Lansing coming on heavily in her wake. The path was tortuous, hemmed in by blocks of stone that had fallen in the narrow street.

Several times Lansing heard the screaming again.

He burst out of the street into the plaza. Mary was halfway across it. On the stairs that led up to the camp stood Sandra, waving her arms frantically, still screaming. He tried to force a burst of speed, but his legs would not respond.

Mary flew up the stairs and caught Sandra in her arms, the two of them standing together, clinging to one another. Out of the corner of his eye, he saw the Brigadier pop out of a street into the plaza. Lansing kept on doggedly, reached the bottom of the stairs and dashed on up.

"What goes on?" he panted.

"It's the Parson," Mary said. "He has disappeared."

"Disappeared! Sandra was supposed to watch him."

"I had to go to the bathroom," Sandra yelled at him. "I had to find a place to go. It was only for a minute."

"You've looked?" asked Mary.

"I've looked for him," Sandra shrilled. "I've looked everywhere."

The Brigadier came puffing up the stairs. Behind him, still out in the plaza, Jurgens came, hopping along, flailing with his crutch in an attempt to hurry.

"What's all the racket?" the Brigadier demanded.

"The Parson's gone," said Lansing.

"So he ran off," said the Brigadier. "The little scut ran off."

"I tried to find him," Sandra screamed.

"I know where he is," said Mary. "I am sure I know."

"So do I," said Lansing, charging for the entrance.

Mary yelled after him, running as she called, "You'll find a flashlight by my sleeping bag. I kept it there all night."

Lansing saw the flash and scooped it up, scarcely pausing in his stride. He ran for the basement stairs. As he went down them, he was talking to himself. "The fool!" he said. "The terrible, awful fool!"

He reached the basement and plunged for the central corridor, the bobbing flashlight beaming the way before him.

There still might be time, he told himself. There still might be time, but he was sure there wasn't.

He was right—there wasn't.

The big room at the end of the corridor was empty. The row of peepholes gleamed faintly in the dark.

He reached the first door, the one that opened on the crabapple world, and flashed the torch upon it. The lugs that had held the door securely against opening dangled on their bolts.

Lansing reached for the door and a terrific force hit him from behind, throwing him to the floor. The flashlight, still lit, went rolling. He had bumped his head against the floor in falling and stars and flashes of light went buzzing through his brain, but still he fought against the weight that held him down.

"You idiot!" yelled the Brigadier. "What were you about to do?"

"The Parson," Lansing mumbled thickly. "He went through the door."

"And you were going to follow?"

"Why, yes, of course. I could have found him . . ."

"You utter fool!" yelled the Brigadier. "That's a one-way door. You go in, but you can't come back. Go in and there is no door. Now will you behave yourself if I let you up?"

Mary had picked up the flashlight and was shining it on Lansing. "The Brigadier is right," she said. "It could be a one-way door." Then she screamed, "Sandra, get away from there!"

As she screamed, Jurgens came out of the dark and lunged with his crutch at Sandra. It struck her in the ribs and flung her to one side.

The Brigadier lumbered to his feet and backed against the door, guarding it against all comers.

"You understand," he said. "No one goes through this door. No one touches it."

Lansing climbed shakily to his feet. Jurgens, after knocking her down, was helping Sandra up.

"There it is," said Mary, shining the torch upon the floor. "There's the wrench he used to loosen the lugs."

"I saw it yesterday," said Jurgens. "It was hanging on a hook beside the door."

Mary stooped and picked up the wrench.

"Now," said the Brigadier, "since all of us have gone through our periods of insanity, let's settle down. We'll put the lugs back in place, then we'll throw away the wrench."

"How do you know it's a one-way door?" Sandra demanded.

"I don't know," said the Brigadier. "I'm just betting that it is."

And that was it, thought Lansing. No one could know, not even the Brigadier. And until they knew, knew without question, no one could go through the door.

"There's no way of knowing," said Jurgens, "until you step through the door. Then it could be too late."

"How right," said the Brigadier. "But no one is going to try."

He held out a hand to Mary, and she handed him the wrench.

"Hold the light on me," he said, "so I can see what I'm doing."

18

"HE ESCAPED," SAID THE Brigadier. "Lansing, when he talked with you last night did he mention escape?"

"No, I'm sure he didn't, but apparently he was hopeless. He said this place was Hell and he meant that it was *Hell,* the actual biblical Hell. He wasn't simply swearing."

"He was a weak man," said the Brigadier. "He took the coward's way out. He was the first of us to go."

"You sound," said Sandra, still tearful, "as if you expect others of us to go."

"There are always casualties," said the Brigadier. "One must count on casualties. Of course, you do your best to hold them down to an acceptable percentage."

Lansing grimaced. "If you think of this as humor, let me say that it's repugnant humor. You'll get no laughs from us."

"And now you're going to tell us," Mary said, "that we must carry on. Even with the Parson gone, we must carry on."

"Of course we must," said the Brigadier. "It's our only chance. If we don't find something here—"

"If we find something here, you'll think it is a trap," said Sandra. "You'll be scared to use it. We can't use the doors because they may be traps."

"I'm sure they are," said the Brigadier. "I don't want to catch any of you trying to find out."

"I looked through the peephole," said Jurgens, "and there was no sign of him."

"What did you expect to see?" asked the Brigadier. "Him standing there, thumbing his nose at us? As soon as he stepped through the door, he lit a shuck. He got out as fast as he could manage. He didn't want to take a chance."

"Maybe it was for the best," said Mary. "He may be happy there. I remember his face when he first looked through the peephole. He looked happy, the only time I ever saw him happy. There was something in that world that appealed to him. To all of us, perhaps, but especially to him."

"I remember," said Lansing. "He *was* happy. It was the first time I ever saw him without the corners of his mouth pulled down."

"So what do the two of you want us to do?" asked the Brigadier. "Line up in front of that door and all go marching through?"

"No," said Mary. "It wouldn't be right for us. But it was right for the Parson. It was the one way out for him. I hope that he is happy."

"Happiness should not be our sole goal," said the Brigadier.

"Nor is a death wish," said Mary, "and that is what *you* have. I'm convinced this precious city of yours will kill us one by one. Edward and I are not about to stay and have that happen to us. Come morning, we are leaving."

Lansing looked across the fire at her and for a moment felt the impulse to walk around the circle and take her in his arms. He did not do so; instead he stayed sitting where he was.

"The party can't split up," said the Brigadier, in a desperate tone. "The only strength we have lies in our staying together. You are giving way to panic."

Sandra screamed, "It is all my fault! If I'd stayed and watched him."

"It makes no matter," said Jurgens, trying to comfort her. "He would have waited for his chance. If not today, then another day. He would not have rested until he tried that other world."

"I think that's right," said Lansing. "He was a desperate man, at the end of his tether. I never realized how far gone he was until we talked last night. I honestly don't think any of us can blame ourselves for what took place."

"Then what about this leaving business?" asked the Brigadier. "How about it, Lansing?"

"It is my judgment that all of us should get out of here," said Lansing. "There is something sinister about the city. Certainly you have sensed it. It's dead, but even dead, there is something watching us. Watching all the time. Every move we make. You can forget it for a time and then you feel the watching once again, between your shoulder blades."

"And if we stay, if the rest of us stay?"

"Then you stay alone. I'm leaving and Mary's going with me." Thinking as he said it that not until Mary had spoken earlier had he known they would be leaving. How had she known? he wondered. What unknown, unconscious communication lay between them?

"A few more days," pleaded the Brigadier. "A few more days. That is all I'll ask. If nothing turns up in the next few days, then all of us will leave."

No one answered.

"Three days," he said. "Only three days. . . ."

"I'm not one to push a man to his limit in a bargain," Lansing said. "Mary willing, I'll make a deal with you and give you the benefit. Two days and that is all. There'll be no extension."

The Brigadier threw a puzzled look at Mary.

"All right," she said. "Two days."

Outside, night had fallen. Later the moon would rise, but now, with the sun gone, full night had fallen on the city.

Jurgens rose awkwardly. "I'll get supper started."

"No, let me," Sandra said. "It helps if I keep busy."

From far off came a terrible crying. They stiffened where they were, sitting starkly, listening. Again, as had been the case the night before, on a hilltop above the city a lonely creature was sobbing out its anguish.

19

LATE IN THE AFTERNOON of the second day, Mary and Lansing made the discovery.

Between two buildings, at the end of a narrow alley, they saw the gaping hole. Lansing turned the beam of his flashlight into the darkness. The beam revealed a narrow flight of stairs, a more substantial flight than might have been expected leading from an alley.

"You stay here," he said. "I'll go down and look. It'll probably turn out nothing."

"No," she said, "I'm going with you. I don't want to be left alone."

Carefully he lowered himself into the opening and gingerly descended the steep flight. Behind him clicks and scuffings told him that Mary was very close behind. There was more than one flight of stairs. He came to a landing and a quarter of the way around it another flight plunged down. It was not until he had taken the first few steps down the second flight that he heard the muttering. When he stopped dead in his tracks to listen, Mary bumped into him.

The muttering was soft. Nor was it quite a mutter, which was what he first had thought it was. Rather a throaty singing, as if someone were singing softly to himself. Masculine, not feminine, singing.

"Someone's singing," Mary whispered.

"We'll have to go and see," he said. He didn't want to go on. If he had done what he wanted, he would have turned about and fled. For while the singing (if it was singing) sounded human, there still was about the whole experience an eerie alienness that set his teeth on edge.

The second flight ended on yet another landing and as he went down the third flight, the singing gained some strength, while downward and ahead of him he saw softly glowing lights—cat eyes staring at him out of darkness. Reaching the foot of the stairs, he moved out a few steps on a metal walkway and Mary came to stand beside him.

"Machinery," she said. "Or a machine."

"It's hard to tell," he said. "An installation of some sort."

"And operating," she said. "Do you realize this is the first live thing we've found."

The machinery, Lansing saw, was not massive. Not overpowering. The many glowing eyes scattered all through it furnished enough light so that the machinery could be seen—guessed rather than seen, he told himself, for the light from the eyes was faint.

The whole assembly was a spindly, spidery mass. It seemed to have no moving parts. And it was singing to itself.

When he trained his light ahead, he saw that the metal walkway on which they stood ran straight ahead, forming a narrow path between two conglomerations of machinery. The path ran a long way, well beyond the strength of the flashlight's beam, and as far as he could see, the spindly forms flanked it on either side.

Walking slowly and carefully, he started down the walkway, with Mary close beside him. When they reached the beginning of the machinery they halted and he trained the light on the nearest segments of the installation.

The machines were not only spindly; they were delicate. The polished metal, if it was metal, gleamed brightly; there was no dust or grease upon it. It didn't, in fact, look like any machinery he had ever seen. It looked like a piece of metal sculpture that a slap-happy artist had assembled with a pair of pliers, chortling all the while. But, despite the lack of moving parts, despite any indication of actual operation, it seemed to be brimming with a sense of life and purpose. And all the time it sang, crooning to itself.

"It's strange," said Mary. "As an engineer, I should have some inkling as to what this could be. But there's not a single component that I recognize."

"No notion what it's doing?"

"None at all," she said.

"We've been calling it machinery."

"For lack of a better term," she said.

Lansing found his body unconsciously responding to the rhythm of the song the machines were singing, as if his body, all of his body, was responding to its beat. It seeped into him, formed a background for his life.

It's taking over, he thought, but the thought came from very far away and did not seem to be a part of him, as if another person might be thinking it. He recognized the danger of being taken over and tried to call out a warning to Mary, but the warning took some little time and before he could cry out, he was another kind of life.

He was light-years tall and each step he took spanned many trillion miles. He loomed in the universe, his body wispy and tenuous, a body that flashed like spangles in the glare of flaring suns that swirled and spun about him. Planets were no more than grating gravel underneath his feet. When a black hole blocked his way, he kicked it to one side. He put out his hand to pluck half a dozen quasars and strung them on a strand of starlight to hang about his neck.

He climbed a hill made of piled-up stars. The hill was high and steep and required a lot of scrabbling to get up it; in the process of climbing he dislodged a number of the stars that made up the hill and, once dislodged, they went clattering down, rolling and bouncing to the bottom of the hill, except that it had no bottom.

He reached the summit and stood upon it, straddle-legged to hold himself secure, and all the universe lay spread out before him, to its farthest edge. He raised a fist and shook it, bellowing out a challenge to eternity, and the echoes of his shouting came back to him from infinity's farthest curve.

From where he stood he saw the end of time and space and remembered how once he had wondered what lay beyond the end of time and space. Now he saw and recoiled upon himself. He lost his footing and went tumbling down the hill, and when he reached the bottom (but not the bottom, for there was no bottom), he lay spread-eagled in a drift of interstellar dust and gas that surged all about him and tossed him mercilessly, as if he were in the clutches of an angry sea.

Remembering what he had seen beyond the end of time and space, he groaned. And groaning, he came back to where he was, standing on a metal walkway, flanked by spidery machines that were crooning to themselves.

Mary had him by the arm and was tugging to get him turned around. Stupidly, not too sure as yet of where he was, he went along with the tugging and got turned around. The lighted torch, he saw, was lying on the floor and he stooped to pick it up. He did pick it up, but in doing so almost fell upon his face.

Mary tugged at him again.

"We can stop now. How are you?"

"I'll be all right," he said. "I seem to be confused. I saw the universe—"

"So that is what you saw."

"You mean that you saw something, too."

"When I came back," she said, "you were standing frozen. At first I was afraid to touch you. I thought that you might break into a million pieces."

"Let's sit down," said Lansing. "For a minute, let's sit down."

"There's no place for us to sit."

"On the floor," he said. "We can sit on the floor."

They sat upon the hard surface of the walkway, facing one another.

"So now we know," she said.

"Know what?" He shook his head as if to clear his mind. The haze was clearing slightly, but he was still muddled.

"Know what the machines are supposed to do. Edward, we can't tell the Brigadier about this place. He'd go hogwild."

"We've got to tell him," Lansing said. "We made a deal with him. We must be fair with him."

"Once again," she said, "something we don't know how to handle. Like the doors."

He looked back over his shoulder at the spidery machines. He could see them more clearly now. The fuzziness was going.

"You said you saw the universe. What do you mean by that?"

"Mary, Mary, Mary! Will you, please, wait a minute."

"It hit you hard," she said.

"I think perhaps it did."

"I came out of it easy."

"That's your strong sense of self-perception."

"Don't joke," she said. "Don't try to make a joke of it. This is serious."

"I know that. I'm sorry. You want to know. I'll try to tell you. I visited the universe. I was tall and big. I had a body of shining starlight, maybe a puff of comet tail. It was like a dream, but not really like a dream. I was there. It was all ridiculous, but I was there. I climbed a hill made up of shoveled-together stars and, standing on top of it, I saw the universe, all of the universe, out to the end of time and space, where time and space pinched out. I saw what lay beyond time/space, and I don't now remember exactly what I saw. Chaos. Maybe that's the name for it. A churning nothingness, a raging, angry nothingness. I'd never thought of nothing as a raging anger. That's what shook me. When I say raging I don't mean hot. It was cold. Not just cold by temperature, for there was no way to know the temperature. Cold in a deadly, venomous way. Uncaring. Worse than uncaring. Angry against everything that exists or ever existed. Raging to get at anything that is not nothingness and put an end to it."

She made a sympathetic motion with her hands. "I shouldn't have asked you. I shouldn't have insisted. I'm sorry I forced you into telling me. It wasn't easy for you."

"I wanted to tell you. I would have told you, but maybe not right yet. But now it's over with and I feel easier about it. Telling you, I gave some of it away. What they did to me—to us. You said you saw it, too."

"Not what you saw. Not as devastating. I'm sure the machine did it to us. It takes your mind, your ego, the life force, the personality, and rips it out of you and sends it somewhere else. You said it was like a dream and still it was not a dream. I think it's actuality, not a dream. A machine would not have a dream concept. If it were possible for someone to go where you went, in all actuality, of course, they'd see what you saw. There were absurdities, of course. . . ."

"I kicked a black hole out of the path. I climbed a starry mountain. Planets crunched like gravel when I stepped on them."

"Those are the absurdities, Edward. The reaction, rebellion of your mind. A defense mechanism meant to keep you sane. The laughter element. The big guffaw to show you didn't mind."

"You mean you think I was really there? That my mind was really there?"

"Look," she said, "we have to face it. The people who lived in this city were sophisticated scientists, uncanny technicians. They had to be to produce this apparatus and the doors and the Brigadier's graphics tank. Their minds, their aims, canted in a different direction than yours or mine. They performed chores, sought out answers we'd never think about. Absurd as they may be, the doors are understandable. But what we have here is not understandable. In certain ways, it may be scientific heresy."

"If you talk that way long enough, you'll talk me into it."

"We have to face facts. We're dealing with a kind of world we do not understand. We're dealing with what is left of it. God knows what you would have found here at the height of their culture. These may be human concepts. I think they are. They are the kind of heady projects the human race might do. But because of the very fact that they are so far-out human, they may seem more alien to us than something put together by a race on some distant solar system."

"But their culture failed. Despite all they did or could do, it all came down to nothing. They're gone and their city's dead."

"They might have gone elsewhere. To a world they found."

"Or they may have overreached themselves. Have you thought of that? They lost their souls—is that what the Parson said?"

"It sounds like him," said Mary.

"And now yourself. Where did they send you?"

"I caught just a glimpse of it. You must have stayed longer than I did. Just a glimpse was all. Another culture, I think. I really saw no one. I talked with no one. I was like a ghost that no one saw. A shadow that walked in and then went out again. But I sensed the people, the sort of lives they lived, the thoughts they thought. It was beautiful.

"They were godlike. Truly godlike. There is no doubt of that. Stay there long enough, sensing them, seeing how far they stood above you and you would have been reduced to a crawling worm. Gentle gods, I think. Although they were sophisticated. Civilized. Entirely civilized. They have no government. There is no need of one. And no economic sense, no need of economics. It would take a true civilization, the highest concept of civilization, to need no government and no economic system. No money, no buying or selling, no borrowing or loaning, therefore no interest rates, no grubby bankers, no attorneys. There may even have been no such a thing as law."

"How do you know all that?"

"It soaked into me. All of it was there for one to know. Not to see, of course. To know."

"Instead of telescopes," said Lansing.

"Telescopes?"

"I was just thinking aloud. Back in my world, and I suppose in yours as well, men use telescopes in an attempt to ferret out the secrets of space. But these people—they had no use of telescopes. Instead of looking out, they *went* out. They could go out there themselves. I suppose wherever they might wish. Having built the sort of installation that is here, they certainly would have known how to use it and control it, so they could go to specific targets. But now the machines—what else can I call them?"

"Machines is good enough."

"Now they are running wild. They sent us out at random."

"Somewhere in this city," she said, "there must be a control room from which this installation can be handled. Maybe booths in which people who are to be subjected to its operation can be placed—although I guess I'd doubt that. The system would be something far more subtle than that."

"Even if we found such a place," he said, "it might take years before we could learn to operate it."

"Could be, but we could have a shot at it."

"Maybe this is what happened to the people here. Maybe they found another world, a better world, and sent all their people there."

"In body as well as in mind?" she asked. "That would take some doing."

"That's right. I didn't think of that. Even if they could that wouldn't explain everything else being gone. Unless they sent along all their possessions as well."

"I would doubt that," Mary said. "Unless they used this apparatus to find another place and they could build another door to it. The two could be related, these machines and the doors, although I'd be more inclined to view the installation here as a research tool to be used to learn from alien worlds. Imagine what could be done with it. You could get all kinds of data that could be adapted to your culture. You could revise political and economic systems, steal technological procedures previously unknown to you, overhaul sociological structures, perhaps even learn of new scientific approaches, even entirely unknown scientific disciplines. For any civilized race, it would be a cultural shot in the arm."

"You touched on it exactly," he told her. "An intelligent race, you said. Was the race that lived here intelligent enough? Would your culture or mine be intelligent enough to use what we could find by the proper use of this installation? Or would we simply hunker down, clinging to our old ways, the life we were accustomed to, and misuse or abuse what we found on other worlds— perhaps misuse it disastrously?"

"That's not up to you or me," she said. "Not at the moment, it's not. I think we should go out and see if we can locate that hypothetical control room."

He rose and reached down a hand to help her to her feet. Once up, she still held to his hand.

"Edward," she said, "the two of us have been through an awful lot together. Even in so short a time . . ."

"It's not seemed short to me," he told her. "I can't seem to remember a time without you."

He bent to kiss her and she held him briefly, then stepped away. They climbed the stairs back to the alley and began their search. They stayed at it until darkness began to fall. They found no control room.

Back at the building where they were camped, they found Sandra and Jurgens busy preparing the evening meal. The Brigadier was not around.

"He went off by himself," Sandra explained. "We haven't seen him since."

"We found nothing," Jurgens said. "How about you?"

"No business talk, please, until after supper," Mary pleaded. "By that time the Brigadier should be back."

He arrived half an hour later and sat down heavily on his rolled-up sleeping bag. "I don't mind telling you I'm bushed," he said. "I covered a good part of the northeast section. For some silly idea I had the hunch that if we were to find anything, we would find it there. I found not a thing."

Sandra dished up a plate of food and handed it to him. "Let's eat," she said.

The Brigadier took the plate and began eating, without waiting for the rest of them, shoveling the food into his mouth. He looked tired, Lansing thought. Tired and old. For the first time, the Brigadier showed a touch of age.

When they had finished eating, the Brigadier dug a bottle out of his pack and passed it around the circle. When it came back to him, he took a long pull at it, recapped it and sat cuddling it in his lap.

"This is two days," he said. "That is what you promised me. I am a man of my word. I will not try to hold you further. Mary, I know you and Lansing will be moving on. How about you other two?"

"I think we'll go with Mary and Lansing," Sandra said. "I know I will. The city frightens me."

"How do you feel?" the Brigadier asked Jurgens.

"With all due respect," the robot told him, "there seems no point in staying."

"As for myself," said the Brigadier, "I'll stay on for a while. Later I may catch up with you. I'm sure there is something to be found here."

"Brigadier," said Lansing, "we found it this afternoon. But I must warn you that—"

The Brigadier leaped to his feet and the bottle went flying from his lap. It hit the floor but did not break. It went rolling across the floor, and Lansing caught it.

"You found it!" yelled the Brigadier. "What is it? Tell me what you found."

"Brigadier, sit down," said Lansing, speaking sharply, as one might address a naughty child.

Apparently astonished at the tone of Lansing's voice, the Brigadier sat down meekly. Lansing leaned forward and handed him the bottle. He took it and placed it back in his lap.

"Now let's talk about this quietly," Mary said. "Let us consider it. Let's not go charging off. I suggested to Edward that we should say nothing of our discovery, but he said we had made a bargain—"

"But why?" shouted the Brigadier. "Why say nothing?"

"Because what we found is beyond our understanding. We know at least one thing that it can do, but there is no way to control it. It's dangerous. It's nothing to fool around with. We told ourselves that somewhere there must be a control room, but we couldn't find it."

"You're an engineer," said Jurgens. "You, of all of us, should know the most about it. Why don't you go ahead and tell us what you found."

"Perhaps you, Edward," Mary said.

Lansing said, "No, it's yours to tell."

She told them and they listened intently. There were a few questioning interruptions, but not many.

After she had finished, a long silence ensued. Finally Jurgens turned to Mary. "What you are saying is that the people here had a thrust toward other worlds. Alien worlds, most likely, rather than alternate Earths."

"They may not have been aware of the alternate Earths," said Lansing.

"They wanted to get away from here," said Jurgens. "The installation that you found and the doors are tied together, part of the same research effort."

"It seems likely," Mary told him.

The Brigadier said, quietly, quite unlike his earlier shouting, "You two are the only ones who have seen it. The rest of us, all five of us, should have a look at it."

"I'm not saying we should not investigate," said Mary. "What I do say is that we should be careful what we do. Both Edward and I were taken over, but only for a moment. That may be no more than a sample of what it can do."

"You have searched for a control room?"

"We searched till dark," said Lansing.

"It would seem the control should be housed with the apparatus," said the Brigadier.

"We thought of that, of course. But there is no room. All the space is taken up by the installation. Then we figured that in a building close by . . ."

"That would not necessarily be the case," said Mary. "I know that now. The control room could be anywhere in the city. Anyplace at all."

"You say the mechanism is unrecognizable? That you have no idea what it is?"

"There is not a single piece of it," said Mary, "that I recognized as anything that would correspond to any kind of mechanism familiar to my world. Of course a closer look, a closer examination might make for a marginal understanding. The point is that I wouldn't want to get that close, get that involved with it. That would be sticking your neck out. Edward and I did not experience the full effect, I'm sure. Get more involved, closer to it, I can't imagine what might happen."

"The feature of this city that worries me the most," said Sandra, "is the flatness of it. Not of the city itself, but the culture that it represents. It exhibits a cultural poverty that is simply impossible. There are no churches, no recognizable places of worship, nothing that ever seems to have been a library or an art gallery or a music hall. It seems impossible to me that any people could have been so destitute of sensitivity, could have been satisfied to live out such flat lives."

"They may have been a one-idea people," said Lansing. "Absorbed, the entire body of them, in one area of research and endeavor. This, of course, is hard to understand, but we cannot know their motives. It would be possible, I suppose, to have so strong a motive . . ."

"This discussion is getting us nowhere," growled the Brigadier. "We'll have a look in the morning. Or at least *I* will have a look. The others of you will be taking off."

"We'll stay with you," said Lansing, "long enough to have that look."

"But, for God's sake," said Mary, "everyone be careful."

20

"I DOUBT," THE BRIGADIER observed, "that there is as much danger here as would appear to be the case. The machines may be able to affect a sensitive, whereas a man of stronger fiber who had his feet solidly planted on the ground . . ."

"I suppose," said Lansing, "you are thinking of yourself. If that is the case, don't let me hold you back. Go ahead and walk straight into it."

"You're dead wrong," Mary told the Brigadier. "I'm not a sensitive. It's just possible Edward may be and Sandra certainly. The Parson was and—"

"The Parson," said the Brigadier, "could not have been a sensitive. Unstrung, perhaps, unstable, but otherwise a clod."

Mary sighed in resignation. "Have it your own way," she said.

The five of them stood on the metal walkway, well clear of the machines, which still were glowing with their cat eyes, still singing to themselves.

"I had anticipated," said Jurgens, "that being half machine myself I might be able to discern some affinity with this installation. I could not know, of course, for on my world there are only the simplest machines. Nothing remotely like these. As I say, I had looked forward to a possibly interesting experience, but I am deeply disappointed."

"You feel nothing?" Sandra asked.

"Not a thing," he said.

"Well, now that we have seen these machines," the Brigadier asked, "what do we do about them? What do we do next?"

"We promised you nothing," Lansing said, "except that we would come along with you to have a look at them. For my part, that's all I'm going to do. Have another look at them."

"Then what's the use of finding them?"

"We told you," Mary said, "that at the moment there is no way of understanding them. You were looking for something—you had no idea what it was—so we went out and found it for you. I told you the other night that this city will kill us one by one. The Parson told you it was evil and he fled the evil that he saw. If the Parson was right and there is evil in this city, the machines may be a part of it."

"You don't think this, do you?"

"No, I don't. I don't think machines have a capacity for evil. But the city is no place to stay and I am leaving it, right now. Are you coming, Edward?"

"You lead the way. I'll be right behind you."

"Now wait a minute!" stormed the Brigadier. "You can't desert me now. Not when we are on the brink."

"The brink of what?" asked Jurgens.

"The brink of finding the answer we seek."

"It's not here," said Jurgens. "The machines may be a part of it, but they're not all of it and you can't get the solution from them."

The Brigadier sputtered at him, but no words came out. His face was puffed and red with anger and frustration. Then suddenly his sputtering stopped and he shouted at them. "We'll see about that! I'll show you. I'll show all of you!"

As he shouted at them he leaped forward, running down the walkway, straight between the two banks of machines.

Jurgens took two quick steps in pursuit, struggling to get solid footing with his crutch on the smoothness of the metal walkway. Moving deliberately, Lansing kicked the crutch out from under him and sent the robot sprawling.

The Brigadier still was running. He was far down the walkway when suddenly he sparkled all along his entire body. The sparkle flared for a small fraction of a second and the Brigadier was gone.

Blinded by the flare, they all stood stockstill, horrified. Jurgens, using the crutch to pull himself erect, scrambled to his feet.

"I think," he told Lansing, "that I must thank you for my life."

"I told you, long ago," said Lansing, "that if you ever tried another stupid trick, I'd clobber you with whatever was at hand."

"I can't see him," said Sandra. "The Brigadier's not there."

Mary directed a flashlight beam down the walkway. "Neither can I," she said. "The beam doesn't carry far enough."

"I think it does," said Jurgens. "The Brigadier is gone."

"But it wasn't that way with us," Mary said to Lansing. "Our bodies stayed behind."

"We weren't as far down the walkway as the general was."

"That may be it," she said. "You spoke of the machines being able to take over the body as well as the mind. I told you it would be impossible. Maybe I was wrong."

"Two of us gone," said Sandra. "The Parson and the Brigadier."

"The Brigadier may come back," said Lansing.

"Somehow I don't think so," said Mary. "There was a lot of energy involved. The Brigadier could very well be dead."

"You can say this for him," said Jurgens. "He went out in a blaze of glory. No! No! I'm sorry. I apologize. I did not mean that; I should not have said it."

"You're forgiven," Lansing said. "You just beat another one of us to saying it."

"Now what?" asked Sandra. "What do we do now?"

"That's a problem," Mary told her. "Edward, do you have any kind of hunch that he'll be coming back? As we came back."

"No hunch. Since we came back, I thought . . ."

"But this was different."

"The damn fool," said Lansing. "The poor, pitiful damn fool. The leader to the end."

They stood, huddled together, looking down the walkway in all its emptiness. The cat eyes glowed, the machines kept up their crooning.

"Maybe we should wait awhile," said Mary, "before we leave the city."

"I think we should," said Jurgens.

"If he does come back, he'll need us," Sandra said.

"Edward," Mary asked, "what do you think?"

"That we should wait," he said. "At a time like this, we can't desert the man. I can't imagine he'll come back, but if he should . . ."

They moved their camp into the alley, near the stairs that went down into the cavern where the machines sang softly to themselves. Each night the lonesome beast came out on the hills above the city and cried out its bitterness and lostness.

On the morning of the fourth day, after consulting the map that might have represented this part of the world, they left the city and found the westward continuation of the road they'd walked to reach it.

∽21∽

EARLY IN THE AFTERNOON they reached the summit of the hills that ringed in the city and entered a grotesque world of erosion carving. The trail plunged downward through a colorful nightmare of earthen turrets, castles, battlements, towers and other fantastic shapes, tinted by the unending range of hues exhibited by the many geological layers of the different earths.

The going was slow; they did not try to hurry. The trail no longer could claim the distinction of being called a road. At times they would come out into the flatness of small floodplains, but then they would leave them to drop again into the weird, color-riotous madness of the tortured terrain.

Well before night closed in, they chose a camping place in the angle of a soaring clay cliff. Wood they found in tangled heaps of drift, deposited at some time long ago when great trees had come riding on the crests of the raging torrents that had carved the land. Wood, but no water. The day had not been excessively hot, however, and their canteens were almost full.

Vegetation grew sparse. Except for occasional patches of stout grasses and a few clumps of small conifers, hugging close against the ground, the sculptured earth was bare.

After supper they sat and watched the glory of the colors fade. When night fell, the stars came out bright and hard. Searching the skies, Lansing spotted familiar constellations. There could be no doubt, he told himself, that this place was Earth, but not the old familiar Earth that he had known. It was not another planet in another solar system; it was one of the alternate Earths that Andy had talked about, never for a moment suspecting there could be such other Earths.

The time factor bothered Lansing. With the constellations so little changed, if changed at all, the time differential between this Earth and the one that he had known must be no greater than a few tens of thousands of years at most. And yet, on this Earth, a great civilization had risen to heights as great or greater than had been the case on his Earth—had risen, developed, flourished and died. Could it be, he asked himself, that here man had gotten an earlier start? Could the race of man here have developed some millions of years earlier? Was it possible, he wondered, that the crisis point between the two had been the dying out of mankind on his Earth, necessitating a starting over? That idea bothered him. If man died out on one Earth, what would be the chance of starting over again, of being given a second chance? Reason told him that the chance would be well nigh impossible.

"Edward," Mary called, "you've scarcely said a word. What is going on?"

He shook his head. "A few random thoughts. Nothing of any great importance."

"I'll never feel quite right," said Sandra, "for having left so soon. We really didn't give the Brigadier much chance of getting back."

"Why didn't you speak up?" asked Mary. "You never said a word. We would have listened to you."

"I was as anxious as the rest of you to get away. I couldn't bear the thought of spending another day in the city."

"For my part," said Jurgens, "I think we wasted time waiting for him. He's gone and gone for good."

"What will happen to us now?" asked Sandra.

"Because the Parson and the Brigadier are gone?" asked Jurgens.

"Not that the two of them are gone, not those two alone. But there were six of us and now there are four. When will there be only three of us, or two?"

"We'll have a better chance out here than we had in the city," Mary said. "The city was a killer. We lost our people in the city."

"We'll be all right," said Jurgens. "We'll feel our way along. We'll keep close watch and we won't take chances."

"But we don't know where we're going," Sandra wailed.

"We never have," said Jurgens. "Not since we were first thrown into this world have we known where we were going. Maybe the next bend down the trail will tell us. Maybe the day after tomorrow or the day after that."

That night the Sniffler came back again. It sniffed all around the camp but did not intrude. They sat and listened to it. There was something comforting about its presence, as if an old friend had come back, as if a straying dog had come home again. There was no terror in the sniffling. The Sniffler had not entered the city with them; perhaps it liked the city no more than they had. But now that they were on the trail again, it had returned to join them.

Well before dark on the second day, they came on a tumbled ruin that sat on a small terrace above the trail.

"A place to spend the night," said Jurgens.

They climbed the terrace and came to a rubble of fallen stones, soft sandstone blocks that at one time had formed a low wall around the small, ruined building that stood in the center of the rectangle formed by the scattered wall.

"Sandstone," said Lansing. "Where could it have come from?"

"Over there," said Jurgens, pointing to a low clay cliff that formed a backdrop for the place. "A strata of sandstone in the clay. There are signs, old signs, of quarrying."

"Strange," said Lansing.

"Not so strange," Jurgens told him. "Here and there, along the way, there have been sandstone outcrops."

"I hadn't noticed."

"You have to look sharp to see them. They are of the same color as the clay. I saw the first one by accident and then kept looking for them."

The area within the shattered walls might have covered half an acre, scarcely more. The ruin standing in its center at one time had been a one-room structure. The roof had fallen in, part of the walls had tumbled down. Some broken crockery was scattered about on what once had been a well-trodden earthen floor, and in one corner of it Jurgens found a tarnished, battered metal pot.

"A stopping place for travelers," said Sandra. "A caravansary."

"Or a fort," said Jurgens.

"A fort against what?" asked Lansing. "There is nothing here to fort up against."

"At one time there might have been," the robot said.

Outside the ruined building they found evidence of an old campfire, a bed of ash and smoke-blackened stones placed at intervals around it, perhaps to serve as cooking hearths. Beside the fire site was piled some driftwood.

"The last party through," said Jurgens, "gathered more than was needed. It should last us out the night."

"How about water?" Lansing asked.

"I think we have enough," said Mary. "We'll have to find some tomorrow."

Lansing walked out to the ruined wall and stood, looking out over the monstrously sculptured terrain. Badlands, he thought, that was the word he had been searching for during the last two days and that had eluded him till now. Out in the western area of the two Dakotas were stretches of such lands as these that the first explorers—French, perhaps, although he could not remember with any certainty—had called badlands, bad lands to travel through. Here, unknown years ago great freshets of water, probably originating in torrential rains, had chewed up the land, gouging it out, washing it away, with a few areas of more resistant material withstanding the raging waters to finally turn into the twisted shapes that now remained.

Here, once, in days long gone, this trail they followed might have been an artery of trade. If Sandra had been right, if this ruin once had been a caravansary, then it had been a stopping place for caravans that carried precious freight, perhaps from the city, perhaps to the city. But if to the city, where had been the origin of the caravans? Where lay the other terminus of the route?

Mary came up from behind and stood beside him. "Other nonimportant thoughts?"

"Only trying to look back into the past. If we could see the past, what this place was like some thousands of years ago, we might know somewhat better what is happening now. Sandra suggested that this once had been a stopping place for travelers."

"It is a stopping place for us."

"But before us? I just now was speculating that caravans could have passed this way, perhaps many centuries ago. To them it would have been a known land. To us it is unknown."

"We'll be all right," she reassured him.

"We're moving deeper into the unknown. We have no idea what's ahead. Someday our food will come to an end. What do we do then?"

"We still have the food the Parson and the Brigadier were carrying. It'll be a long time before we'll run out of food. Water is our big concern right now. We must find water tomorrow."

"Somewhere this desolate land must end," he said. "We'll find water when it does. Let's go back to the fire."

The moon came up early, a full moon or almost full, flooding the badlands with its unearthly, ghostly light. On the other side of the trail lay a mighty butte, the side presented to them still in darkness, but its shape sharply outlined by the rising moon.

Sitting close beside the fire, Sandra shivered. "It's a fairyland," she said, "but a vicious fairyland. It never occurred to me that a fairyland could have a vicious aspect."

"Your viewpoint," Lansing said, "is colored by the world you lived in."

Sandra flared at him. "There is nothing wrong with the world I lived in. It was a beautiful world, filled with beautiful things and beautiful people."

"That's what I meant. You have no comparison."

His words were blotted out by a sudden wail that seemed to come from almost on top of them.

Sandra leaped to her feet and screamed. Mary took a quick step forward, seized her by the shoulders and shook her.

"Shut up!" Mary yelled at her. "Keep quiet!"

"It followed us!" Sandra shrieked. "It is trailing us!"

"Up there," said Jurgens, pointing toward the butte. The wail had died and for a moment there was silence.

"Up on the rim," said Jurgens, speaking quietly.

And there it was, the thing that wailed, a monstrous creature outlined against the rising moon, a black cutout against the big face of the moon.

It was wolflike, but much too large to be a wolf, heavier, more full-bodied than a wolf and yet it held the sense of strength and agility that was the mark of a wolf. It was a great shaggy beast, unkempt, as if it might have fallen on hard times, foraging desperately for the little food it found, skulking to locate a place to sleep and raked by an agony that drove it to lament against the world.

It flung back its head, lifting its muzzle, and cried again. Not a wail this time, but a sobbing ululation that wavered across the land and quivered among the stars.

Lansing felt a chill run through him and he struggled to remain erect, for his knees were buckling. Sandra was crouched upon the ground, her head shielded by her arms. Mary was bending over her. Lansing felt an arm thrown around his shoulders. Turning his head, he saw that Jurgens was beside him.

"I'm all right," said Lansing.

"Of course you are," said Jurgens.

The Wailer howled and whimpered, bawled and brayed its grief. It went on forever, or seemed to go on forever, and then, as suddenly as it had come, was gone. The moon, swimming up the east, showed only the smooth, humped line of the looming butte.

That night, after the three humans were in their sleeping bags and Jurgens stood on watch, the Sniffler came out of the night and sniffed all about the firelit circle of the camp. Lying in their bags, they listened to the sniffling and were undismayed. After the Wailer on the butte top, he was a welcome friend come visiting.

The next afternoon they came out of the badlands into a narrow but widening green valley and found water in a stream that ran through it. As they traveled along the stream, the valley widened further and the flanking badlands' skyline drew off and off until it was only a white smudge on the left and right horizons, finally to fade out entirely.

Just before sunset they came upon another stream, a somewhat larger one, flowing from the west, and on the point of land between the two streams, where they flowed together, the travelers came upon an inn.

22

WHEN THEY PUSHED THE door open, they found themselves in a large common room, with a fireplace at one end. Before the fireplace was a large table ringed with chairs. With their backs toward the new arrivals, two people sat in chairs, facing the fire. A dumpy little woman with a moonlike face hurried from the kitchen, wiping her hands on a checkered apron tied about her middle.

"So you are already here," she gasped. "You catch me by surprise. You arrive sooner than I thought."

She halted in front of them, still wiping her hands, and squinted at them out of her moon face. She put up a hand to brush a straggling lock of hair out of her face.

"My, my," she said, in mild exclamation, "there are four of you! You lost no more than two in passing through the city. The people sitting by the fire lost four, and there are bands that are all gobbled up."

Some small sound made Lansing glance toward the other end of the room, the shadowed area away from the fire, and there he saw the card players crouched around a table, intent upon their game and paying no attention to the arrival of the party. The noise he had heard, he realized, had been the soft slapping-down of cards upon the tabletop.

He nodded toward the players.

"When did they show up?" he asked.

"They came last night," said the woman. "They went straight to the table and sat down. They've been playing ever since."

The two who had been sitting before the fire had gotten to their feet and were advancing across the room. One of them was a woman, blond, tall and willowy; the other was a man who reminded Lansing of a bond salesman who at one time had tried to sell him a portfolio that was, at best, highly questionable.

The woman held out her hand to Mary. "My name is Melissa. I am not a human, although I may look like one. I'm a puppet."

She made no further explanation, but shook hands all around.

"I am Jorgenson," said the man, "and extremely glad to see you. The two of us, I must confess, are frightened. We've been cowering here for days, unable to convince ourselves that we should continue on this senseless journey to which we, unwillingly and unwittingly, seem to have been committed."

"I can appreciate how you might feel that way," said Lansing. "All of us, I think it safe to say, have felt similar touches."

"Let's go back to the fire," said Jorgenson. "We have a bottle on which we have not been able to make appreciable progress. You, perhaps, can help us."

"Most willingly," said Lansing. "Thanks for the invitation."

The aproned woman, who apparently was the proprietor of the inn, had disappeared. The card players paid them no attention.

Settled in chairs before the fire and with the drinks all poured, Jorgenson said, "And now, perhaps, we should become better acquainted with one another and exchange experiences and thoughts. So far as I am concerned, I am a time traveler. When I first came to this place I thought I was just traveling through—which, if that had been the case, would have seen me long gone from here. It turns out, however, that this is not the case. Why it's not, I do not know. I'm not at all sure what happened; this is the first instance that I have been stuck in time."

Lansing tasted the drink and it was passing good; he took another swallow.

"As I told you," Melissa said, "I am a puppet. I do not have it quite straight in mind what a puppet is, although I am made to understand it is an imitation human. Why there should be need of imitation humans, I am not exactly sure. There are only a few of us or, rather, there were only a few of us, since I am no longer there—a few of us residing in what I suppose might be called the ultimate city, a place of great comfort and convenience, in which we live what could be described as good lives except that our lives seem to have no purpose, which at times can be mildly depressing. There are, as I have said, only a few of us and it may well be that all of us are puppets, although I have always been afraid to ask—

fearing, you see, that I might be the only puppet among the lot of them, and if that should turn out to be true, it would be just dreadful."

"For years," said Jorgenson, "I have been seeking for a certain time and place. Once, long ago, I was there for a while and then, without meaning to, I slipped out of it. I've sought it ever since and no matter how hard I try, always seem to miss it. I have wondered if, for some reason, it may be closed to me. And if that should be true, I have wondered why."

"If you had it well in mind," said Mary, "that might help you find it. I mean, if you knew the time and place—"

"Oh, I know the time and place fairly well. It is in the 1920s, the so-called Roaring Twenties, although at the time I was there, there was no roaring in them. There was peace and quiet, the peace and quiet of a never-ending summer's day. The world as yet had not arrived at the cynical sophistication that came upon us some decades later on. I think, as a matter of fact, I have it pegged quite well. I think it was 1926 and the month was August. The place was a sleepy seaside town on the eastern coast. Massachusetts, maybe, more likely Delaware or Maryland."

"None of the names you speak mean anything to me," Melissa complained. "You've told me North America, but I know no North America. All I know was the place where we lived. It was magnificently built and we had little, scurrying mechanical servitors who kept it clean and neat and attended to our needs. But there were no place names, not even a name for where we lived. There was no need for us to know if it had a name and there was nowhere else that we wished to go, so there were no place names, either, for the other places if, in fact, there were other places."

"There were six of us," said Jorgenson, "when we came to this place."

"There were six of us as well," said Mary. "I wonder if such groups as ours always are made up of six."

"I would not know," said Jorgenson. "Our group and your group are the only ones I know of."

"There was an idiot," said Melissa, "not a drooling idiot, but a most engaging one. He was full of fun. He was always clowning and making the most outrageous puns. And there was the Mississippi gambler. I have never asked before because I didn't want to display my ignorance. But I'll ask now. Can anyone tell me what a Mississippi is?"

"It is a river," Lansing told her.

"The landlady said that you lost the other four in the city," Mary said. "Can you tell us how you lost them?"

"They did not come back," Melissa said. "All of us went out one day, looking for something. What we were looking for, we had no idea. Well before night, the two of us came back to where we were camping in the plaza. We built up the fire and cooked a meal and waited for the others. We waited through the night and they did not return. Then, shaking in our fear, we went out and hunted for them. We sought them for five days and there was no trace of them. And every night a giant beast came out on the hills above the city and cried out against its fate."

"So you found the trail west of the city and finally reached this inn," said Sandra.

"That is what we did," said Jorgenson. "Since then we have been cowering here, afraid to travel further."

"The landlady," said Melissa, "has been hinting that it is time for us to go. She knows we have no money. Two of our group had money, but with them, the money's gone."

"We have some money," Lansing said. "We will pay your bill and you can travel on with us."

"You will travel on?" she asked.

"Of course we will," said Jurgens. "What else is there to do?"

"But it's all so senseless!" cried Jorgenson. "If we only knew what we're here for, what we're supposed to do. Have you any information?"

"None at all," said Mary.

"We're rats running in a maze," said Lansing. "Maybe we'll get lucky."

"When I was home," Melissa said, "before I was transported here, we had gaming tables. We'd play the games for hours, even for days. There were no rules to the games, the rules developed as we went along. Even when the rules were established, or we thought they had been, then they'd change again. . . ."

"Did anyone ever win?" asked Mary.

"I can't seem to remember. I don't think we ever did. Not a one of us. But we didn't mind, of course. It was just a game."

"This game is real," Jorgenson said, glumly. "We all have bet our lives."

"There are certain skeptics," said Lansing, "who will tell you there is no abiding principle in the universe. Just before I left my world, I talked with a man—a friend of mine, a loud-mouthed friend of mine—who suggested that the universe might operate at random, or worse. This I can't believe. There must be an element of reason in it. There must be cause and effect. There must be purpose, although that does not mean we are capable of grasping the purpose. Even if some other, more intelligent form of life should set us down and explain it to us in considerable detail, we still might not understand it."

"Which doesn't hold out too much hope for us," said Jorgenson.

"No, I suppose it doesn't. Although it could mean that there is some hope. We're not entirely sunk."

"There are mysteries," said Jurgens, "and I speak in the best sense of the word—not the shoddy, sensational connotation of it—that can be unraveled if one puts his mind to it."

"We've asked the landlady what lies ahead," Melissa said, "and she can tell us almost nothing."

"Exactly like that great lout at the first inn," said Jorgenson. "He could tell us only of the cube and city."

"The landlady," said Melissa, "says that some distance ahead, we'll come to a singing tower. And that is all. Except that she warns us we should only travel west, not north. To the north, she says, lies Chaos. Chaos, with a capital."

"She knows not what Chaos is," said Jorgenson. "She only knows the word. She shivers when she says it."

"So then we'll travel north," said Jurgens. "I tend to get suspicious when someone warns you off from a certain place. I get the feeling that something may be found there we're not supposed to find."

Lansing finished his drink and set the mug upon the table. He got slowly to his feet and walked across the room until he stood beside the table where the four were playing cards.

He stood for a long moment, with none of them paying him the slightest heed, as if they had not noticed his approach. Then one of them raised his head and turned it, looking at him.

Lansing stepped back a pace, horrified at what he saw. The

eyes were dark holes in the skull, out of which peered two black obsidian pebbles. The nose was not a nose, but two breathing slots, slashed into the area between the eyes and mouth. The mouth was another slash, without benefit of lips. There was no chin; the face sloped down to the neck in a slanting line.

Lansing turned about and left. As he approached the table before the fire, he heard Sandra saying, with a strange lilt in her voice, "I cannot wait until we reach the singing tower!"

THEY REACHED THE SINGING tower on the fourth day after they left the inn.

The tower was not a tower; it was a needle. Standing on top a high hill, it jabbed a finger heavenward. At the base it measured a good six feet across, tapering to a sharp point a hundred feet or more above the ground. It was of a rather nasty pinkish color and was made of a substance that appeared similar to the substance of which the cube had been constructed. Plastic, Lansing told himself, although he was fairly sure that it was not plastic. When he laid his hand flat against its surface, he could feel a slight vibration, as if the wind out of the west, playing upon it, was causing it to vibrate along its entire length as a freestanding, tapering, most unlikely violin string would vibrate to the bow.

With the exception of Sandra, all of them were disappointed with the music it made. Jorgenson said, in fact, that it wasn't music—that it was simply noise. It was not generally loud, although at times it did become a little louder. It sounded, Lansing thought, somewhat like chamber music, although his exposure to chamber music had been slight. Long ago, he recalled, Alice on a Sunday afternoon had enticed him to a chamber music concert and he had suffered, silently but acutely, through two solid hours of it. Yet, despite the fact that more often than not it was a soft music, it had fantastic carrying power. They had heard the first wind-blown snatches of it on the afternoon of the third day out.

Sandra had been instantly entranced; even hearing only snatches of it, she had been captivated. She had balked at stopping to camp that night.

"Can't we press on?" she'd asked. "Perhaps we can reach the tower before the night is done. None of us is really all that tired and it will be cool walking in the night."

Lansing had ruled out, rather brusquely, any thought of traveling by night.

Sandra had not argued. She had not helped fix supper, as had been her habit, but had walked out on a small knoll above the camping place and had stood there, a small, slender, wind-blown figure, tensed with listening. She had refused to eat, she did not sleep; she had stood upon the knoll all night.

Now that they had climbed the high hill to its top, where stood the so-called tower, she still was in her trance. She stood to one side, head thrown back, staring upward at the tower, listening with every fiber of her being.

"It stirs me not at all," said Jorgenson. "What does she find in it?"

"It stirs you not at all," Melissa said, "because you have no soul. No matter what you may say, it still is music, although a strange music at the best. I like music you can dance to. I used to dance a lot. This is not music one can dance to."

"I'm worried about Sandra," Mary said to Lansing. "She hasn't eaten since we heard the first notes of the music and she hasn't slept. What shall we do about it?"

Lansing shook his head. "Leave her alone for a while. She may snap out of it."

When the evening meal was cooked, Melissa took a plate of food to Sandra and coaxed her into eating, although she did not eat a great deal and spoke scarcely at all.

Sitting by the fire and watching the woman, outlined against the sunset color of the west, Lansing recalled how anxiously she had looked forward to the singing tower. On that first night out from the inn, she had said, "It could be beautiful. How I hope it is! There is so little that is beautiful in this world. A world deprived of beauty."

"You live for beauty," he had said.

"Oh, indeed I do. All this afternoon I have tried to make a poem. There is something here from which a poem might be made —a thing of beauty in itself springing from a place that is most unbeautiful. But I cannot get it started. I know what I want to say, but the thought and word will not come together."

And now, sitting by the fire and watching her, so bewitched by music that bewitched no one else, he wondered if she had made any progress with her poem.

Jorgenson was saying to Jurgens, "Back at the inn you said we should travel north. We had been warned against the north. You said you were suspicious whenever you were warned, that if one were told not to go somewhere, one must always go. There are always attempts, you said, to mislead one in his quests."

"That's quite right," said Jurgens. "I think my reasoning is sound."

"But we went west, not north."

"We traveled toward the known; now we'll travel to the unknown. Now, having reached the tower, we'll swing north and have a look at Chaos."

Jorgenson looked questioningly at Lansing and Lansing nodded at him. "That's what I had in mind as well. Do you have comment?"

Jorgenson shook his head, embarrassed.

"I wonder," said Melissa, "what Chaos possibly could be."

"It could be almost anything," said Lansing.

"I don't like the sound of it."

"You mean you are afraid of it?"

"Yes, that's it. I'm afraid of it."

"People put different names to the selfsame thing," said Mary. "Chaos might mean one thing to us and a totally different thing to someone else. Different cultural backgrounds make for varying perceptions."

"We are grasping at straws," said Jorgenson. "Desperately, unthinkingly grasping. We first grasped at the cube, then at the city. Now it's the singing tower and Chaos."

"I still think the cube was significant," Mary said. "I still have the feeling—I can't get rid of it—that we messed up with the cube. The Brigadier thought it would be the city, but the city was too pat, too patently misleading. It would be a natural reaction for anyone to expect the answers from the city." She said to Jorgenson, "You found no answers there?"

"Just empty rooms and dust over everything. The four who were lost may have found an answer; that may have been the reason they didn't return. You found more than we did—the doors and the installation. Still, they told you nothing; they were valueless."

"Not entirely without value," said Mary. "They told us much about the inhabitants of the city. A sharply scientific people, technologically inclined, very sophisticated. And what we found pointed the way that they had gone—into other worlds."

"As we have gone into another world?"

"Precisely," said Jurgens. "With one exception—they went on their own."

"And now are snatching us."

"We can't be sure of that," said Lansing. "Someone, some agency, as you say, snatched us, but we can't be sure who it might have been."

"This experience," Mary said to Jorgenson, "can't be entirely foreign to you. You have been such a traveler. You voluntarily went to other worlds, traveling in time."

"But no longer," said Jorgenson. "I have lost my ability. In this place my procedures do not work."

"Perhaps if you concentrated on how you did it, the mechanism that you used. What you said or did, your state of mind."

Jorgenson cried at her, "Don't you think I've tried? I tried back there in the city."

"Yes, he did," Melissa said. "I have watched him try."

"If I could have," said Jorgenson, "if I only could have, it would have been possible to go back in time to that period before the city was deserted, while the people still were there, engaged in whatever work they may have been attempting."

"That would have been neat," Melissa said. "Don't you see how neat it would have been."

"Yes, we see how neat," said Lansing.

"You don't believe in my time traveling," Jorgenson challenged him.

"I didn't say that."

"No, you didn't. You haven't. Not in so many words."

"Look here," said Lansing, "don't try to start a hassle. We have all the trouble that we need. We can get along without personality clashes. You say you travel in time and I don't contradict you. Shall we leave it at that?"

"Fair enough," said Jorgenson, "if you keep your mouth shut."

With some effort, Lansing did not answer.

"We've struck out," said Mary, "on most of what we've found. I had held a hope the tower might give us a clue."

"It has given us nothing," said Jorgenson. "It is like all the other stuff."

"Sandra may come up with something," Jurgens said. "She is letting the music soak into her. After a while—"

"It's nothing but tinkly, seesawing sound," said Jorgenson. "I can't see what she could find in it."

"Sandra comes from an artistic world," Mary told him. "She is attuned to aesthetic qualities that in other worlds are only marginally developed. The music—"

"If it is music."

"The music may mean something to her," Mary said, unperturbed by his interruption. "After a while, she may get around to telling us."

24

SHE DID NOT GET around to telling them.

She ate only a little. She did not refuse to talk, but her talk was short and noncommittal. For the first two days, for almost forty-eight hours, she stood upright, tense with listening, paying no attention to her companions of the trail or, indeed, even to herself.

"We're wasting time," Jorgenson complained. "We should be moving north. Chaos, if we find Chaos there, whatever it may be, may tell us something. We can't be stuck here forever."

"I won't go north," shrilled Melissa. "I'm afraid of Chaos."

"You're a flighty bitch," said Jorgenson. "Not even knowing what it is, you are scared of it."

"This kind of talk," said Lansing, "is getting us nowhere. Bickering doesn't help. We should talk, most certainly, but we should not be yelling at one another."

"We can't just march off and leave Sandra," Mary told them. "She was with us from the start. I will not desert her."

"North is not the only way to go," said Jurgens. "We have been told we'll find a condition there called Chaos, but if we continued, we might find something farther west. At the first inn we heard of the cube and city, but nothing else. At the second inn it was the tower and Chaos. The innkeepers are not too generous with their information. We have a map, but it is worthless. It points the way from the city into the badlands, but nothing more. It does not show the second inn or the tower."

"Perhaps," said Lansing, "they tell us all they know."

"That may be right," Jurgens agreed, "but we can't rely on them."

"The point's well made," said Jorgenson. "We should go both west and north."

"I won't leave Sandra," Mary said.

"Maybe if we talked with her," suggested Jorgenson.

"I've tried," said Mary. "I've told her we can't stay here. I've told her we can come back again and then she can listen to the tower. I doubt she even hears me."

"You could stay with her," said Jorgenson. "The rest of us split up. Two go west, two go north, see what we can find. Agree all of us will be back in four or five days."

"I don't think that's wise," protested Lansing. "I am against leaving Mary here alone. Even if I were not, I'm inclined to think we should not split up."

"So far, there's been no danger. No real threat of physical danger," said Jorgenson. "It would be safe. Leave Mary here, the rest of us take a quick run out. I can't bring myself to hold much hope, but there's always a chance we will turn up something."

"Maybe we could carry Sandra," Jurgens suggested. "If we get her away from the music, she might be all right."

"I suppose we could," said Lansing, "but the chances are she'd fight us. She's not in her right mind. Even if she didn't fight us, if all we had to do was haul her along, she would slow us up. This is bad country. There are long stretches between water. We have water here, but between here and the last water was two days."

"Before we left we'd fill the canteens," said Jorgenson. "We'd drink sparingly. We'd be all right. Farther on the water situation may improve."

"It seems to me that Jorgenson may be right," said Mary. "We can't leave Sandra. I'll stay with her. There seems to be no danger. The land is empty of any kind of life—only the Sniffler, and he is one of us."

"I will not leave you here alone," said Lansing.

"We could leave Jurgens," suggested Jorgenson.

"No," Mary told him. "Sandra knows me best. I'm the one she always turned to." She said to Lansing, "All of us can't stay here. We are wasting time. We must know what is north and west. If there is nothing there, then we'll know and can make other plans."

"I won't go north," Melissa said. "I simply will not go."

"Then you and I'll go west," said Jorgenson. "Lansing and Jurgens north. We'll travel light and fast. A few days only and then we'll be back. By that time Sandra may be herself again."

"I still have hopes," said Mary, "that she is learning something, hearing something to which the rest of us are deaf. The answer, or part of the answer, may be here and she the only one to find it."

"We stay together," Lansing insisted. "We are not breaking up."

"You're being obstinate," said Jorgenson.

"So I'm being obstinate," said Lansing.

Before the end of the day, Sandra had abandoned her standing position and fallen to her knees. Every now and then she crawled, hitching herself closer to the singing tower.

"I'm worried about her," Lansing told Mary.

"So am I," said Mary, "but she seems to be all right. She talks a little, not much. She says that she must stay. The others of us should go on, she says, but she can't leave. Leave her some food and water, she told me, and she'll be all right. She did eat something this evening and drank some water."

"Does she tell you what is happening?"

"No, she's not told me that. I asked her and she either wouldn't or couldn't tell me. Couldn't, I would guess. She may not as yet know herself what's happening."

"You're convinced there is a happening, that it's not just sheer fascination with the music?"

"I can't be certain, but I think there is a happening."

"It's strange," he said, "that we can gather no significant information from the tower. There's nothing here, absolutely nothing to put a handle on. Like the cube. The two of them. Nothing from either one of them. Both of them are constructions. Someone built them for a purpose."

"Jorgenson was talking about that, too. He thinks they are false clues. Constructions to confuse us."

"The maze syndrome. Running in a maze. A test to sort us out."

"He doesn't say so, but that is what he means."

They were sitting apart from the others, a short distance from the fire. Jurgens stood to one side, doing nothing, simply standing there. The other two were beside the fire, talking to one another occasionally, but mostly sitting silent.

Mary took Lansing by the hand. "We have to make some move," she told him. "We can't just sit here, waiting for Sandra. The man back at the first inn talked about winter coming. He said he closed up for the winter. Winter could be dreadful here. Our time may be short. This is already autumn. Maybe deep into autumn."

He put an arm around her, drew her close. She rested her head on his shoulder.

"I can't leave you here," he said. "Not alone. It would tear me up inside to leave you here alone."

"You have to," she said.

"I could go north alone. Leave Jurgens here with you."

"No, I want Jurgens with you. It's safe here; there may be danger in the north. Don't you see? It must be done."

"Yes, I know. It makes sense. But I simply cannot leave you."

"Edward, you must. We have to know. What we are looking for may be in the north."

"Or in the west."

"Yes, that's true. It may even be here, but we can't be certain. Sandra is a poor reed to lean upon. There is a chance she'll come up with something, but only a chance. Nothing to wait around for."

"You'll be careful? You'll stay right here? You'll take no chances?"

"I promise you," she said.

In the morning she kissed him good-bye and said to Jurgens, "You take care of him. I'm counting on you to take care of him."

Jurgens told her, proudly, "We'll take care of one another."

25

FROM THE INN TO the tower the land had grown increasingly arid. North from the tower the aridness turned to desert. It was hard traveling. The sand slid underneath the feet, there were dunes to be climbed. The wind blew steadily from the northwest and swirled sand into their faces.

They did no talking. Heads bent against the wind, Jurgens checking compass readings and setting the course, they made dogged progress north. The robot limped ahead and Lansing staggered after him. At first Lansing had gone ahead, the robot limping behind him. But, as Lansing tired, Jurgens, his mechanical body never tiring, had taken the lead.

After several hours the dunes, in large part, disappeared and they came to firmer, although still sandy, footing.

Watching Jurgens as the robot hitched energetically ahead of him, Lansing fell to wondering about him. Jurgens was still a mystery—as, he admitted, all the rest of them were mysteries. He tried to bring into mind what he knew of each of them, and the facts that he could muster were sketchy. Mary was an engineer in a world where the old empires of the eighteenth century still persisted, making for a stable, but noncompassionate, world. Other than that he knew little about her except for one important fact—he loved her. No idea of what kind of job she may have worked in, what kind of engineering she might have practiced, nothing about her family or her former life, less, perhaps, about her than any of the others.

Sandra's world was a fuzzy place, a culture that he could not understand, although, he told himself, the culture that she mirrored might be no more than a small subculture in which she had existed. The overall culture of her world might be something else entirely and she almost as unaware of it as he. They had not, he thought, been entirely fair to Sandra. The group, as a whole, largely had ignored her. Given a chance, she might have been able to make a significant contribution. If she had been exposed to the machines of the installation, rather than he and Mary, she might have brought back from her experience more than they had brought. Even now, through her close rapport with the music tower, she might supply the key to what they all had sought.

The Parson had been, it seemed to Lansing, an open book, although, once again, he might have been a reflection of a subculture. There was no evidence to suggest that the Parson's entire world had been as bigoted, as narrow and as vicious as the Parson saw his world. Given time, they might have had a chance to comprehend the Parson, to have found with him some level of understanding, knowing his background, to have found some measure of sympathy with his cross-grained thinking.

The Brigadier, he told himself, had been another matter. Secretive—he had not attempted to explain his world, had refused to tell how he had been pitchforked into the present situation—domineering, with a fierce urge to mastery and command, unwilling to listen to reason other than his own, he had been an enigma. Undoubtedly he had not been a member of a subculture; his world sounded like a place of military anarchy in which hundreds of contending little warlords had battled one another. A game, he had said, not more than a game, but at best a deadly one.

And Jurgens? No subculture there, but a world that had been abandoned for the stars, with the rejects left behind to slide down into an uncomprehending barbarism. Freedom, Jurgens had said— he finally had gained freedom from the implicit responsibility he and the other robots had felt toward the sad remnants of humanity. Freedom? Lansing wondered. He wondered if Jurgens even now realized he had not regained his freedom. He still played shepherd to his humans, even as he played it now, plunging ahead through this desert heading for a Chaos that he or no one else could claim to understand. Ever since they had come to this unlikely world, he had stood by, always ready to serve, always with the needs and hopes of others, of his humans, foremost in his mind.

For some reason, however, he had not put his entire trust in these humans of his. To him, Lansing, he had told at least part of his story—what his world was like, his hobby of making humanoid puppets, fashioned from the old tales of mankind. (Puppets, Lansing wondered, like the puppet Melissa?) To all the others he had not told a thing, had remained stubbornly silent even when Mary had asked him, more or less, point blank.

That was puzzling, Lansing told himself. Why had the robot confided in one of them and no one else? Was there between the two of them a bond that the robot saw and the man could not?

Up ahead of him, Jurgens had halted at the foot of a small dune. When Lansing came up, the robot pointed at an object protruding from the dune. It was a heavy glass or clear plastic bubble, resembling the helmet of a space suit, and inside it, facing them, was a human skull. The grinning row of teeth flashed a wide-spaced smile at them and one of the teeth, Lansing saw, was gold, glinting in the sun. Hunched out of the dune was a rounded piece of metal and farther along the dune, toward the right, another chunk of metal.

Jurgens took a shovel from his pack and began to dig away the sand. Lansing, saying nothing, stood and watched.

"In a minute we will see," said Jurgens.

In a few minutes they did see.

The metal contraption was vaguely human-shaped. There were three legs, not two, and two arms, a torso. It measured ten or twelve feet in length, and in the upper part of it was a space in which a skeleton that once had been a man had ridden. The bones that belonged to the skeleton were jumbled all about, disarticulated, in that space the man had occupied. The skull was captured in the bubble.

Jurgens, squatting beside it, looked up at Lansing.

"A guess?" he asked.

Lansing shuddered. "Your guess, not mine."

"All right," the robot said. "A walking machine."

"A walking machine?"

"It could be. That's the first thing that came to mind."

"But what is a walking machine?"

"Something akin to this was developed by the humans of my planet. Before they went out to the stars. To be used on other planets. In a hostile environment, I suppose. I never saw one. I only heard about them."

"A machine to move about in on a hostile planet?"

"That's right. Tied in with the human nervous system. Intricate circuitry that would respond in the same way as a human body would respond. The human wants to walk, so the machine walks. The arms the same."

"Jurgens, if this is true, we may be looking at one of the original people of this planet. No other human could have been brought here as we were brought, encased in a contraption such as this. We came in the clothes we stood in, of course, but . . ."

"You can't rule it out, however," Jurgens said.

"Perhaps," said Lansing, "but such a man, if he came from elsewhere, would have had to come from an alternate world that had become hostile to man. So polluted, so dangerous . . ."

"A world at war," said Jurgens. "Full of dangerous rays and gases."

"Yes, I suppose that would be possible. But once he reached this world, he would have needed it no longer. The air here is not polluted."

"You must realize," said Jurgens, "that it might have been impossible for him to separate himself from it. He may have been so biologically tied to it that there was no escape from it. He probably would not have minded it too much. He would have been accustomed to it. And such a machine would have some advantages. In a place like this it would."

"Yes," said Lansing, "yes, it would."

"Here he came to grief," said Jurgens. "Here, in all his arrogance, he came to final grief."

Lansing looked at the robot. "You think that all humans are arrogant. That it's a mark of the human race."

"Not all humans," Jurgens said. "You can understand if I hold some bitterness. To be left behind . . ."

"It has festered all these years?"

"Not festered," Jurgens said.

They were silent for a time, then the robot said, "Not you. You are not arrogant. You never have been. The Parson was, so was the Brigadier. Sandra, in her gentle way . . ."

"Yes, I know," said Lansing. "I hope you can forgive them."

"You and Mary," Jurgens said. "I'd lay down my life for you and Mary."

"And yet you would not tell Mary about yourself. You refused to tell her."

"She would have pitied me," said Jurgens. "I could not have withstood her pity. You have never pitied me."

"No, I haven't," Lansing said.

"Edward, let us leave the arrogance behind. The two of us now should be upon our way."

"You lead, I follow," Lansing said. "We have no time to waste. I didn't like leaving Mary. Even now I find it hard not to turn back."

"Three days more and we'll be back. We'll find her safe and sound. Four days is all we'll give ourselves."

They found no wood along the way. The land was scoured bare of everything. That night they made camp without a fire.

In a hard, enameled way, the night was beautiful. Empty sand and a soaring moon, while out toward the edges of the sky, undimmed by the white brilliance of the moon, the stars shone with a fierce intensity.

Lansing felt the essence of the night soaking into him—the hard, the cruel, the classic beauty of it. Once he heard what he thought was wailing. It came from the south, and it sounded like the wailing of the great lost beast that had wailed above the city and again from the badlands butte. He listened intently, not certain he had heard it, but it did not come again.

"Did you hear anything?" he asked Jurgens.

Jurgens said he hadn't.

The robot woke Lansing well before dawn. The moon was hanging just above the western horizon and the stars were paling in the east.

"Eat something," Jurgens told him, "and we'll be on our way."

"Nothing now," said Lansing. "A drink of water's all. I'll eat later while we walk."

The going was fairly easy to start with, but by noon they began to encounter dunes again, small ones at first, growing larger as they went along. They were in a world of shifting yellow sand, with the pale blue of the sky a dome that came down and enclosed the sand. The land ahead of them gradually sloped upward until it seemed they were climbing into the hard blue sky. Ahead of them a narrow strip of sky above the northern horizon assumed a darker, deeper shade of blue, and as they climbed over the treacherous dunes, the sand sliding underneath their feet, so did the darker strip climb higher in the sky, turning from dark blue at its top to black a little lower down.

Vague, muted mumblings came from the north. As they fought to make their way against the dunes, the mumbling grew louder.

Jurgens stopped at the top of one high dune and waited for Lansing to catch up. Lansing pulled up beside him, panting with the climb.

"That sounds like thunder up ahead," said Jurgens. "A heavy storm may be coming up."

"The color of the sky looks right," said Lansing, "but it doesn't look like a storm cloud. I never saw one with an edge that runs straight across. There usually are big thunderheads boiling up, and I see no thunderheads."

"I thought awhile ago," Jurgens said, "that I saw a lightning flash, not the bolt itself, but a flicker, like the reflection of a flash."

"Heat lightning," Lansing told him. "A reflection against the clouds of lightning far away."

"In a while we'll see what it is," said Jurgens. "Are you ready to go on? Or shall we rest awhile?"

"Go on. I'll tell you when I need to rest."

By midafternoon, the great black cloud had climbed well above the horizon. In places it had tinges of deep purple and was, in all, a frightening phenomenon. It appeared to have no motion, no roiling clouds, no wind-driven banks of scudding vapor, although at times it seemed to Lansing, when he stopped for a moment to watch it, to have an almost imperceptible downward movement, as if a thin film of some substance was running down across the blackness, as a thin sheet of water would run down a windowpane during a summer shower. A sense of terrible violence seemed inherent in the cloud itself, the overwhelming threat of heavy weather, and yet there was no visible violence or even threat of violence except for the massive lightning strokes that at intervals ran across the face of darkness. Now the rumble of thunder was continuous.

"Most unusual," Jurgens said. "I have never seen the like of it."

"Chaos?" Lansing asked. Asking it, he remembered the chaos, or the sense of chaos (for he doubted now that he'd really seen it) he had glimpsed when he had stood for a moment on the hill of suns above the universe. And that glimpsed chaos, that glimpsed universal chaos had not been anything like this, although he realized that if he were called upon to describe it, he would be unable to tell a single thing about it.

"Perhaps," said Jurgens. "I ask you: What is Chaos?"

Lansing did not attempt to answer.

They climbed on, and now the way was steeper than it had been at any time since they had started out. They toiled upward over a series of ever higher dunes, and ahead of them the horizon curved away from them to both left and right, as if they were climbing one continuous dune, the rim of which ran in a semicircle, either side of it impinging on the blackness in the sky.

Late in the afternoon they reached the top of the great ridge they had been climbing. Lansing, exhausted, slumped down to the sand, leaning against a large boulder. A large boulder? he asked himself. A boulder here when there had been up to this time nothing larger than a grain of sand? He staggered to his feet, amazed, and the boulder was there—not one boulder, but a clump of them, perched just below the ultimate height of the dune they had been climbing. Resting in the sand, as if someone had, perhaps in ages past, carefully placed them there.

Jurgens stood on top of the dune, straddle-legged, with his crutch dug deep into the sand to prop him up and keep his balance.

To right and left swept the curving edge of the dune that they had climbed, while in front of them the surface broke sharply to plunge downward in an unbroken slope until it reached the bottom of the massive cloud that loomed in front of them.

Looking directly at the cloud, Lansing saw that it was not a cloud, although what it was he did not know. It was a massive wall of utter blackness that rose from where it met the surface of the downward-sloping sand far into the sky, so far that he was forced to crane his neck to see the top of it.

Lightning bolts still slashed across its face with devastating ferocity, and thunder crashed and rumbled. The wall, he saw or thought he saw, was a monstrous dam raised against the sky, and over the lip of it was pouring something that was not water, a gigantic waterfall of a blackness that was not water, crashing down across the face of it, a waterfall so solid and unbroken that he did not see the actual falling of it, but only had the hypnotic sense of its falling. Watching it, he realized that it was not only thunder that he heard, but the deep, awful roar of whatever was falling over the lip of the dam, the Niagara-like rushing sound of something falling from great height, falling from the unknown into the unknown. It seemed to him that the very ground beneath him was trembling with the roar.

He turned his head and looked at Jurgens, but the robot did not notice him. He was leaning heavily upon his crutch, staring at the blackness, seemingly entranced and hypnotized by it, rigid with his watching.

Lansing shifted his gaze back to the blackness and now, clearer than ever, it seemed to be a dam, although a moment later he was not sure it was a dam. First a cloud and then a dam and now, he wondered, what could it be now?

One thing he knew—it was not the answer that they sought or even a clue that in time might provide the answer. Like the cube and doors, like the installation and the singing tower, it was meaningless. Perhaps not meaningless entirely, but meaningless to him and Jurgens and the other humans, to the intelligence and perception that resided in the human mind.

"The end of the world," said Jurgens, speaking with a strange catch in his voice.

"The end of this world?" asked Lansing, and having said it, was sorry that he had, for it was a silly thing to say. Why he had said it, he could not imagine.

"Perhaps not only of this world," said Jurgens. "Not of this world alone. The end of all worlds. The end of everything. There goes the universe. Eaten by a blackness."

The robot moved forward a step, lifting his crutch and probing for a solid place to set it. He did not find a solid place. The crutch skidded and went flying from his hand. The bad leg collapsed under him and sent him lurching forward. He fell and somersaulted on the slope. His pack came off his shoulders and went skidding down the slope before him. Jurgens's hands were working frantically, clawing at the slope to stop his slide, but there was nothing he could grasp. There was only sand to grasp and it was sliding all about him, sliding with him. His clutching hands left long print marks in the sand.

Lansing, who had been crouching, came swiftly to his feet. If he could remain upright, he thought, driving his feet deep into the sand beneath the sliding surface, there would be a chance to reach Jurgens and halt his slide, drag him back to safety.

He took a downward step and his forward-reaching foot found no solid footing. The sand was like so much powder. There was no walking on it, no standing on it. He tried to throw himself backward, stretching desperately to reach the top of the dune, hoping to use it to lever himself off the moving surface. But his foot was slipping faster now, plowing a deep furrow in the sand, and he came down on the face of the slope and slid, slowly, ever so slowly, but with no hope of stopping. Not only was he sliding, but all the sand about him made a slow but inexorable response to the pull of gravity.

He thrust out his legs and arms to present a wider resistance to the surface on which he slid, and it seemed, when he did so, that he might be moving just a bit more slowly, although it was hard to tell. It was hopeless, he told himself, being honest with himself. Any effort on his part to claw his way upward would do no more than disturb the sand, making it slide the faster, carrying him with it.

But now he knew that the downward movement had slowed somewhat and for a moment it seemed that the slide had stopped. He lay spread-eagled on the sand, fearful of moving, apprehensive that any movement on his part would start the slide again.

He did not know where Jurgens was, and when he did try to move his head in an effort to look down the slope, in the hope of catching a glimpse of him, the sand began to slide again, so he threw back his head and held it hard against the surface and the sliding stopped.

Eternities passed, or what seemed to be eternities. The ground still seemed to shiver with the thundering of the great black waterfall. The noise blotted out much of his perception of who or where he was. Lying as he did, he could see, just barely, the top of the dune up which he and Jurgens had climbed. A couple of hundred feet away, he estimated. If he could only crawl those two hundred feet—but the two hundred feet, he knew, were impossible.

He concentrated his attention on that impossible dune top, as if by concentrating on it, he somehow could achieve it. It stayed unmoving and empty, a sandy line against the blueness of the sky.

For a moment he swiveled his eyes to look away, to peer along the seemingly never-ending expanse of slope to which he clung. When he looked back to the top of the dune, someone was standing there—four someones lined against the sky, standing there and peering down at him out of faces that were silly, devastating travesties of human faces.

Only slowly did he realize who they were—the four card players who had sat around a table, set apart from the others who were there, in two different inns and now staring down at him with their skull-like faces.

Why should they be here? he wondered. What had brought them? What could possibly be here that would be of any interest to them? He thought momentarily of calling out to them, then decided there would be no point in doing so. If he did, they would only ignore him and that would make the situation worse. For a moment he wondered if they were really there. Could his imagination be playing tricks on him? He looked away and then looked back; they were still there.

One of them, he saw, held something in his hand, and he tried to make out what it was but was unable to. Then the player who was holding whatever it was he had in his hand lifted it above his head and twirled it. When he did that, Lansing knew what it was; it was a coil of rope. The card players were throwing him a rope!

Then the rope was in the air, uncoiling as it flew toward him. He'd have just one chance, he knew, certainly no more than a couple. If he had to lunge to catch the rope, that would start him sliding once again, and by the time the rope had been pulled in, coiled again and thrown, he would be beyond its reach.

The rope seemed to hang in the air, scarcely moving, uncoiling as it came. When it struck, it was on top of him; a perfect throw. He reached out more desperately than was needful, grasped it in one hand, rolled over to get into position to grasp it with the second hand. He was sliding while he did this, and sliding very fast. He tightened his one-handed hold upon the rope in a death-stricken grip. Then he had the second hand upon it and was stopped with a tooth-rattling jolt as the length of the rope ran out. He hung to it with a fierce grip and slowly began to pull himself up the slope. He kept his body low, not risking any accident that might cause him to lose the rope. Foot by foot he hauled himself along. Finally he halted to regain his breath and looked up the slope. The ridge was empty; the card players were gone. Who, then, he wondered, was holding the rope? He had a sudden, sickening vision of the far end of the rope coming free, to send him hurtling down the slope. Breath sobbing in his throat, he climbed like a madman, unthinkingly, carelessly. The only thing that mattered was to get to the top of the dune before the rope came free. He felt his body slide over the ridge. Only then did he quit climbing.

He rolled over and sat up. He did not let loose of the rope until he was sitting flat upon his bottom, on the solid surface on the safe side of the slope. Then he did let loose of it. He saw that the rope was tied around one of the boulders that he had noticed with some surprise when he and Jurgens had climbed to reach the ridge that stood above the deadly slope.

Jurgens! he thought. Jurgens, oh, my God! During the last few minutes of his desperate climb (could it have been only minutes rather than hours?), all thought of Jurgens had been wiped out of his mind.

He went on hands and knees up the slope to reach the dune top and lay there, gazing down over the long, smooth chute of sand. The trail that he had left in hauling himself to the top was rapidly being smoothed out by the slow creep of the flowing sand. In a few more minutes there would be no evidence that he had ever been there.

There was no sign of Jurgens, no evidence of the track that he had made in his slide down the slope. Jurgens, he knew, was gone —gone into whatever had awaited him in that boundary area where the great blackness came down to the sand.

The robot had not cried out, he remembered, had not cried for rescue, had not called his name for help. He had gone silently to his doom—or, if not doom, whatever waited for him at the bottom of the slope. This, Lansing was certain, had been out of consideration for him, out of a wish not to involve him, the human Lansing, in the accident.

Had it been an accident? he wondered. He remembered once again how Jurgens had stood entranced before the face of the awful thundering darkness—even as Sandra had stood entranced before the singing tower. Lansing remembered, too, how Jurgens had taken that first step forward even as he stood—as he must have known he stood—on the final edge of safety, but taking the step, nevertheless, to draw closer to this terrible thing that fascinated him.

Had he been lured as Sandra had been lured? Had there been something in the curtain of blackness that had called out to him? Had he taken that step quite willingly, not expecting that he would be plunged down the slope, but quite willingly now that it had happened—in an unconscious, an unknowing but all-engrossing urge to come closer to whatever it had been that had captured him?

Lansing shook his head. There was no way to know.

But if all this should be true, he thought, then at last the robot, Jurgens, had made a move upon his own, acting for himself and not for the humans who were in his custody. He had acted as he had always wanted, not as his loyalty to humans had insisted. In that final moment Jurgens had found the freedom that he sought.

Lansing climbed slowly to his feet. He flipped the tied end of the rope off the boulder and methodically began to coil it. There was, perhaps, no need to coil it, he could simply have dropped it and left it where it fell. But coiling it gave him a job to do.

Having coiled it, he laid it on the ground and looked around to see if he could locate the card players. But they were not there, there was nothing to indicate they ever had been there. Later on, he told himself, he would worry about them. He had no time now to puzzle over them. There was a task he had to do and as swiftly as he could.

He had to get back to the singing tower, where Mary still was standing watch over the entranced Sandra.

26

HE STUMBLED SOUTH, FOLLOWING the trail that he and Jurgens had made in coming north. Some stretches of it already had been wiped out by the drifting sand, but in each instance he was able to pick it up a little farther on. He still heard the rumble back of him, the receding sound of Chaos. And what, he asked himself as he crept along the trail, had Chaos been? Not that it mattered now. All that mattered now was to get back to Mary.

Night fell and the moon came out, a bloated globe swimming out of the east, and the first stars shone. Doggedly he kept on. It should be easier now than it had been earlier in the day, he told himself, because now he was traveling downhill. It did not, however, seem any easier.

He collapsed and lay upon the sand, unable to go on, unable to lift himself to his feet again. He rolled over on his back and fumbled for his canteen. While he fumbled for it, he fell into sodden sleep.

He woke in a blaze of sun, wondering for a moment where he was. He propped himself on an elbow to look about; there was nothing to be seen except the blinding sand, reflecting back the shimmer of the sun. He put up a fist and rubbed his eyes—remembering where he was and that he must go on.

He surged to his feet and shook himself. Standing unsteadily, for he still was only half awake, he hitched his canteen in front of him and drank of the tepid fluid. Then, recapping the canteen, he started walking, heading down the trace that earlier he himself had made. He clawed food, any kind of food, the first his searching fingers found, out of his pack, and munched it as he walked. There was nothing that could be allowed to stop him going south. His legs, stiffened by sleep, cried out against his going, but he drove them on and gradually they became good legs again. His throat cried out for water, but he didn't drink, for the water in his canteen was low and he must conserve it. (Hours later he realized that a second canteen, filled with water, was tucked into his pack-sack.) The sand ahead of him rippled and swam in the harsh blaze of the sun. He had slept longer than he should have, losing valu- able time, and he used this as a lash to drive himself on.

He thought of Jurgens at times, but not too often or too much. That again was something that he could do later on. He tried to concentrate on the thought of Mary, waiting for him at the singing tower. But at times even the thought of Mary slipped away and he plunged on into a vacuum, knowing only one thing, holding fast to one thing in his mind—that he must reach the singing tower.

He came to the end of the dunes and while the trail was now fainter, he still was able to follow it, for the ground still was sandy. The sun reached zenith and went down the west. With the going better—more level ground and fewer and smaller dunes—he tried to hurry, but was unable to move his legs the faster. The best that he could manage was a steady plodding. Which was not to be wondered at, he reasonably told himself. This was the third full day of tortuous travel. Still he blamed himself, raged at himself for not going faster.

The sun went down and to the east the stars blazed out and the sky lighted as the moon came up. Still he drove himself. If he kept going, if he only could keep going, he could be at the singing tower by dawn.

His body betrayed him. His legs gave out and finally he had to call a halt. He hauled himself into protection against the wind afforded by the lee of a small dune and unstrapped his pack. He found the extra canteen and had all the water that he needed, being careful not to drink too much. He found hard sausage and soft cheese and gulped it down, half starved.

He'd sit and rest awhile, he promised himself, but he would not go to sleep. In an hour or so he could go on again. He dozed and when he woke, the first light of dawn was dimming the eastern stars.

Cursing himself for sleeping, he staggered up, shouldered the pack and started south again. He had promised Mary he would not be gone longer than four days, and he would keep his promise.

Dunes lay ahead of him and the end of easy travel. On this

stretch of land before he reached the dunes, he must cover as much ground as possible, for the dunes would slow him up.

Why was he so frantic? he asked himself. There was not this much need to hurry. Mary was all right. She was waiting for him and she was all right. These reassurances gave him no comfort; he did not slacken his pace.

Shortly after noon he came again to the dune where they had found the wrecked walking machine. The skull, with its gold tooth glinting, grinned idiotically at him. He did not linger.

He came to the dunes and attacked them like a man berserk. Only a few hours more, he told himself. He'd be at the tower before the sun had set, with Mary in his arms. An hour or so later he caught a glimpse of the tower as he topped one of the higher dunes, and the sight of it drove him even harder.

All the time that he had been making his way across the desert he had held in mind a rather hazy vision of Mary running toward him, calling out joyously to him, with her arms outstretched, as he came down the final length of ground. This did not happen. She did not come running to greet him. There was no evidence of her at all. No smoke trailed up from the campfire. There was no one, not even Sandra.

And then, as he came running down toward the camp, he saw Sandra. She lay huddled close against the base of the singing tower. She did not move. The wind fluttered a scarf that she wore about her neck and that was all.

Lansing came to a stumbling halt. A chill hand reached out from somewhere to touch his heart and a shiver of panic ran through his body.

"Mary!" he shouted. "Mary, I'm back! Where are you?"

Mary did not answer. Nothing answered.

Sandra would know, he told himself. Apparently she was asleep, but he would shake her awake and she would tell him.

He knelt beside her and shook her gently. There was something very wrong—she had no weight. He shook her again and the thrust of the shake turned her so that he could see her face. It was a wizened mummy face.

He jerked his hand from her shoulder and the face dropped back, no longer looking at him. Dead, he thought—as if she had been dead a thousand years! Shriveled inside her clothing, flutter-

ing in the wind, a husk from which all life and substance had been
sucked!

He stood again and wheeled about. He stumbled to the fire and
held his hands above the gray ash. He felt no heat. He dug into
the ashes and the fire was dead, there was no lingering coal at the
bottom of the ash. A packsack lay beside the dead fire, only one
packsack. Sandra's more than likely. Mary's pack was gone.

He let himself down to a sitting position and his mind was
numb—numb to horror and grief, just numb.

Sandra dead and Mary gone and the fire—the fire, he thought, it
would have taken hours for the fire to burn completely out. Mary
had been gone for hours.

His brain lost some of its numbness and the terror came rushing
in, but he fought it back.

There was no time to submit to terror or to panic. This was the
time to sit quietly and think, to try to think it out, to pull all the
pieces together and see what might have happened.

The camp was deserted. Jorgenson and Melissa were not here,
but that meant nothing. They might be late in coming back. They
all had agreed, when they left the camp, to return in four days,
and the fourth day had not ended.

Sandra was dead, with the appearance of having been dead a
long time, although that was not possible. She had been alive four
days ago, less than four days ago. The tower, he told himself bit-
terly and with no logic, had sucked her dry, and fed upon her,
consumed her until there was nothing left of her. Sucked her dry,
perhaps, because she had willed that it should do so, willingly giving herself to it, a devotion paid to her perception of the beauty
she'd found in it.

Mary was gone, but she had not fled. She had not run, screaming, into the wilderness. Her pack was gone. She had taken it and
left. But why had she not left something to tell him where she'd
gone? A note, perhaps, weighed down by a rock.

He rose to his feet and searched the area, finding nothing, then,
to be certain, he searched it again and the second time found
nothing.

She could have gone north, he thought, thinking to meet him
and Jurgens on their way back. Or she could have gone west, hoping to find Jorgenson and Melissa, although that seemed unlikely,
for she had not liked either one of them. Or perhaps she had

taken the trail back to the second inn and was waiting there for him.

First things first, he told himself, surprised at how calmly he could think. First he'd go back to the beginning of the dunes and make a wide sweep to see if he could find her track. If she had gone north, she probably would have found their tracks and followed them, but if that had been the case, he'd have met her when he was coming back, for he'd backtracked all the way.

Still he went and made the sweep and found no tracks other than his own and Jurgens's. He examined the tracks they had made carefully for evidence of a third person. There was no evidence. There were only their two tracks going north and his set of tracks on his return. No other person had passed that way.

Night was settling in when he returned to the camp. For a time he stood and thought, trying to reach some decision. At last he made one, and it was a hard one for him to make. But, trying to suppress his guilt at making it, he told himself it was the one thing he could do.

He was bushed. He had been four full days upon the trail with no rest and little sleep. He needed a chance to become whole again. He'd not be helping either Mary or himself by charging off again, half dead from sleep, his thinking dazed, his perceptions dulled. By morning Jorgenson and Melissa might have returned and could help him in his search. Although that, he told himself, was no great factor in his thinking; he thought no more of the two of them than Mary had. At best they were poor sticks.

He found wood and started a fire, boiled coffee, fried bacon, made some pancakes and opened a can of applesauce—the first square meal he had had for days.

The thought of Mary never left his mind, but he persisted in assuming that she was all right, that no matter where she might be she was safe. He tried to wipe the terror and the worry from his mind, but succeeded only partially.

He wondered what might have caused her to leave. Whatever the reason might have been, it must have been persuasive, for under almost any circumstance she would have waited his return. There must have been pressing reason for her going, and he tried to summon up in his mind some possibilities. But that was fruitless and sometimes terrifying and he did his best, once started, to quit thinking of it.

He wondered, too, about Sandra. Should he bury her, digging a hole and covering her and saying some awkward and futile words when it all was done? Somehow, for some reason that he could not clearly comprehend, it seemed not quite the thing to do. It seemed, the more he thought about it, that disturbing her in any way would be sacrilegious. Better, perhaps, to leave her as she was, a shriveled (and holy?) sacrifice at the base of the singing tower. He thought about it and his thinking made no sense at all, but in a crazy, convoluted way it seemed to have some logic in it. What would Sandra have wanted? he asked himself, and there was no answer. He had not known Sandra well enough to guess what she might have wanted, and that, he thought, was a pity. Perhaps he had not known any of them well enough, as well as he should have known them. Despite the many days he had spent with them, he had not known them well. Did it, he wondered, require a lifetime to know a person well?

Of the six of them, four were gone, only he and Mary left. Now Mary, too, was gone, but he'd find her, he told himself, he'd find her.

After he had eaten, he crawled into his sleeping bag and was almost asleep when he was jerked awake by the sobbing of the Wailer. The sobbing was not nearby; it came from some distance down the trail, but still, in the silence of the night, it was loud.

He sat and listened to it, remembering the night of that first day, going north with Jurgens, when he had thought he heard the crying and had asked the robot, who had said that he heard nothing.

When the wailing all was done, he lay down again, pulling the bag up around him. Before he went to sleep, the Sniffler came and prowled all about the campfire. He spoke softly to it and it did not answer him, although it kept on with its sniffling.

Before the sniffling ended, he had gone to sleep.

27

EARLY ON THE MORNING of the second day after Lansing
had headed for the inn, the Wailer appeared. It was on the summit
of a hill that paralleled the trail and as Lansing strode along, the
Wailer kept slow pace with him. When, on occasion, Lansing fell
behind, the Wailer halted and sat down ponderously to wait for
him. When once he had forged ahead a little, the Wailer loped
easily to catch up.

To say the least, this was mildly disconcerting. Lansing did his
best not to let it show. Other than a sidelong glance from time to
time to keep track of the animal, Lansing attempted to pretend
that he was ignoring it. After a while, he told himself, it will give
up the game it's playing with me and go trotting off somewhere.
The Wailer, however, did not appear to be of this mind at all.

The mighty beast, more wolflike than it had seemed when
they'd seen it on the butte top, had a look of reprehensibility. It
was, Lansing figured, an arrant vagabond. So far it had made no
hostile move, but that was not to say it wouldn't. Any moment it
could turn into a raging fury. If such should happen, no one could
hope to stand against it. Lansing undid the guard of his belt knife
so it would be easy to his hand, but had no hope that it would
count for much if the animal should charge.

Mary, he thought. Was this great beast the reason that Mary
had left the camp? Had it harried her out of it? And where had
she gone? Or had she gone anywhere? Had the beast, after playing
a silly game with her, finally charged? He bent over, retching at
the thought of it.

If she had fled under pressure from the beast, without doubt she
would have headed for the inn, for that was the only place that

would afford protection. God grant, he prayed, that she had reached it.

The beast was coming closer, edging down the hillside toward him, wagging its tail at him (and a wolf, he remembered, never wags its tail), laughing at him with its lips pulled back, showing a lot of teeth. To gain some distance from it, he left the trail, slanting south and east. The Wailer crossed the trail and followed, paralleling his progress, not coming directly at him but continually edging closer. It drove him south and east.

The game went on for hours. The sun reached noon and started sliding west. Somewhere ahead of him, Lansing knew, flowed the river that, coming from the west, flowed into the badlands stream they had followed. On the point of land between the two rivers stood the inn. He could not allow this beast to drive him beyond the river. If that happened, he would not reach the inn and it then could herd him on and on, until he dropped from exhaustion.

Topping a low ridge late in the afternoon, he saw the river. He went down the slope toward it, the Wailer following. When he reached the river he halted and faced about. The Wailer stood not more than fifty feet away. Lansing lifted the knife from his belt and stood waiting.

"All right," he asked the Wailer, "what is it going to be?"

The Wailer was huge. It stood ten feet at the shoulder. It lowered its head and thrust out its muzzle and came toward him, pacing slowly, first one slow step and then another. It was shaggy and disreputable. It looked like an unmade bed. And it was big—God, was it big! One snap and it would have him.

Lansing tightened his grip upon the knife, but did not raise it. He did not move a muscle, standing rigid and rooted in the face of the beast's advance. It edged closer and closer. It thrust out its muzzle, almost reaching him, and snarled.

With an effort, Lansing did not move. He wondered vaguely, marginally, what might have happened had he moved. And was surprised he hadn't.

The beast took another step. The muzzle now was only a foot or so away. This time there was no snarl. Still gripping the knife, Lansing lifted his free hand and laid it on the muzzle. The ragged beast groaned with pleasure. It moved closer, so that its muzzle pressed against his chest, forcing him back a short step. He stroked the muzzle, reached up and scratched an ear. The beast cocked its head to one side so that ear was easier to reach.

Lansing scratched the ear, and the Wailer held its head so it could be scratched. It mumbled a little in its throat and pushed Lansing back another step as it moved affectionately against him.

"That's enough," said Lansing. "I can't go on petting you all day. I have traveling to do."

Almost as if it had understood, the great beast grumbled at him. Lansing took another backward step into the river. Then, deliberately, he let his hand fall from the mighty head and, turning about, began to wade the stream.

He kept on wading. The water was like ice. He did not look back until he reached midstream, with the water to his knees. Then he did look back. The Wailer stood forlornly on the shore, looking after him. It took a step, putting one foot in the water, then pulled it back and shook it.

Lansing laughed and went on wading. When he reached dry land, he turned again. The beast still was on the other shore. Seeing Lansing halt and look back, it took two steps into the water, then pulled back and shook itself.

"So long, friend," said Lansing. Briskly he set out down the river. Half a mile farther on he had another look. The beast still had not crossed the river. Apparently it did not like cold water.

Lansing hurried. Despite what had happened, he told himself, it would not be a bad idea to put as much distance between himself and the Wailer as was possible. It was the sort of beast one could not place much reliance on.

The sun went down, but he did not pause for the night. He kept on walking, occasionally jogging, running at times, intent on covering as much ground as he could. The moon, now slightly past full, shed a cold, white light upon the wilderness. The river gurgled eastward. At dawn he stopped and built a fire, boiled coffee, had something to eat. There was no indication the Wailer was anywhere about.

He was tired and wanted sleep, but after a short time set out again, driving himself down the river. The sun was slanting well into the west when he reached the inn.

The common room was empty, dark and chilly. No blaze burned on the hearth. The card players were not at their table.

Lansing called and there was no answer. Going across the

room, he collapsed into a chair before the dead fireplace. He huddled in the chair, worn by fatigue.

After a time, the moon-faced woman in the checkered apron came out of the kitchen.

"Oh," she said, "so it's you again."

He croaked at her. "Was a young woman here? In the last day or two?"

"Oh, yes, indeed she was."

"And where is she now?"

"She left this morning. Early in the morning."

"Did you notice where she went? What direction she took?"

"No, I didn't, sir. I happened to be busy."

"Did she leave any word? Could she have left a note?"

The woman said, "I believe she did. I put it away. I'll go and get it."

She bustled off and Lansing waited. After a time she came back, carrying a bottle and a mug, which she set on the table beside him.

"I don't know what happened," she said, "but I cannot find the note. I must have mislaid it."

He surged to his feet and roared at her. "How could you have mislaid a note? A note that was given you this morning?"

"I do not know how I could have, sir. Apparently I did."

"Well, look for it, then. Have another look."

"I've looked everywhere," she said. "It's not where I thought I put it. It's not anywhere."

Lansing sank into the chair. She poured a drink and handed it to him. "I'll start a fire to warm you and then I'll cook you something," she told him. "You probably are hungry."

"Yes, I am," growled Lansing.

"The lady," she said, "had no money . . ."

"Goddammit," Lansing shouted, "I'll pay her bill. Are you sure about that note?"

"Quite certain, sir," she said.

He sat morosely, drinking, watching her start a fire.

"You'll be staying the night?" she asked.

"Yes, I will," he said. "I'll leave early in the morning."

Where could Mary have gone? he asked himself. Back to the singing tower to wait, knowing he'd show up? Or back through the badlands to the city? Not back to the city, he thought, certainly not back to the city. Although, perhaps, she might. Just possibly she might. Maybe she had thought of something there that needed more looking into, some facet of the city they had overlooked. But the question was why she hadn't waited here; certainly she knew that he would follow her.

He sat pondering, turning over and over the thoughts that came to mind. By the time the landlady brought in the food, he'd made his decision. He'd go back to the singing tower and if she were not there, he'd start over again—from the tower back here again and then on to the city. If she was not in the city, he'd go back to the cube. He kept remembering that Mary had always thought the answer lay somewhere in the cube.

HE WAS WITHIN A few hours of the tower when he met the other two—Jorgenson and Melissa—coming down the trail. There had been no sign of the Wailer.

"My God," said Jorgenson, "I'm glad we found you. There was no one at the tower."

"No one but Sandra, and she was dead," Melissa said.

"Where are the other two?" asked Jorgenson.

"Jurgens was lost at Chaos," Lansing told him, "and I am hunting Mary. You are sure you saw no sign of her?"

"None at all," said Jorgenson. "Where do you think she could be?"

"She had been at the inn. I thought she might have come back to the tower. Since she hasn't, I would imagine she is heading for the city."

"She would have left word for you at the inn," Melissa said. "You two were very close."

"She did leave a note. The landlady couldn't find it. Claimed that she had lost it. I helped her search for it before I left."

"That's strange," said Jorgenson.

"Yes, very strange. Everything here seems to work against us."

"What happened to Jurgens?" Melissa asked. "I liked him. He was a sweet old soul."

Swiftly Lansing told them, then asked, "What is in the west? Did you find anything?"

"We found nothing," Jorgenson told him. "We stayed out a couple of days longer than we had intended, hoping we'd find something. The land is arid, not quite desert. Almost desert. We had water trouble, but we got along."

"Just empty land," Melissa said. "You could look for miles— and nothing."

"Finally we came to the edge of the escarpment we had been traveling across," said Jorgenson. "Not knowing, of course, we were traveling an escarpment. The land broke down, a long line of cliffs, and there, far as we could see, was desert. Real desert; sand and that was all. It stretched away as far as we could see and it was emptier, if that was possible, than the land we'd crossed. So we came back."

"Chaos north and nothing west," said Lansing. "That leaves the south, but I'm not going south. I'm going to the city; I think that Mary's there."

"It's almost sunset," said Jorgenson. "Why don't we camp? Start out in the morning. Decide what we should do and start out in the morning."

"I'm willing," Lansing said. "There's no sense in going to the tower since you just left. Tell me about Sandra. Did you bury her?"

Melissa shook her head. "We talked about it, but we couldn't. To bury her seemed not quite right. We decided we should leave her where she was. She is little better than a mummy. I think she died as she would have wanted to. We thought it best to leave her."

Lansing nodded. "My thoughts were much the same. I even wondered if she'd died. It seemed to me, looking at her, that she had only gone away. The life of her, the spirit of her, going some- where else, leaving a withered, worthless husk behind."

"I think that you are right," Melissa said. "I can't put it into words, but I think that you are right. She stood apart from all of us; she was never one of us. What would be right for us would not be right for her."

They built a fire, cooked food, boiled coffee and ate, crouched around the fire. The moon came up, the stars came out and the night was lonely.

Holding the coffee mug in both his hands, sipping occasionally at the brew, Lansing thought back to Chaos and to Jurgens, principally to Jurgens. Had there been, he asked himself, anything that he could have done to save the robot? Had there been some way, if he only had been able to think well and fast enough, that he could have walked down the sloping sand to catch his sliding friend and haul him back to safety? His mind was blank as to any suggestion of how he might have done it. Yet he could not escape the sense of guilt that rose up to choke him; he had been there. Certainly there had been some action that he could have taken. He had tried, of course; he had ventured out on the sliding sand slope, he had had a try at it, but that had not been good enough. He had tried and failed, and failure itself spelled out to guilt.

And what of Jurgens now? Where had he gone, where was he now? He, Lansing, had not even paid his friend the courtesy of watching where he'd gone. He had been busy at the time, trying to save himself, but be that as it may, he somehow should have managed to note what had happened to the robot. It seemed, he told himself sourly, that there was no end to guilt. Whatever a man might do, there was always guilt.

The assumption must be that Jurgens had kept on sliding, unable to stop the slide, until he came to that point where the black curtain of roaring Chaos (whatever Chaos might be) came down to meet the sand. And what happened then? What was it Jurgens had said just before the fall? *The end of everything. There goes the universe. Eaten by the blackness.* Had Jurgens known? Or had he been only talking? There was no way to know.

It was strange, Lansing thought, the ways they had been lost. The Parson walking through a door. The Brigadier being taken up (taken up?) by the two banks of machines crooning to themselves. Sandra sucked dry of life by a singing tower. Jurgens sliding into Chaos. And Mary—Mary walking off. But as yet Mary was not gone—at least so far as he knew, she was not gone as the others now were gone. There still was hope for Mary.

Jorgenson asked, "Lansing, what is going on? You seem deep in thought."

"I've been thinking," Lansing said, "of what we should do come morning."

He had not been thinking that, but it was something he could say to answer Jorgenson.

"I suppose back to the city," said Jorgenson. "That's what you indicated."

"You will come with me?" Lansing asked.

"I won't go to the city," Melissa said. "I was in the city once and—"

"You won't go to the city and you won't go north," said Jorgenson. "There are too many places you refuse to go. Much more of this, by Jesus, and I'm walking off and leaving you. You're bitching all the time."

"I think we could save some time," said Lansing, "by going cross-country."

"What do you mean, cross-country?"

"Well, look," said Lansing. He put down the cup and with the palm of one hand smoothed out a place in the sand. With an extended forefinger he began to draw a map. "When we left the city we traveled the badlands trail. We were going slightly west, but mostly north. Then when we left the inn, we traveled straight west to the tower. It seems to me there should be a shorter way."

He had drawn one line to represent the badlands trail, another, at right angles to it, between the inn and tower. Now he made another mark, connecting the tower and city. "If we went that way, there'd be less ground to cover. A triangle, you see. Instead of traveling two legs of it, we'd travel only one. Head southeast."

"We'd be in unknown country," Jorgenson protested. "No trail to follow. We'd get tangled in the badlands. We would lose our way."

"We could maintain our bearing with compass readings. It might be we would miss the badlands. They may not extend this far west. It would be a shorter way to go."

"I don't know," said Jorgenson.

"I do. That's the way I'm going. Will you come along?"

Jorgenson hesitated for a long moment, then he said, "Yes, we'll come along."

They set out at early dawn. An hour or so later they crossed the eastward-running river that some miles later would flow past the inn. They crossed at a shallow ford, barely getting wet.

The character of the land began to change. It went in a gentle slope upward from the river, marked by long ridges, each ridge rising higher than the last. It became less arid. There was less sand, more grass. Trees began to appear and as they climbed each successive ridge, the trees increased in number and in size. In some of the small valleys that separated the ridges, tiny creeks made their way, clear, sparkling water chattering over rocky courses.

Toward the end of the day they topped one ridge that stood considerably higher than those they had been crossing and saw, spread out before them, a valley somewhat wider and more lush than the others they had seen—a green valley with many trees and, far below, a river of respectable size. A short distance up the valley, toward the west, thin curls of smoke spiraled up into the air.

"People," said Jorgenson. "There must be people there."

He started moving forward, but Lansing put out a hand to halt him.

"What's the matter?" asked Jorgenson.

"We don't go rushing in."

"But I tell you, there are people."

"I suppose there are. But we don't go rushing in. Neither do we sneak up. We let them know we're here and give them a chance to look us over."

"You know about everything," said Jorgenson, sneering.

"Not everything," Lansing told him. "Only common sense. Either we give them a chance to look us over or we sneak around them, pass them by."

"I think we should go in," Melissa said. "Mary may be there. Or someone might know something of her."

"That's unlikely," Lansing said. "I'm convinced she headed for the city. She'd have no occasion to come this way."

"We're going in," said Jorgenson, a belligerent tone in his voice. "Someone may know what is going on. If so, it'll be the first time we've known since we came here."

"Okay," said Lansing. "We'll go in."

They went down the hill until they reached the valley, went slowly up it, toward the smoke. Up ahead someone saw them and shouted warning. The three halted and stood waiting. In a short time a small group of people, ten or so, appeared, making their way down the valley toward them. The crowd stopped and three men walked forward.

Lansing, standing in front of Jorgenson and Melissa, studied the three as they approached. One of them was old. His hair and beard were white. The other two were younger—one a blond youth with yellow beard and hair that hung down to his shoulders, the other a grim, dark-visaged, dark-haired man. He wore no beard, but the stubble on his face was heavy; he had not shaved for several days. Their clothing was in tatters, elbows out, holes in the knees of their trousers, rips and tears inexpertly sewed together. The old man wore what appeared to be a vest of rabbit fur.

The three halted only a few paces away. The yellow-haired man spoke in a strange tongue.

"Heathen talk," said Jorgenson. "Why can't he speak English?"

"Foreign, not heathen," Lansing said. "German, at a guess. Do any of you speak English?"

"I speak it," the old man said. "I and a couple of others in the camp. Your guess is correct. My young friend does speak German. Pierre, here, speaks French. I can understand both fairly well. My name is Allen Correy. I would suppose you might have come from the tower. You must have lost your way."

"As a matter of fact," said Lansing, "we are heading for the city."

"For what reason?" Correy asked. "There is nothing there. All of us know that."

"He's hunting for a lost girl friend," said Jorgenson. "He has the idea she may be going there."

"In that case," Correy said to Lansing, "I sincerely hope you find her. You know how to get there?"

"Southeast," said Lansing. "That should get us there."

"Yes, I think it will," said Correy.

"Do you know anything about the country up ahead?"

"Only for a few miles. We stay fairly close to camp. We do not wander far."

"You are people, I suppose, the same as us. I don't know what to call us. I've never thought about that. But people who were brought here."

"We are part of them," said Correy. "There may be other bands like us, but if so, we don't know where they are. You know, of course, that few of us survive. We are a small group of survivors. There are thirty-two of us here. Twelve men, the rest are women. Some of us have been here for years."

The dark-visaged Frenchman spoke to him, and Correy said to Lansing, "You will pardon me. I forgot my manners. Will you not come into camp and join us? It will be dark before too long and supper now is cooking. We have a huge pot of rabbit stew and plenty of fish to fry. I wouldn't be surprised if there should be a salad, although we are long since out of dressing and must do with hot cooking fat. I must warn you also we are short of salt. Long since we have become accustomed to the lack, and it no longer bothers us."

"Nor will it bother us," Melissa told him. "We accept your invitation gladly."

A short distance up the valley, as they rounded a grove of trees that had hidden it, they came upon a cornfield with a few shocks of harvested stalks still standing in it. Beyond the field, in a sheltered cove formed by a sharp bend in the river's course, stood a collection of rude huts and a few tattered, weatherbeaten tents. Fires were burning and small groups of waiting people stood about.

Correy gestured at the cornfield. "It's a poor thing at the best, but we take good care of it and each season harvest enough to take us through the winter. We also have a rather extensive garden plot. Mrs. Mason secured for us the seed corn and the seeds we needed to plant the garden."

"Mrs. Mason?" Melissa asked.

"She is the landlady at the inn," said Correy. "A grasping soul, but she has cooperated with us. At times she sends recruits, people of our sort who have nowhere else to go and gravitate back to the inn. She doesn't want them there unless they have money they can spend. Few of them do, so she gets rid of them by sending them to us. However, our population does not grow by any appreciable number. There are deaths, especially in the bitter winter months. We have, among other things, a growing cemetery."

"There's no way back?" asked Jorgenson. "No way back to the worlds you came from?"

"None that we have found," said Correy. "Not that we have sought extensively. A few of us have. Most just hunker down."

The evening meal was ready to be dished up by the time they

arrived at the camp. They sat down, the three of them, in a circle with all the others about the central campfire and were given bowls of stewed rabbit and others of boiled, mixed vegetables and platters of crisp-fried fish. There was no coffee or tea, only water to drink. There was not a salad, as Correy had said there might be.

Many of the people in the camp, perhaps all of them (Lansing tried to keep count, but lost the count) came to shake their hands and welcome them. Most of them spoke in foreign tongues, a few in broken English. There were two other than Correy for whom English was a native language. Both of them were women, and immediately they squatted down with Melissa and the three of them jabbered away at an alarming rate.

The food, despite the lack of salt, was good.

"You said you lack salt," Lansing said to Correy, "and probably a number of other things. Yet you say that Mrs. Mason secured seed for your garden and your patch of corn. Won't she get you salt and other necessities you need?"

"Oh, most willingly," said Correy, "but we have no money. The treasury has run out. Perhaps earlier we spent it more freely than was wise."

"I have some left," said Lansing. "Would a donation be in order?"

"I would not wish to solicit funds," said Correy, "but if, of your own free will . . ."

"I'll leave a small sum with you."

"You're not staying with us? You are welcome, as you must know."

"I told you I was going to the city."

"Yes, I do recall."

"I'll be glad to spend the night," Lansing told him. "In the morning I will leave."

"Perhaps you will come back."

"You mean if I don't find Mary."

"Even if you find her. Any time you wish. She'll be welcome if she returns with you."

Lansing looked about the camp. It was not the sort of place where he would care to settle down. Life here would be hard. There would be unremitting labor—chopping and bringing in wood, taking care of the garden and the cornfield, the never-ending scrounging for food. There would be bitter little rivalries, the flaring of tempers, incessant squabbling.

"We have worked out a primitive way of life," said Correy, "and we manage rather well. There are fish to be taken from the river, the valleys and the hills have game. Some of us have become experts at trapping—there are a number of rabbits. More some years than others. A couple of years ago, when a drought hit us, all of us worked hard and long, carrying water from the river for the garden and the corn. But we managed; we had a splendid harvest."

"It's amazing," Lansing said, "such a varied mix of people. Or I suppose it's varied."

"Very much so," Correy said. "In my former life I was a member of a diplomatic corps. We have, among others, a geologist, a farmer who once owned and worked thousands of acres, a certified public accountant, a noted and once-pampered actress, a woman noted as an eminent historian, a social worker, a banker. I could go on and on."

"Have you, in the time that you and the others have had to think about it, arrived at any conclusions as to why we all may have been brought here?"

"No, not actually. There are many speculations, as you may guess, but nothing solid. There are those who think they know, but I'm quite certain that they don't. There are people, you understand, who find a certain stability in convincing themselves they are right about even the most fantastic notions. It gives them something they can cling to, a certainty that they know what is going on, that they know while all the rest of us are groping in the dark."

"And you? Yourself?"

"I am one of those people who is cursed by being able to see both sides, or the many sides, of a question. As a diplomat, it was imperative that I should. I find it necessary to be strictly honest with myself; I will not allow myself to fool myself."

"So you have no hard conviction?"

"Not a single one. All of it is as much a mystery to me as the day that I arrived."

"What do you know of the country we'll be traveling to reach the city? How about the badlands?"

"It's rough and hilly," said Correy, "so far as we have ventured. Forest mostly. But not hard going. The badlands I do not know about. We have not come upon them. They must lie east of here."

"You are quite content to stay here? You have not ventured farther? You have not looked?"

"Not content," said Correy, "but what is there to do? Some of us have gone north to Chaos. Did you go that far?"

"I did. I lost a good friend there."

"The north is closed by Chaos," Correy said. "There is no getting past it. What it is, I do not know, but it blocks the way. For a hundred miles or more beyond the tower is nothing but man-killing desert. To the south, so far as we have gone, there seems no promise. So now you go back to the city, hoping you will find something that you missed."

"No," said Lansing. "I am going to find Mary. I *must* find her. She and I are the only ones of our band who are left. The other four were lost."

"The two who are with you?"

"They were not with us to start with. They are from another group. We found them at the inn."

"They seem to be nice people," said Correy. "Here they come, to join us."

Lansing looked up and saw Jorgenson and Melissa walking around the circle. Jorgenson, coming up, squatted down in front of him. Melissa remained standing. "Melissa and I want to tell you something," Jorgenson said. "We're sorry, but we're not going with you. We've decided to stay here."

29

IT WAS JUST AS well, Lansing told himself. He could travel easier and faster by himself. Since morning he had covered a lot of ground—more, he was convinced, than he would have covered if the other two had been tagging along. More than that, he hadn't liked either one of them. Melissa was a whining bitch and Jorgenson was an unlovely bastard.

If he had regretted leaving anyone, it had been Correy. Though he had spent only a few hours with him, he had liked the man. He had given him somewhat more than half of the coins that still were left and had shaken hands with him. In accepting the donation, Correy had been studiously gracious, thanking him not for himself but for the band.

"I shall husband this sudden wealth in the common interest," he had said. "I know, given the chance, everyone would thank you."

"Think nothing of it," Lansing had told him. "Mary and I may be back."

"We'll keep a place beside the fire for you," Correy had told him. "I hope most sincerely you don't have to come back. Life here is not a good prospect. Maybe you'll find a way out. Some of us must. I hope you do."

He had not thought until Correy had spoken so that there remained any hope of finding a way out of the situation. Long ago, he realized, he had given up such hope. His one hope had been to find Mary so that together they could face whatever was in store for them.

He thought about it as he trudged along. Correy, he knew, had spoken more cheerfully than he'd really thought, but the question still remained—could there yet remain some hope? Logic said that hope was slight, and he was a trifle disgusted at himself for entertaining any thought of it. Yet, as he walked along, he still could detect, deep inside himself, that small, faint glimmer of it.

The travel was comparatively easy. The hills were steep, but the forest was open. There was no water problem. Time after time he came on small creeks and rills running between the hills.

By nightfall he came upon the badlands. They were not, however, the colorful nightmare his band had traversed after leaving the city. These were small badlands, the beginning of badlands that had stopped before going far. Here the action of primeval water had not finished with its job. The rains had stopped, the massive erosion had been ended before full badlands had developed. There were small floodplains, a few deeply channeled gulches, fantastically carved formations that were not complete, as if a sculptor had thrown away his mallet and chisel, in frustration or disgust, before his work was done.

"Tomorrow," Lansing said, speaking aloud to himself, "I will reach the city."

He did reach it the next day, just after the sun had marked off noon. He stood on one of the high hills that ringed it in and looked out over it. Down there, he thought, Mary could be waiting for him, and when he thought it, he found that he was trembling.

He plunged down the hill and found a street that led to the city's heart. It all had the old, familiar look to it—the red, eroded walls, the blocks of fallen stone cluttering the street, the dust over everything.

In the plaza he halted and looked around to orient himself. Once he had gotten his directions straightened out, he knew where he was. Over there to the left was the broken facade of the so-called administration building, with the single tower still standing, and down a street cater-cornered to it he would find the installation.

Standing in the plaza, he called for Mary, but there was no answer. He called a few more times and then he called no more, for the haunting echo of his voice, reverberating back to him, was terrifying.

He walked across the plaza to the administration building and climbed the broad stone stairs to reach the entrance hall where they had camped. His footsteps raised booming echoes that sounded like querulous voices crying out to him. He prowled about the hall and found evidence of their having been there, an emptied can or two, an emptied cracker box, a mug that someone had forgotten. He wanted to go down into the basement and look at the doors, but he was afraid to. He started several times and each time turned back. What was he afraid of? he asked himself— afraid that he would find one of the doors, perhaps the one to the apple-blossom world, had been opened? No, he told himself—no, no, Mary never would do that. Not now would she do it, maybe later on when all hope of finding him was gone, that and all other hope, but certainly not now. Perhaps, he thought, it would be impossible for anyone to do it. The Brigadier had carried away the wrench, probably had hidden it somewhere. Never again, the Brigadier had vowed, would a door be opened.

Standing silently, unmoving in the entrance hall, he seemed to hear their voices, talking not to him, but to one another. He tried to shut his ears to them, but the voices still persisted.

He had planned to camp there, but decided that he couldn't. There were too many voices, the memories were too thick. So he moved out into the center of the plaza and began hauling in wood from wherever he could find it. All the rest of the afternoon he worked, building a good-sized woodpile. Then, as dark came down, he made a fire and fed it to make it bright and high. If Mary should be in the city, or approaching it or somewhere watching it, she would see the fire and know that someone was there.

On a smaller fire he boiled coffee and cooked some food. As he ate, he attempted to work out a plan of action, but all that he could think of was to search the city, every street if need be. Although, he told himself, that would be wasted effort. If Mary was in the city, or even now be coming up on it, she would head straight for the plaza, knowing that anyone else who came to the city would do the same.

The Wailer came out on the hills when the moon came up and cried out its agony of loneliness. Lansing sat beside the fire and listened, crying out and answering with his own loneliness.

"Come down here to the fire, with me," he told the Wailer, "and we can mourn together."

It was not until then that the realization struck him that the loneliness might keep on and on, that he might never find Mary. He tried to envision how it might be to never see her again, to continue life without her, and how it might be for her. He quailed at the thought of it and huddled closer to the fire, but there was no warmth in it.

He tried to sleep; he slept but little. In the morning he started his search. Gritting his teeth against the fear, he visited the doors. None of them had been opened. He searched out the installation and went down the stairs that led to it. For a long time he stood listening to the song the machines were crooning to themselves. He searched streets haphazardly, inattentively, knowing that he was wasting time. But he kept on, for there was a need to keep busy, to keep himself distracted and somehow occupied.

For four days he searched and found nothing. Then he wrote a note to Mary and left it, weighed down by the mug someone had forgotten, beside the old campfire in the administration building, and took the trail back to the cube and inn.

How long had it been, he wondered, since he first had found

himself upon this world? He tried to count the days, but his memory was hazed and he lost track each time he tried to count. A month, he wondered, could it have been no more than a month? Thinking back, it seemed half of all the time there was.

He tried to spot landmarks along the trail. Here we had camped, he'd tell himself, here is where Mary had seen the faces in the sky. Over there is where Jurgens had found the spring. Here is where I had cut the wood. But he was never sure if he was right or not. It was too deep into the past, he told himself, a month into the past.

Finally he came to a hilltop from which he could sight the cube. It still was there, as bright and classically beautiful as he remembered it. For a moment he was surprised to see it—not that he hadn't expected to find it, but he would not have been greatly surprised if he had not found it. This world, during the last few days, had seemed to assume a phantom quality, with him walking through a vacuum.

He walked down the switchbacks that wound down the long, steep hillside and reached the hill-rimmed bowl where the cube was sited. As he came around the final bend in the road before it reached the cube, he saw that someone was there. He had not seen them before, but now there they were, the four of them sitting on the stone slab that he and Mary had uncovered, the slab that was located at the edge of the circle of white sand surrounding the cube. They sat there, cross-legged, and played their unending game of cards.

They did not notice him when he walked up to them, and he stood for a while to watch them at their play.

Then he said, "I think I should thank you gentlemen for throwing me the rope."

At his words, they looked up and stared at him out of their white-china faces with the round, browless eyeholes and the black agates suspended in the eyeholes, the twin slashes for nostrils and the one slash for the mouth.

They said nothing, only stared at him, expressionless, although he thought that he saw some annoyance and rebuke in those smooth white faces, like white, round doorknobs with faces painted on them.

Then one of them said, "Please move on. You are standing in our light."

Lansing backed up a step or two, then after a pause backed away until he was standing on the road. The four card players already had gone back to their play.

Mary had not been in the city, he thought; had she been she would have seen his fire and come to it. And she was not here. There was one more place to look.

Doggedly he went on down the road, with no hope left, but still driven by the necessity to continue his search until there was no place else to go.

Night had fallen when he reached the inn. No light showed in the windows, no smoke issued from the chimney. Somewhere in the woods a lonely owl was hooting.

Walking up to the door, he seized the latch. It did not respond to the pressure of his thumb; apparently it was locked. He knocked on the door and there was no answer. He ceased his knocking and listened for the scuff of feet across the floor within. Hearing nothing, he knotted his fists and hammered at the door. Suddenly the door came open and, leaning as he had been in his vigorous pounding, he stumbled across the threshold.

Mine Host stood just inside, one hand on the open door and the other holding a stubby candle in his massive fist. He lifted the candle so that its light fell full on Lansing's face.

"So it's you," said Mine Host, in a terrible voice. "What is it that you want?"

"I am looking for a woman. Mary. You remember her?"

"She is not here."

"Has she been here? Did she come and leave?"

"I have not seen her since you left."

Lansing swung about and walked to the table by the dark fireplace, sat down in a chair. The wind was out of him. Quite suddenly he felt weak and worthless. This was the end of it. There was no place else to go.

Mine Host closed the door and followed him to the table. He set the candle on it.

"You cannot stay," he said. "I'm leaving. I'm closing for the winter."

"Mine Host," said Lansing, "you forget your manners and neglect your hospitality. I am staying here for the night and you'll find me food."

"There is no bed for you," said Mine Host. "The beds are all

made up and I'll not make one up again. If you wish, you may
sleep upon the floor."

"Most willingly," said Lansing, "and how about some food?"

"I have a pot of soup. You can have a bowl of that. There is a
mutton roast, or what is left of a mutton roast. I think I can find a
heel of bread."

"That will do quite well," said Lansing.

"You know, of course, you cannnot stay. In the morning you
must leave."

"Yes, of course," said Lansing, too weary to argue.

He sat in the chair and watched Mine Host lumber toward the
kitchen, where a dim light shone. Supper, he thought, and a floor
to sleep upon and in the morning he would leave. Once he left,
where would he go? Back up the road again, most likely, past the
cube and then on to the city, still searching for Mary, but with
slight hope of finding her. More than likely in the end he would
wind up in the camp beside the river, with the other lost ones who
were scratching out a life of sorts. It was a dismal prospect and
one that he did not care to face, yet it probably was the only option that was left to him. If he should find Mary, what then?
Would the two of them in the end be forced to seek refuge in the
camp? He shivered, thinking of it.

Mine Host brought in the food and thumped it on the table in
front of Lansing, then turned to leave.

"Just a moment," Lansing said. "I'll need to buy supplies before I leave."

"I can let you have all the food you wish," said the innkeeper,
"but the rest of the merchandise is packed away."

"That's all right," said Lansing. "It's mainly food I need."

The soup was tasty; the bread was days old and hard, but he
dipped it in the soup and ate it. He had never cared for mutton,
let alone cold mutton, but he ate several thick slices of it and he
was glad to have it.

The next morning, after a bad night's sleep and a breakfast of
oatmeal, grudgingly provided by Mine Host, Lansing, after some
haggling over payment, bought a supply of food and started up the
road.

The weather, which had been fine and sunny during all the time
since Lansing had first come into the world, turned cloudy and
blustery. A sharp, cruel wind blew out of the northwest and at

times there were short sleet squalls, the pellets of ice stinging his face.

As he came down the steep plunge into the bowl where the cube sat, a dull gray under the clouded sky, he saw that the card players were no longer there.

He reached the bottom of the hill and started across the level ground, aiming for the cube, head bent against the wind.

At the sound of a shout, he jerked his head up and there she was, running down the road toward him.

"Mary!" he shouted, breaking into a run.

Then she was in his arms, clinging to him. Tears ran down her cheeks as she lifted her head to take his kiss.

"I found your note," she said. "I hurried. I was trying to catch up with you."

"Thank God you're here," he said. "Thank God I found you."

"Did the landlady at the inn give you my note?"

"She said you'd left one, but she lost it. Both of us looked for it. We tore the inn apart; we couldn't find it."

"I wrote you I was going to the city and would meet you there. Then I got lost in the badlands. I got off the trail and couldn't find it again. I wandered for days, not knowing where I was, then all at once I climbed a hill and the city lay below me."

"I've been hunting you ever since I got back to the singing tower. I found Sandra dead and—"

"She was dead before I left. I would have stayed, but the Wailer showed up. He kept edging in on me, closer all the time. I was afraid—Lord, how frightened I was. I headed for the inn. He trailed me all the way. I knew you would come to the inn to find me, but the landlady ordered me out. I had no money and she wouldn't let me stay, so I wrote the note to you and left. The Wailer didn't show up and it was all right, then I got lost."

He kissed her. "It's all right now," he said. "We found one another. We are together."

"Where is Jurgens? Is he with you?"

"He's lost. He fell into Chaos."

"Chaos? Edward, what is Chaos?"

"I'll tell you later. There'll be lots of time. Jorgenson and Melissa came back from the west, but they didn't come with me."

She stepped away from him.

"Edward," she said.

"Yes, what is it, Mary?"

"I think I know our answer. It's the cube. It was the cube all the time."

"The cube?"

"I just thought of it, just awhile ago, walking down the road. Something that we overlooked. Something that we never thought of. It just came to me. I wasn't even thinking of it, then suddenly I knew it."

"Knew it? For God's sake, Mary . . ."

"Well, I can't be sure. But I think I'm right. You remember the flat stones that we found, the slabs of stone, the three of them, set into the sand? We had to brush them off to find them. They were covered with sand."

"Yes, I remember. Yesterday the card players were sitting on one of them."

"The card players? Why should the card players—"

"Never mind that now. What about the stones?"

"What if there were other stones? Stones forming a walk that led up to the cube? Three walks up to the cube. Put there so that anyone who wanted could walk up to the cube, safe from whatever it is that guards it. But covered by sand so the walks can't be seen."

"You mean . . ."

"Let's have a look," she said. "We could cut a tree branch or a bush and use it as a broom."

"I'll use it as a broom," he said. "You stay back, out of the way."

She said, meekly, "All right. I'll be right behind you."

They found a bush and cut it down.

As they approached the circle of sand, she said, "The sign is down. The warning sign, in Russian. You pounded it in again and now it's down, mostly covered by the sand."

"There's someone here," he said, "who works hard to make it tough on people. Notes are lost, signs are down, walks are covered. Which of the stones should we start with?"

"I don't think it matters. If one doesn't work out, we'll try another."

"If there *are* other stones, if there *is* a walk. What do we do when we get up to the cube?"

"I don't know," she said.

He walked out on the slab and crouched cautiously at the end of it, reached out with the bush to brush at the sand. Underneath the brushing another slab showed through. He brushed some more.

"You are right," he said. "There is another stone. Why didn't we think of this to start with?"

"A mental lapse," she said. "Brought on by apprehension. Jurgens had been crippled and that business with the Parson and the Brigadier had us scared."

"I still am scared," he said.

He cleaned the near end of the second slab, stepped out on it and swept the sand off the rest of it. Leaning out, he brushed at the sand in line with the second slab. Another slab appeared.

"Steppingstones," said Mary. "Right up to the cube."

"Once we get there, what happens?"

"We'll find out then," she said.

"What if nothing happens?"

"Look," she said, "at least we will have tried."

"I suppose there's that," he said.

"One more slab," he said, wondering if there would be another slab. It would be just like the jokers who ran this business to lay out a path and leave it one stone short.

He leaned out and brushed, and there was another slab.

Mary moved up beside him and they stood together, facing the deep-blue wall of the cube. Lansing put out a hand and ran his palm flat across the wall.

"There is nothing," he said. "I've been thinking all this time there might be a door. But there isn't. If there were, you'd see at least a hairline crack. Just a wall, that's all."

"Push on it," said Mary.

He pushed on it and there was a door. Quickly they stepped through it and the door hissed shut behind them.

∽ 30 ∼

THEY STOOD IN AN enormous room filled with blue light. Tapestries hung about the walls, and between the tapestries were windows—those portions of the walls not masked by the tapestries. Scattered all about the room were groupings of furniture. In an upholstered basket close to the door a curled-up creature slept. It resembled a cat, but was not a cat.

"Edward," said Mary, breathlessly, "those windows look out on the world we left. There could have been people in here watching us both now and the other time that we were here."

"One-way glass," said Lansing. "A visitor can't see in, but can be seen from inside the room."

"It isn't glass," she said.

"Well, of course it's not, but the principle's the same."

"They were sitting here," said Mary, "laughing at us while we were trying to get in."

The room, in all its emptiness, seemed to be unoccupied. Then Lansing saw them. Sitting in a row on a large couch at the far end of the room were the four card players, sitting there and waiting, their dead-white, skull-like faces staring fixedly at them.

Lansing nudged Mary and gestured at the players. When she saw them, she shrank back against him.

"They're horrible," she said. "Will we never get away from them?"

"They have a way of turning up," he said.

The tapestries, he saw, were not normal tapestries. They moved —or, rather, the scenes that were depicted on them moved. A brook sparkled in the sun and the little waves and eddies brought about as the water gurgled down a rocky incline were actual, moving waves and eddies, not cleverly painted waves and eddies. The branches of the trees that grew along the brook moved in the wind and birds flew about among them. A rabbit crouched, nibbling in a patch of clover, then hopped to another place and resumed its nibbling.

On another of the tapestries young maidens, clothed in gauze-like veils, danced blithely in a forest glade to the piping of a faun who, in his playing, danced more energetically, although less gracefully, than the maidens, his cloven hoofs thumping on the sod. The trees that surrounded the glade, great misshapen, not quite ordinary, trees, were swaying to the music, also dancing to the pipe.

"We might as well," said Mary, "go across the room and see what it is they want of us."

"If they'll talk to us," said Lansing. "They may just sit and look at us."

They started walking down the room. It was a long, awkward length of space to cover with the card players watching, without a muscle moving in their faces. These could be the kind of men, if they were men, who might find it impossible to move their lips to smile, impossible to laugh, impossible to be human.

They sat, unmoving, in a row upon the couch, their hands placed firmly on their knees, with never a flicker of expression to indicate they saw anything at all.

They were so alike, so like four peas in a pod, that Lansing could not think of them as four, but only as a single entity, as if the four were one. He did not know their names. He had never heard their names. He wondered if they might, in fact, have no names. To distinguish one from the other, he assigned them identities, mentally tying tags upon them. Starting from the left, he would think of them as A, B, C and D.

Resolutely, he and Mary marched down the length of the room. They came to a halt some six feet from where the players sat. They came to a halt and waited. So far as the card players were concerned, it seemed, they were not even there.

I'll be damned if I'll be the first to speak, Lansing told himself. I'll stand here till they speak. I'll make them speak.

He put his arm around Mary's shoulder and held her close against him, the two of them standing side by side, facing the silent players.

Finally A spoke to them, the thin slash of mouth moving just a little, as if it were an effort to force out the words.

"So," he said, "you have solved the problem."

"You take us by surprise," said Mary. "We are not aware a problem has been solved."

"We might have solved it sooner," Lansing said, "if we had known what the problem was. Or even that there was a problem. Now, since you say we've solved it, what happens? Do we get to go back home?"

"No one ever solves it the first time round," said B. "They always must come back."

"You've not answered my question," said Lansing. "What happens now? Do we go back home?"

"Oh, my, no," said D. "No, you don't go home. We could not let you go."

"You must realize," said C, "that we get so few of you. Out of a few of the groups we may get one, almost never two, as is the case with you. Out of the most of them, we get none at all."

"They go fumbling off in all directions," said A. "They go bolting off, seeking sanctuary in the apple-blossom world or they become entranced with the translators or they—"

"By translators," Mary said, "you mean the machines in the city that keep crooning to themselves?"

"That is our name for them," said B. "Perhaps you can think of a better name."

"I wouldn't even try," said Mary.

"There's Chaos," Lansing said. "That must gobble up a lot of them. Yet you threw me a rope at Chaos."

"We threw you the rope," said A, "because you tried to save the robot. At the risk of your own life, never hesitating, you tried to save the robot."

"I thought he was worth saving. He was a friend of mine."

"He well might have been worth saving," said A, "but he used poor judgment. Here we have no place for those who have poor judgment."

"I don't know what the hell you're getting at," said Lansing, angrily. "I don't like the way you sit in judgment. I don't like anything about the four of you and I never have."

"As we go," said D, "we are getting nowhere. I grant you the privilege of the animosity that you bear us. But we cannot allow petty bickering to sway us from the need to talk with one another."

"Another thing," said Lansing. "If the talk promises to be of any length, we do not propose to stand here before you like supplicants before a throne. You at least might have the decency to provide us a place to sit."

"By all means, sit," said A. "Drag over a couple of chairs and be comfortable."

Lansing walked to one side of the room and came back with chairs. The two of them sat down.

The creature that had been sleeping in the basket came strolling across the floor, sniffling as it came. It rubbed affectionately against Mary's legs and lay down on her feet. It gazed up at her with eyes of liquid friendliness.

"Can this be the Sniffler?" she asked. "It prowled about our campfires, but we never caught a glimpse of it."

"This is your sniffler," said C. "There are a number of snifflers; this one was assigned to you."

"The sniffler watched us?"

"Yes, it watched you."

"And reported back?"

"Naturally," said C.

"You watched us every minute," Lansing said. "You never missed a lick. You knew everything we did. You read us like a book. Would you mind telling me what is going on?"

"Willingly," said A. "You've earned the right to know. By coming here, you have earned the right to know."

"If you'll only listen," said B, "we shall attempt to tell you."

"We're listening," said Mary.

"You know, of course," said A, "about the multiplicity of worlds, worlds splitting off at crisis points to form still other worlds. And I take it you are acquainted with the evolutionary process."

"We know of evolution," Mary said. "A system of sorting out to make possible the selection of the fittest."

"Exactly. If you think about it, you will see that the splitting off of alternate worlds is an evolutionary process."

"You mean for the selection of better worlds? Don't you have some trouble with the definition of a better world?"

"Yes, of course we do. That's the reason you are here. That's the reason we have brought many others here. Evolution, as such, does not work. It operates on the basis of the development of dominant life forms. In many cases the survival factors that make for dominance in themselves are faulty. All of them have flaws; many of them carry the seeds of their own destruction."

"That is true," said Lansing. "On my own world we have developed a mechanism which enables us, if we wish or blunder into it, to commit racial suicide."

"The human race, with its intelligence," said B, "is a life form too finely tuned to be allowed to waste itself—to commit, as you say, racial suicide. It is true, of course, that when, and if, the race dwindles to extinction, a successor will arise, some other life form with a survival factor greater than intelligence. What that factor might be, we cannot imagine. It would not necessarily be superior to intelligence. The trouble with the human race is that it has never given the intelligence it possesses the opportunity to develop to its full potential."

"You think you have a way to develop that full potential?" Mary asked.

"We hope we have," said D.

"You have seen this world you now are on," said A. "You have had the opportunity to guess at some of its accomplishments, at the direction in which its technology was trending."

"Yes, we have," said Lansing. "The doors that open on other worlds. A better concept than world-seekers in my world have come up with. Back home we dream of starships. Only dream of them, for they may not be possible. Although, come to think of it, on Jurgens's world Earth was empty because its people had gone out to the stars."

"Do you know," asked C, "if they ever got there?"

"I assume they did," said Lansing. "But no, I don't know they did."

"And there are what you call the translators," said Mary. "Another way to travel—to travel and to learn. I suppose you could utilize the method to study the entire universe, bring back ideas and concepts the human race might never have dreamed of on its own. Edward and I were only caught on the edges of it. The Brigadier rushed in and was lost. Could you tell us where he went?"

"That we cannot do," said A. "Used improperly, the method can be dangerous."

"Yet you leave it open," Lansing said. "Callously, you leave it open, a trap for unwary visitors."

"There," said D, "you have hit exactly on the point. The unwary are eliminated from consideration. In our plan we have no use for those who act as fools."

"The way you eliminated Sandra at the singing tower and Jurgens on the slopes of Chaos."

"I sense hostility," said D.

"You're damned right you sense hostility. I *am* hostile. You eliminated four of us."

"You were lucky," A told him. "More often than not an entire band is eliminated. But not by anything we do. They are eliminated by the faults within themselves."

"And the people at the camp? The refugee camp near the singing tower?"

"They are the failures. They gave up. Gave up and 'hunkered down.' You two did not give up. That's why you are here."

"We're here," said Lansing, "because Mary always believed the answer lay within this cube."

"And by the force of her belief, you solved the riddle of the cube," said A.

"That's true," said Lansing. "Being true, then why am I here? Because I tagged along with Mary?"

"You're here because, along the way, you made the right decisions."

"At Chaos I made a wrong decision."

"We don't think you did," said C. "A matter of survival, while important, is not always a correct decision. There are decisions that can ignore survival."

Sniffler, resting on Mary's feet, had gone fast asleep.

"You make moral decisions," said Lansing, angrily. "You're great decision makers. And with such certainty. Tell me, just who the hell are you? The last survivors of the humans who lived upon this world?"

"No, we're not," said A. "We can't even claim that we are human. Our home is on a planet on the far side of the galaxy."

"Then why are you here?"

"I don't know if we can tell you so you'll understand. There's no word in your language that adequately expresses what we are.

For the want of a better term, you might think of us as social workers."

"Social workers!" said Lansing. "For the love of Christ! It has come to this. The human race has need of social workers. We've sunk so low in the galactic ghetto that we need social workers!"

"I told you," said A, "that the term was not precise. But consider this: Within the galaxy there are few intelligences that have the potential promise of you humans. Yet, unless something can be done about it, you are headed for extinction—all of you. Even so great a civilization as once existed on this alternate world went down to nothing. Folly brought it down—economic folly, political folly. You, Lansing, must know that if someone presses a button, your world is gone as well. You, Miss Owen, lived on a world that is heading for a great disaster. Someday soon the empires will fall and from the wreckage it will take thousands of years for a new civilization to arise, if it ever does. Even if it does, it may be a worse civilization than the one you know. On all the alternate worlds, disasters loom in one guise or another. The human race got off to a bad start and has not improved. It was doomed from the first beginning. The solution, as we see it, is to recruit a cadre of selected humans from all the many worlds, using them to give the race a new beginning and a second chance."

"Recruit, you say," said Lansing. "I don't call this recruitment. You snatch us from our worlds. You impress us. You bring us here and, telling us nothing, turn us loose, on our own, in this silly testing area of yours, to see how we make out, watching all the time to see how we make out, making judgment on us."

"Would you have come if we'd asked you? Would you have enlisted?"

"No, I would not have," said Lansing. "Neither, I think, would Mary."

"On all the many worlds," said B, "we have our agents and recruiters. We handpick the humans that we want—the ones we think may have a chance to pass the tests. We don't take just anyone. We are very choosy. Through the years we have collected some thousands of the humans who have passed the test, the kind of humans we think are best equipped to build the sort of society that such a race should build. We do this because it seems to us that it would be a waste for the galaxy to lose the kind of people that you are. In time, working with other intelligences, you will help to form a galactic society—a society beyond any present imagination. We feel that intelligence may be the crowning glory of fumbling evolution, that nothing better can be found. But if intelligence falls of its own weight, as it is falling, not only here but elsewhere, then evolution will turn, blindly, to some other set of survival factors and the concept of intelligence may be lost forever."

"Edward," said Mary, "there may be validity in what he says, in what they've done."

"That well may be," said Lansing, "but I don't like the way they go about it."

"It may be the only way," said Mary. "As they say, no one would enlist. Those few who possibly might probably would be the very ones for whom they'd have no use."

"I am glad to see," said A, "that you are approaching some acceptance of our view."

"What else," asked Lansing, sourly, "is left for us to do?"

"Not much," said B. "If you wish, you still are free to walk out the door into the world you left."

"That I wouldn't want," said Lansing, thinking of the camp of refugees in the river valley. "How about our own—"

He cut off what he had meant to say. If they went back to their own worlds, it would mean that he and Mary could not be together. Groping, he found her hand and clasped it tightly.

"You meant to ask if you could go back to your own worlds," said D. "I'm sorry, but you can't."

"Where we go," said Mary, "does not matter, so long as Edward and I remain together."

"Well, then," said A, "that's settled. We're very glad to have you. Whenever you are ready to go, you can walk through the door in the corner to the left. It does not open on the world you just left, but into a brand-new world."

"Another alternate world?" asked Mary.

"No. It opens on an Earthlike planet very far from here. Looking up at night, you'll see strange stars and constellations that are unfamiliar. A second chance, we said—a brand-new planet to go with that second chance. There is one city only—actually not a city, but a university town made up almost entirely of the university. There you'll teach the things you know and sit in classes to study the things you do not know. Perhaps a number of matters you have never heard or thought about. This will go on for many years, probably your entire lifetimes. Finally, perhaps a century or more from now, a highly intellectual and educated group, equipped with more and better tools than any Earth society has had before, quite naturally will begin to formulate a world society. It's too soon to do so now. There still are many things to learn, many attitudes to absorb and study, many viewpoints to ponder, before that can be done. You'll be under no economic stress during the training period, although in time it will be necessary for the community to develop an economic system. For the moment everything will be taken care of. All we ask is that you study and give yourself the time to become fully human."

"In other words," said Lansing, "you will still be taking care of us."

"You resent that?"

"I think he does," said Mary, "but he'll get over it. Given time, he'll get over it."

Lansing rose from his chair, Mary rising with him.

"Which door did you say?" asked Mary.

"That one over there," A said, pointing.

"One question before we go," said Lansing. "Tell me, if you will, what Chaos is."

"On your world," said D, "you have a Chinese wall."

"Yes, I would suspect on both Mary's world and mine."

"Chaos is a sophisticated Chinese wall," said D. "An utterly stupid thing to build. It was the last and greatest folly performed by the former people of this planet. It contributed to their downfall. The full story is far too long to tell."

"I see," said Lansing, turning toward the door.

"Would you take it badly," asked A, "if we said you go with all our blessings?"

"Not at all," said Mary. "We thank you for your kindness and for the second chance."

They walked to the door but, before they opened it, turned to look back. The four still were sitting in a row upon the couch, the white, blind, skull-like faces watching after them.

Then Lansing opened the door and the two of them passed through.

They stood upon a meadow, and in the distance saw the spires and towers of the university, where evening bells were tolling.

Hand in hand they walked toward mankind's second chance.

About the Author

Clifford D. Simak is a newspaperman, only recently retired. Over the years he has written more than twenty-five books and has some two hundred short stories to his credit. In 1977 he received the Nebula Grand Master award of the Science Fiction Writers of America and has won several other awards for his writing.

He was born and raised in southwestern Wisconsin, a land of wooded hills and deep ravines, and often uses this locale for his stories. A number of critics have cited him as the pastoralist of science fiction.

Perhaps the best known of his work is *City*, which has become a science-fiction classic.

He and his wife, Kay, have been happily married for more than fifty years. They have two children—a daughter, Shelley Ellen, a magazine editor, and Richard Scott, a chemical engineer.